FICTION RIVER: CHANCES

An Original Anthology Magazine

EDITED BY DENISE LITTLE & KRISTINE KATHRYN RUSCH

Series editors
DEAN WESLEY SMITH & KRISTINE KATHRYN RUSCH

ISBN-13:978-1-56146-381-7
ISBN-10: 1-56146-381-7

CONTENTS

FOREWORD

Worth Taking a Chance

The stories you are about to read might remind you of your own great love story. They certainly remind me of mine.

For many years, I thought true love was a construct of fiction. And I made decisions accordingly. When you don't believe you'll find love, you settle. And settling, I've found, never goes according to plan.

I settled twice before I met my true love. I was on my second marriage. He was engaged to the woman who would become his third wife (and his most regrettable choice). We worked together for a while back then. We connected on a deep level, but as neither of us were unattached, we focused on what it could be —friendship.

It would be a decade before the timing was right for us to take a chance on love. And a chance it was: me with two divorces and him with three. That's one of the many ways I knew I had found true love: it was so very worth the risk.

And those are the very best love stories, after all. The ones that inspire hope.

Because true love is out there. You just need to find it.

You can start with the stories in this book, because each of them proves that finding love is worth taking chances.

And we could all use a few more happy endings these days.

—Allyson Longueira
Lincoln City, OR
December 18, 2020

INTRODUCTION

Chancy Propositions

Putting together *Fiction River: Chances* was an unusually chancy proposition, and I'm not just being punny here. The brainchild of the great editor Denise Little (who once edited her own book line for Kensington called [you guessed it] *Denise Little Presents*), this anthology went through a few struggles of its own.

Denise conceived of the anthology pre-pandemic. She picked the stories pre-pandemic. Then life happened, and now I find myself selecting story order and writing introductions...and trying to read Denise's brilliant mind.

I started with Denise's pitch to the authors when she solicited stories for this volume. She wrote:

I'm looking for stories with strong characters who tug at your heart-strings with the chances they take to find themselves together.

The tales you weave can have any trimmings you please—contemporary, historical, mystery, urban fantasy, horror, space opera, teen, time travel, science fiction—anything that makes a believable and interesting world for your characters to play in.

The story can fall into any genre, time frame, or setting. But the heart of the story should be literally the heart of the story: how two fascinating people throw themselves against the whims of fate to find themselves together.

Literature is full of tropes to inspire you. Anthony and Cleopatra (conqueror and conquered), Romeo and Juliet (Montague and Capulet), Buffy and Angel (slayer and vampire), Han Solo and Princess Leia (smuggler and aristocrat).

History, too, has its lessons—Henry VIII alone had six various wives and a number of mistresses. The characters can be as simple as the guy or girl next door or as extravagant as your imagination can make them.

But something is keeping them apart. And chance—whether arranged by the gods or tempted by fate or forced into shape by strong wills—is about to change everything.

Or you can feel free to invent your own chances. Just make sure they are integral to the story....The stories need to be well written and emotionally engaging. I prefer happy endings, but have bought any number of stories with very untraditional versions of a happy ending, including ghosts and graves and tragic solitude when the tale merits it.

I just want to say "ahhhh" when it is all over.

Make me sigh with repletion.

I'm looking forward to it.

All of the stories in this volume meet that criteria and then some. They all made me say "ahhhh" when they ended. Clearly, they inspired a similar reaction in Denise. So, turn the page for something that will tug your heartstrings. You'll find many genre "trimmings" as Denise mentioned, but at the core of each story is a couple who needs to take a chance with each other.

Will they or won't they? Is there a happy ever after or just the whisper of one? Did happiness pass these poor lost souls by?

Well, maybe. You'll have to read each story to find out.

—Kristine Kathryn Rusch
Las Vegas, NV
August 2, 2020

BAKED WITH LOVE

ANNIE REED

Annie Reed leads off the volume with a love letter, not only to the magic of love, but to a bakery in her neighborhood that closed a few years back. That's part of the magic of writing. We can conjure up beloved places from our past, just by putting words on the page.

Annie's brilliant at putting words on the page. She's contributed to 22 Fiction River volumes (so far) as well as to WMG Publishing's Pulphouse Magazine. *Her short fiction has also found its way into our* Holiday Spectacular *and our* Year of the Cat *series. Her award-winning story "The Color of Guilt," chosen as one of* The Best Crime and Mystery Stories of 2016, *originally appeared in* Fiction River: Hidden in Crime.

Annie also writes sweet romance under the pen name Liz McKnight. Find out more at www.annie-reed.com.

Selene stood on the sidewalk in front of Lemon Box Bakery contemplating her imminent demise.

Her stomach rumbled at the whiff of sugary, yeasty, cinnamony goodness seeping out the bakery's front door. A trickle of sweat that had nothing to do with the warm spring morning ran down the back of her neck.

What was she, nuts? Thinking about actually buying a donut? From a place she'd never been to before?

She was a sensible person. She didn't eat ready-made baked goods anymore. Or go out to eat at restaurants if she didn't know the cook. And fast food? A thing of the past.

Her hips thanked her for that last one, although she really missed the fries at Mickey D's.

Ever since a sudden outbreak of culinary magic had changed life on good old planet Earth, eating out—and especially eating fast food—was just too risky. What if the high school kid in charge of the deep fryer had just broken up with his girlfriend? All that angst pouring into the cooking oil along with the frozen fries. The mere idea made Selene shiver.

Culinary magic—and yes, even government officials called it "magic" although with implied air quotes just so people knew the jury was still out on whether magic actually existed—turned every stray emotion of the person making the food into part of the food, and then passed those emotions on to those who ate it.

Most people made their own food these days just to be on the safe side. After all, they were already experiencing their own emotions, so any stray bit of love or contentment, anger or jealousy they consumed along with their homemade buttermilk pancakes couldn't hurt them.

In theory.

Unfortunately, Selene hadn't been able to duplicate the taste of Mickey D's fries at home. Either she sliced the potatoes too thick or didn't fry them long enough or didn't put the right amount of seasonings on them. And the mess! All that hot oil spattering her stovetop.

When her next paycheck came around, she'd have to invest in a deep fat fryer. Or else give up the idea of having fries with her homemade, bun-free burgers.

She hadn't been that successful making bread, either.

Sure, some people had bread machines. Some people had Porsches, too, but that didn't mean everyone could afford them.

Mickey D's was still in business, of course, if not thriving as much as it used to. Ditto for most franchise restaurants and the companies that produced all the ready-made food that the foolhardy bought at the grocery store.

And coffee shops were still around. Those places would never die.

People took crazy risks for coffee. Or brick-oven pizza. Or French fries.

Like she should talk. Here she was, standing in front of a bakery she'd never been to before, contemplating taking her life in her hands for an apple fritter.

At least Lemon Box Bakery looked like a small, family-owned business. Family-owned restaurants were supposed to be the safest to eat at since the cooks were always the same, and if they messed up the food too badly they knew they'd be out of business.

She wasn't too sure about the bakery's slogan printed in flowing script on the front window: *Donuts Baked With Love.*

Either the sign dated to before culinary magic invaded the world, or the owners thought a little love never hurt anyone.

Sure.

The last time she'd thought that, she'd nearly gone to bed with her blind date on the first date. Major mistake! The guy had turned out to be a real creep, and she found out later that he'd tipped the chef at the new-to-her restaurant he'd taken her to so that a little lust went into Selene's salmon alfredo.

Never again, she'd promised herself. If she was going to eat at someplace new, she'd do it alone and then go home immediately afterward to suffer whatever emotional consequences the food brought by herself.

"That's a lonely way to live," her best friend Monica said during their last marathon phone call.

Monica lived three states away now, but she said her dream job was worth it. Selene's job wasn't exactly dreamy—processing paperwork at a construction supply company wasn't anyone's idea of a dream job, but it paid the bills—and sure, she was alone, but at least she knew the emotions she experienced were her own.

She didn't want someone else's idea of love.

She'd rather be lonely.

But she really wanted an apple fritter.

And if she couldn't make yeast behave enough to bake a decent loaf of bread, how in the world was she going to make an apple fritter that was at least a little bit edible?

Her stomach rumbled again.

A middle-aged man came out of the bakery carrying a pink cardboard box in one hand and a croissant in the other. The pastry had a big bite missing from one end, and the man had flakey pastry crumbs on his lips.

"Marvelous," he said with a contented smile.

A full-force assault of humid, richly scented air hit Selene in the face, and for a moment she was lost in memories of standing in her mother's kitchen during the holidays. Her mother had loved to bake, and every day between Thanksgiving and Christmas seemed to bring with it a new type of cookie or quick bread or pastry.

If only Selene had inherited her mother's talents when it came to the kitchen.

She realized the man was holding the bakery door open for her with one shoulder.

"It's safe?" she asked him.

The man shrugged. "Never had a problem. Besides..." He gazed at the croissant like it was the most beautiful thing in the world. "I just love these things."

Baked with love, indeed.

"Do they have apple fritters?" she asked.

He nodded toward the pink box in his hand. "Best in the city."

Damn.

"Going in?" he asked.

She could always just bag the fritter and eat it at home. That way if she experienced an unexpected flush of emotion, she wouldn't be tempted to do something she'd regret later.

And her hips deserved a treat.

She smiled at the man. "Yes, I am."

She just hoped it wasn't the biggest mistake of her life.

"The dough is my friend. The dough is my friend."

Chris glared at the unresponsive lump in the rising bowl.

This particular batch of dough was definitely *not* his friend.

He had no clue what he'd done wrong. Warm water and yeast, butter, sugar, flour. The right music channel playing on the little sound system in the kitchen, the one that played all the songs that reminded him of the first girl he'd fallen in love with.

Everything should have worked. He'd placed the dough in the warming cabinet, set the timer, mixed the glazes, but when he retrieved the dough, it hadn't risen.

Chris took a deep breath and repeated the mantra essential to Lemon Box's success.

"The dough is my friend."

Baking had been so much easier before the rise—pun intended—of culinary magic in the world. Making food back then had been a science. So much of this interacted with so much of that to produce the desired effect when the right amount of heat energy was applied.

Follow the recipe to the letter and you got the end product the recipe was designed to produce. Chris had liked the certainty of that.

So, when his father suggested that Chris take over the business, he'd said yes. Sure, he had to get up before the crack of dawn to make sure he had ample products for the day, but he'd always been an early riser, even back in college, and he'd never been afraid of hard work.

He'd grown up working summers in the bakery with his dad. The yeasty smell of the dough and the sweet fried aroma of the donuts was home to him. He even liked that his dad's bakery had been old school, with all the donuts and pastries and cookies created by hand, not through some cookie-cutter automated process.

These days? Any little frustration could totally screw up a recipe. That's what most people didn't realize. Negative emotions did more than just pass on through the food to whoever ate it. You could do everything exactly right—like Chris had done with the dough that refused to rise—and if you didn't have the right feeling about what you were making, the things wouldn't turn out right.

He used to have a part-time pastry chef working for him, but the woman had gone through a divorce and he'd had to let her go. She'd said she understood, but he'd still felt so bad he'd closed the bakery for a week to give himself time to sort out his own feelings about the loss.

After all, Lemon Box specialized in donuts made with love, and he just hadn't been feeling it.

That must have been what was wrong. He thought he'd buried his feelings after he got the text from his best friend, but apparently he hadn't.

Dude, I found the one! the text had read.

Eric always thought he'd found the one.

The one this week? Chris had texted back along with the appropriate smiley face icon.

No. Dude. The one! I can't wait for you to meet her.

A few more texts established that True Love hadn't been served along with the beef stroganoff and lemon pepper chicken. Eric always prepared his own food and so did his lady love, and they always met in one of the new cafes that offered tables and chairs and ambiance (but no food) for upscale brown baggers.

Chris's college roommate really had found his one and only.

Wedding's next month! Eric had texted. *Better be there, bro.*

Eric, the perpetually single, was getting married.

While Chris had been mixing the dough, he'd mentally run through his list of close friends from college. He and Eric were the last single guys on that list. Even Ronnie, the guy who'd dated a different girl every week, had been married for what—five years now?—and he had three kids already. Chris couldn't remember the last time he had a date.

Well, that wasn't exactly true. It had been before magic invaded the world, back when asking a girl out for a cup of coffee had been easy. All you had to face then was potential rejection, not a potential emotional rollercoaster ride.

Chris had read a lot of Tolkien in high school. He used to think it would be cool if things like elves and dwarves and wizards were real—especially elves because elves would probably be really hot—but that was fiction.

He'd never expected that magic, real magic, would exist someday. And he'd certainly never expected magic to make someone's emotions part of the food they cooked.

At first, he'd been so freaked at the very thought that his emotions could transfer to someone else through a donut he made that he'd considered closing the bakery. His dad had talked him out of it.

"Food has always been a part of celebration," his dad had said. "Of ceremony. What is a birthday without cake and ice cream? What is Thanksgiving without turkey and stuffing? Emotion has always been a part of food."

"But not *in* the food, Pops," Chris had said. "Not my emotion. How can I do that to people? What if I'm having a bad day?"

"What if your customers are having a bad day? You smile at

them now and wish them well as they leave." His dad had shrugged. "Would it be such a bad thing to put that wish in the food? Give them a little emotional lift along with their donut?"

That's how Lemon Box Bakery's new slogan had been born: *Donuts Baked With Love.*

Only Chris wasn't feeling the love now. He was feeling melancholy and lonely and more than a little like life had passed him by while he'd been up to his elbows in flour and powdered sugar.

Or, as Eric would put it, Chris was feeling down.

Was it any wonder the dough wouldn't rise?

He'd have to throw this batch out. Even if he gave the yeast more time to do its thing, he couldn't inflict these donuts on anyone. He'd just have to sell what was already in the display cases out front, go home and have a beer (from a "safe" local brewery), and hope he'd feel more like himself tomorrow.

Or maybe he should just close up for the day and call it a loss.

He was still considering what to do when the sound of his counter bell rang through the bakery. Chris had just waited on one of his regulars a few minutes ago, a pleasant middle-aged man who bought a croissant and five assorted donuts once a week, but he hadn't seen anyone else out front.

"Be with you in a minute," he called out through the open doorway between the kitchen and the front display area.

He dumped the stubborn dough in the trash and washed his hands before he headed out front. He half expected to see his regular back to buy the last remaining croissant in the case. Chris had baked croissants the day before, and he always sold the day-olds to his regular at half price. The guy really loved croissants.

Instead, the most beautiful woman Chris had seen in a long time stood in front of his counter. She was staring at the tray of apple fritters like she'd found the Holy Grail.

And it was about ready to bite her face off.

Oh. My. God.

Selene couldn't believe how wonderful the inside of the bakery smelled. Sure, the grocery store where she shopped every week still had a small bakery area. But the smell of baked goods competed with the hot-oil scent of fried chicken and onion rings from the deli (for people who still had the nerve to buy things like that from a grocery store) and the overpowering fake-floral odors from the air fresheners on aisle three.

She was in heaven. She wanted one of everything in the display case. Blueberry cake donuts. Cherry turnovers. Lemon bars. Oatmeal raisin cookies. Cinnamon twists.

And the most luscious apple fritters she had ever seen.

She could practically feel her hips expanding, and she didn't care. She'd survived on salads (with homemade vinaigrette dressing), simple stir-fry vegetables, crock pot stews and soups, and the occasional roast for months and months now. She ate homemade hamburgers without buns. Questionable pasta she made with a pasta machine she borrowed from one of her friends at work. Whatever fresh fruit was in season.

She wanted something rich. Something decadent. Something she didn't have to try to bake and see fail, time and time again.

No one stood behind the counter. Through an open archway behind the glass display case she could see a table where a birthday cake sat half decorated. She could hear someone moving around back there. She was about to call out when she noticed a silver bell on top of the counter, the kind of bell a guest might find in a low-rent motel. Taped to the counter next to the bell was a small sign that advised her to ring the bell for service.

She drew in a breath to steady her nerves and rang the bell.

"Be there in a minute," came a man's voice from the back of the bakery.

A minute. That would give her one last chance to decide if she was really going to do this. She didn't think she'd be able to turn around and walk out if she had to look the baker in the eye. That would just be rude.

But could she trust this place? The middle-aged man who'd held the door for her looked like he'd fallen in love with his pastry.

She zoned in on the exact apple fritter she wanted. "Don't mess with me," she muttered at it. "I'm taking a big chance here, you know."

She was so focused on the fritter that she didn't notice when the baker stepped through the open archway. He just seemed to appear behind the counter.

"Oh!" she said.

She could feel a sudden flush heat up her cheeks. What if he'd heard her talking to an apple fritter? How embarrassing was that?

If he had, he didn't mention it. "What can I get for you today?" he asked instead.

She breathed a small sigh of relief. He wasn't making fun of her. At least, not now. He might laugh about it later, but she decided not to think about that.

All she had to do was look away from the fritters and tell him what she wanted, but she was having a hard time looking away from the display case.

What was up with that?

Were emotions passing through smell now? Because sure, she really wanted a fritter, but this was downright ridiculous.

She told herself to get a grip.

"I'm sorry," she said, intending to apologize for ignoring the baker who clearly was busy working on things in his kitchen. "But I..."

Whatever else she was going to say fled her brain when she caught sight of him.

He wasn't exactly movie-star handsome, but he sure came close. He had a swipe of flour along one chiseled cheekbone and powdered sugar dusting his clean-shaven chin. His eyes were a warm brown, his shoulders were broad beneath his plain white T-shirt, and his smile was pleasant and welcoming without a hint of laughter at her expense.

She found herself smiling back.

"I haven't been in a bakery in a long time," she finished.

"Let me guess," he said. "Ever since donuts came complete with emotions other than guilt?"

"Something like that." She bit at her lower lip. "I've been thinking about baking my own, but I can't even get bread to rise."

He raised one eyebrow. "Believe me. I get that."

"You?" She couldn't believe that. "Everything here looks wonderful."

"Yeast can be tricky."

She found herself staring into those warm brown eyes, the fritter almost forgotten. This man practically exuded warmth and caring. If he was the only baker here, no wonder the bakery's slogan was *Donuts Made With Love.*

"What do you recommend?" she asked just to keep him talking. His voice was nearly as rich as she imagined the fritter would be.

"Well, the lemon bars are our specialty. My dad's recipe."

Hence Lemon Box Bakery.

"Okay, I'll take one," she heard herself say.

She also took a cherry turnover, the last croissant in the display, and an apple fritter. He packed them all in a pink pastry box, and she handed him her debit card.

He seemed to take an extra beat before he handed the card back with her receipt. "Thanks for stopping by, Selene," he said. "And thanks for the vote of confidence."

The way he said her name sent a pleasant little shiver down her spine. "You're welcome…"

She paused deliberately, and he took the hint.

"Chris," he said.

She nodded. "Chris." Good name. Her mom's middle name had been Kris with a K.

"Hope to see you again." The way he said it, he made it sound more meaningful than the usual "Come again soon."

She held up the box. "Have to give these a trial run first."

He chuckled. "At least come back and tell me what you thought. Good or bad."

"I will," she said before she had a chance to think about it.

Would she be able to tell him if the fritter didn't live up to her expectations? She had pretty high expectations, after all.

And what if the food depressed her beyond the normal "I can't believe I ate the whole thing!" guilt she dimly remembered from the days before culinary magic changed her eating habits.

But for whatever reason, she had a good feeling about Chris and his bakery.

She just had to go home and put the apple fritter to the test, then she'd decide if it was safe to eat everything else in her pink pastry box.

After his new customer—Selene—left, Chris decided to give the donuts one more shot.

He changed the channel on his internet radio to something a little more upbeat. A little more modern.

He reset the mixing machine, the one with a big bowl and a dough hook attachment. He poured warm water in the bowl and dumped in the yeast. While the yeast and water got acquainted, he measured out the flour and sugar and gathered up the rest of the ingredients, then added them to the bowl and began the mixing process.

All the while he thought about his new customer.

How her hair framed her perfectly feminine face.

How her eyes had been a luminous hazel, and her lips had formed a perfect bow even without lipstick.

How wonderful her voice had sounded saying his name.

When all the ingredients were thoroughly mixed and kneaded to perfection by the dough hook, he dumped the dough into a rising bowl, covered the bowl with plastic wrap, and put it in the warming cabinet. While the dough raised, he went about cleaning the mixing bowl and the hook, and then finished decorating the special-order cake.

He waited on two more customers, both regulars, barely noticing that he was whistling a half-formed tune while he worked.

When the timer went off, Chris retrieved the dough from the warming cabinet.

This time the dough had more than doubled in size.

"Good little yeast," he said as he pressed the dough down. "You did good this time around."

He wrapped the dough in plastic again, but this time he put it in the refrigerator to rest overnight. He'd finish this batch in the morning.

He had a feeling they might be some of the best donuts he'd made yet.

He was still whistling that half-formed tune and thinking about Selene when he locked up the bakery for the night.

―――――

The apple fritter was quite literally the best thing Selene had ever tasted.

Sweet and slightly crusty on the outside, yeasty and light on the inside with just the right amount of cinnamon swirled through the dough and enough bits of tart apple here and there to give it a zing. Not too sweet, and not the least bit oily.

She could have eaten the whole thing at one sitting, but she made herself save half for later.

All the while she ate, she thought about Chris, the baker.

She'd always thought bakers were older guys with salt-and-pepper hair and a five o'clock shadow at two in the afternoon, with hound dog jowls and bags under their eyes from getting up before dawn to put bread in the oven. She wasn't sure exactly where she'd gotten that impression—maybe from the movies or from the only baker she ever saw at the grocery store—but that certainly didn't describe Chris.

He looked like he was about her age. No ring on his finger, but that didn't mean anything. He worked with dough, after all, so he might take it off to keep it from getting gunked up.

Still, she wouldn't be surprised to see him show up in her dreams some night. She had a feeling those would be very pleasant dreams.

In fact, she was feeling pretty pleasant after eating half of the fritter. Not exactly happy, and certainly not euphoric, but just a nice little contented, warm feeling. Safe. Like she didn't have a care in the world, or she'd just been snuggled by a very lovey puppy.

Was this Lemon Box's version of love, the kind the donuts were supposed to be made with?

If it was, she was surprised the bakery wasn't more popular. This feeling was definitely one she could live with.

And to think she'd been so scared about even going inside.

"Silly," she muttered to herself.

It looked like pastry—and especially apple fritters—were back on the menu.

The fact that the baker was more than easy on the eyes would just be a nice bonus.

Selene came back to the bakery the following week for another apple fritter, another lemon bar, and a maple glazed donut. And the week after that for a peach turnover, a cinnamon roll, and—of course—an apple fritter.

She was always pleasant. Always had a warm smile for him, and always called him by name. She was turning into a regular customer, and Chris found himself looking forward to her visits.

Chris spent the time between her visits baking up a storm and trying to decide whether to ask her out for coffee. He hadn't had any more catastrophes in the kitchen, even after Eric had texted to ask if Chris could be an usher at his wedding. In fact, the yeast had never performed better.

He'd just about decided to take the plunge and ask her out— she could only say no, right?—when his dad came by the bakery late one afternoon holding one of the bakery's pink pastry boxes in his hands. Inside were the remains of one of three croissants Chris had sold to his regular middle-aged customer the day before.

"I think we have a problem," Chris's dad said.

It seemed the customer, a nice man who bowled for another team in the men's league with Chris's dad, had proposed to the counter girl at the bowling alley the night before. It would have been a sweet story except the man had been married—happily, by all accounts—to the same woman for the past twenty-eight years.

"What have you been putting in the dough?" his dad asked.

"The same thing I always do," Chris said. "It's your recipe."

"No," his dad said. "What have you been putting *in* the

dough?" His dad gestured at the *Donuts Baked With Love* sign in the window and raised his eyebrows.

Chris got it.

"Oh, crap," he said.

Ever since culinary magic had become a fact of life, Chris had carefully monitored his emotions while he mixed the dough for all his pastries and donuts. He always listened to the same songs, thought the same pleasant thoughts, and generally kept himself on as even a keel as possible.

Until he'd met Selene.

She'd affected him the way no other woman ever had. He not only looked forward to her visits, he'd been having happy little daydreams about her. Dreams that would no doubt make his friends question his sanity, since they involved nothing more than spending time with her and maybe making bread together so that he could show her how yeast dough was supposed to rise.

"Oh, crap," he said again. "I think I'm in love."

His dad nodded and sighed, and then he smiled. "It happens to us all one day."

Chris's parents had been married for nearly forty years.

"What am I going to do about the business?" he asked. He couldn't have his customers falling in love willy-nilly just because he couldn't control his own emotions while he was baking.

And worse than that—what if he got up the courage to ask Selene out and she said yes? And then they started really dating? How would he ever know if she really had feelings for him, or if it was just the apple fritters?

Chris leaned on the counter and shook his head. "I'm going to have to close up the bakery," he said.

He didn't want to, but he couldn't think of anything else to do.

His dad put the pink pastry box on the counter and patted the back of Chris's hand.

"Let me make a suggestion," he said.

Selene's weekly visits to the bakery had rapidly become something she looked forward to all week, and not just because Chris made the best apple fritters in the world.

Apple fritters only satisfied her sweet tooth. Seeing Chris once a week satisfied something far more important—her need to connect with someone.

Not that he was anything other than friendly toward her. Sure, they talked a little more each time she went to the bakery. For instance, she knew that his best friend was getting married in a couple of weeks, and she'd told him that her best friend had moved away to follow her dream job. He'd told her about how his dad had retired so he could bowl four nights a week, and she told him that her parents were spending their retirement years traveling around the country in an RV.

But even though she had very pleasant dreams about him—very, *very* pleasant—she didn't flirt with him and he didn't flirt with her. They were just baker and customer.

Weren't they?

She had to admit that lately her dreams found the two of them spending lots of time together, holding hands and taking long walks and baking bread together, of all things. Those dreams made her happy in a way she'd never been before, and she found herself thinking about his warm brown eyes at inopportune moments during the day.

Was this what falling in love felt like?

And if it was, did she feel this way because of her own emotions, or was it something in the donuts?

And if it was the donuts, did that mean Chris was in love with someone else and she was just feeling the side effects?

Well, there was only one way to find out. She'd ask him out for coffee at one of those cafes where everyone made their own. If he turned her down, then she'd know that whatever she felt wasn't because he had feelings for her. She could wean herself off the fritters—she'd had enough in the past couple of weeks to last her a while (her hips would be thankful)—and go back to her mostly healthy, mostly edible home cooking.

She didn't let herself daydream about what would happen if he said yes.

Only the next time she went to Lemon Box Bakery, Chris wasn't behind the counter. An older man, one with salt-and-pepper hair and bags beneath his eyes, stood behind the counter.

"May I help you?" he asked, wiping his flour-dusted hands on his apron.

Her heart hitched in her chest. "Is Chris here?"

The older man smiled. "He's taking a few days off, so I came out of retirement."

Oh. That must make the man behind the counter...

"You're Chris's dad," she said. "I'm sorry. I didn't mean to be rude. I just came in for an apple fritter, and I was surprised Chris wasn't here."

Except there weren't any fritters in the display case.

His brown eyes twinkled. "And you must be Selene."

She blinked in surprise.

"Chris told me about you," he said.

She blinked again. Chris had told his *dad* about her?

"He'd like me to extend an invitation." The man retrieved an envelope from his apron and handed it to her.

She opened it. Inside was a gift certificate for a cooking class at a local gourmet shop. The title of the class was "Getting a Rise Out of It: Homemade Bread Made Easy."

At the bottom of the certificate, Chris had written two words: *Join me?*

The class was for a week from the following Saturday.

More than enough time for any emotional overflow from the pastry to have worn off, provided she didn't eat any between now and then.

Was she ready to find out if what she felt was real?

"Can I get you anything while you're here?" Chris's dad asked.

She shook her head and glanced at the spot in the display case where Chris usually had half a dozen apple fritters. In their place was an entire tray of lemon bars. They looked yummy, but she had other things on her mind.

"No, thank you," she said. "The fritters really are my favorites."

Chris waited nervously inside the classroom attached to The New Gourmet, a locally owned gourmet cooking supply store.

He'd never been to a formal cooking school. He'd learned how to bake in the back room at his father's bakery. The New Gourmet's classroom was about as close as he could get without going out of town.

Not that he really needed lessons. He could make bread with the old equipment at the bakery just as easy as he could with the gleaming new equipment set up on each of eight butcher-block tables arrayed in workstations throughout the classroom. Each workstation had its own shiny brushed-aluminum oven and gas cookstove, an array of pricey bakeware and frying pans, and for tonight's class, a brand name mixer fixed with a dough hook.

Chris had purchased gift certificates for himself and for Selene, but he wasn't sure if she'd come. His dad had told him that she'd smiled a little when she'd opened the gift certificate and that she'd put it in her purse, but she hadn't bought anything that day.

And she hadn't been back to the bakery since.

He wiped his damp palms on the apron The New Gourmet supplied along with all the necessary ingredients for bread already set out on his workstation. He'd have to measure everything, of course, according to the recipe written on a white board at the front of the class. And he had a digital thermometer on his workstation to make sure the temperature of the water was just right before he dumped in the yeast. The instructor would probably be horrified to learn that he measured the temperature of the water at the bakery by running it over his wrist, an old trick he'd learned from his father.

Selene didn't arrive until five minutes before the class was scheduled to start. All the other workstations had filled up except for the one next to Chris. He expected Selene to take it, but instead she only took the apron and then joined him at his workstation.

"Is this all right?" she asked.

Her smile looked tentative and nervous, which mirrored how Chris felt. His heart was beating too fast, and he was sure his voice wouldn't work, but he managed to croak out a "yes" before he really embarrassed himself.

The instructor, a thirty-something woman who hosted a cooking segment on the local news, took her place at the front of the class. She wore cook's whites and a spotless red apron with The New Gourmet blazoned across the front. She lifted an eyebrow when she saw Chris and Selene standing at the same workstation, but then she smiled.

"All right, class," she said, her practiced voice filling the room. "Let's get busy making bread, shall we?"

Baking bread, Selene learned, was only halfway about the ingredients. The rest had to do with confidence.

"That's something new these days," the instructor said. "You want the yeast to love working with your bread? You've got to love it first."

That, Selene thought, was a pretty good metaphor for life.

Or at least for this new part of her life.

The last week and a half without pastry had been a real eye opener, and in a good way.

Her feelings for Chris hadn't diminished. In fact, not seeing him had only made her feelings grow stronger.

She really was in love. Or at least she was well on the way to getting there, and if the look in his eyes when she joined him at his table was any indication, he felt the same way about her.

It turned out that they worked well together. They took turns kneading the bread on the butcher block tabletop, and by the time they were ready to put the ball of dough into an oiled bowl to let it rise, they were both dusted with flour.

"The sign of a good cook," Chris said as he wiped a streak of flour off her cheek.

She retaliated by wiping a spot of flour off the tip of his nose.

While the bread was rising in a warm oven, they wandered through the store. Chris explained what some of the more exotic implements were designed for, like the egg separator that looked like a slinky coiled into an ice cream cone shape. They discovered they both had single-serving coffee makers, and he bought her a sample of his favorite coffee blend.

When the class was over, each student got to take their loaf of homemade bread home.

"So, who gets your loaf?" the instructor asked the two of them as the other students filed out. "If you want to split it, I'd recommend waiting until it cools enough to cut easily."

Chris glanced at Selene, a broad grin on his face. "It's a shame to cut it," he said. "It's the best loaf I've ever made."

Selene only had her failed attempts to go by, but the loaf they'd made together looked marvelous. The yeast had done its job all right, and the end result was a gloriously brown, perfectly shaped loaf of bread that smelled like heaven.

"I have strawberry jam at home," she said. "It's the one thing I can make pretty well by myself. Sugar, fruit, boil it down and stick it in the fridge. Want to come over for toast and jam? Or is that too adventurous?"

She'd made the jam back when she was sure she could figure out the bread thing by herself. It had been chilling, uneaten, in her refrigerator, but now she finally had something to put it on.

And someone to share it with.

His smile widened. "Sure."

The instructor left them alone, but they barely noticed.

"You're not afraid of what I might have let slip into my food while I was making it?" Selene asked.

He shook his head. "You trusted me, and look how that turned out."

Pretty darn well, from her perspective. And clearly from his as well.

He walked her out to her car. She stood for a moment holding the warm bread in her hands, unsure of who should actually take custody of the loaf for the trip to her apartment.

She was about to say something when he leaned forward and kissed her lightly on the lips.

"Wow," she said when the kiss ended.

Okay, she hadn't had an apple fritter in a week and a half, so the feeling that zinged through her when he kissed her definitely hadn't come from the pastry.

Speaking of...

"Now that I've mastered yeast bread, thanks to you," she said, putting a flirty tone in her voice, "do you think you can teach me how to make apple fritters?"

He laughed, and she laughed along with him.

"I think I've created a monster," he said. "You're relentless."

He had no idea.

She didn't either, really. It had been too long since she'd had someone in her life. But she had a feeling she was about to find out.

She had a feeling they both were.

AN OCEAN OF SECRETS IN HER EYES

DAYLE A. DERMATIS

I love stories about Hollywood in the 1930s and 1940s, and clearly Dayle A. Dermatis does too. Her Nikki Ashburne series features former Hollywood stars who haunt hotels all over the Los Angeles region. In addition to her novels, Dayle has published more than 100 short stories in multiple genres, appearing in such venues as Fiction River *(twenty-one volumes to date, most recently* Special Edition: Summer Sizzles *and* Superstitious*),* Alfred Hitchcock's Mystery Magazine, *and DAW Books.*

For more information about her and her wonderful fiction, visit DayleDermatis.com, sign up for her newsletter, and/or support her on Patreon.

The studio owned her.

And if Sam wasn't careful, the studio would own him, too.

The year was 1942. Sam Belmont tipped his fedora back against the heat of the Hollywood lights. Full summer, but they still lit the back lot when they were filming, ensuring the proper illumination and shadows to best show off their actors and create the right look.

As if any shadow could detract from the stunning, shining glory that was Tabitha St. Claire. She seemed to emit a light of her own.

The plot of the film, as near as Sam could understand it, was typically farfetched. Tabitha played an heiress who'd run away to the circus to get away from her father, who wanted to marry her to a much older man. Because of her equestrian skills, she'd become the girl who stands atop the ponies as they pranced around the ring. She'd fallen in love with a high-flying acrobat... who of course was also a millionaire hiding from the murderer who'd killed the rest of his family.

This was the final scene, where they met in the middle of the midway, all truths revealed, and kissed as the credits would roll in the completed film. Sam had watched several takes before everything—performance, sound, props, things he couldn't see the difference in—was deemed perfect and the director called it a cut and wrap.

Tabitha, her voluptuous curves highlighted in a circus leotard and tights, whispered something in the lead actor's ear, then patted his cheek and smiled her famous smile, followed by a wink, before she walked away, her dark chestnut hair gleaming in the hot lights.

"She's a stunner, isn't she?" Jack Webster, head of talent management for the studio, asked Sam. Smoke curled around his face from the cigarette in his mouth. He was in his mid-forties, thickening around the middle, his nose leaning toward an unhealthy shade of red, but his dark eyes were shrewd.

"She is," Sam agreed, knowing it was really a rhetorical question. Who didn't love Tabitha St. Claire? It seemed the entire country did—and beyond.

Sam did, too, when it came to her acting. But the falseness and trappings of Hollywood left him cold. He'd seen too much muck and dirt behind the glitz and glamour.

"Gorgeous dame, talented as hell—the whole package," Jack said. "Come to my office. We need to talk."

He led Sam through the back lot to the rows of pink-stuccoed bungalows that served as offices for the studio.

Jack tossed his jacket on the coatrack by the door and indicated with a nod of his head that Sam should do the same. Sam hung his fedora and jacket, but didn't loosen his tie or roll up his sleeves as Jack did. There was a pecking order here, and he understood it.

He was grateful for the fan that stirred the hot summer air, even if it didn't do much. Something was better than nothing.

Jack lit another cigarette, offered one to Sam, who shook his head. But when Jack picked up the crystal decanter of whiskey and shook it in question, Sam said, "On the rocks."

The ice tinkled in the glass as Sam sipped. Finer stuff than he could ever afford.

Jack took a healthier swallow and tipped back in his chair. His desk was covered in papers and photographs, no doubt the submissions from starry-eyed men and women hoping to make it big.

"Here's the thing," he said. "Tabby's one of our top money-makers—for obvious reasons."

Sam didn't like the way Jack called her "Tabby." For the most part, he didn't like Jack at all. Jack had an oily cast to him; money was paramount to him, money and status, not people. Just like the studio itself.

But a job was a job, and the studio would pay better than wives looking for proof that their husbands were stepping out on them, or parents wanting him to find their missing children, or any of the small jobs he performed.

(Small for him. Huge for the parties involved.)

He was good at what he did, which was why he'd been summoned for this audience with Jack Webster, been invited onto the studio lot and allowed to view the filming.

He kept his face schooled, impassive, and Jack Webster plowed on.

"Something's off, though," Jack said. "She's a professional, never misses a call time or her mark, no matter how late she stays up hosting or attending some glamorous shindig—and believe me, the parties she throws are spectacular."

"But?" Sam asked.

"But she disappears some weekends, you know? Says she's visiting her sister in Bakersfield. If she wants to see her sister so much, why doesn't she just move the girl down here? Who the hell wants to live in Bakersfield, anyway?"

Someone with a family, and a home, and roots, Sam thought, but didn't share.

"And you want to know if something's wrong," Sam said.

"Exactly." Jack pointed at Sam, cigarette between his fingers. "Tabby represents the studio. We can't have anything look bad, if you know what I mean."

Sam did. Studios owned their actors—even the actors' personal time, to a large extent. It mattered who they flirted with, who they dated, who they married. It mattered if they did something stupid while drunk. It mattered that they didn't do anything that reflected poorly on the studio.

"What exactly do you need me to do?" Sam asked.

Jack snorted out a sigh of annoyance. "For all she's a party girl, Tabby's tight-lipped," he said. "Keeps her cards close to her chest. And what a chest, eh? Mmph. Anyway, we've had our in-house guy look into things and he came up empty-handed. If there's something brewing, it's gonna take more than making a few calls or chasing paperwork." He pointed with his cigarette again, the smoke curling and dispersing in the fan's stubborn attempts to cool the office. "You get my meaning?"

"I do," Sam said. Jack wanted him to get close to Tabitha, was authorizing him to do so without putting it into words, so he could deny it later if things went south.

"Good man. If things go well, maybe we'll have to put you on retainer. We could use someone like you."

Sam ignored that. "I'll be billing you for expenses above and beyond my regular fee," Sam said. Before Jack's eyebrows could rise all the way up, he continued. "To appear in Miss St. Claire's circles, I have to dress the part, and so forth."

Jack Webster scowled. It was clearly an expression his face fell into regularly. "I'll be looking at every charge," he warned. "Don't play games."

As if what they were discussing right now wasn't a game.

"Of course not," Sam said.

Sam expensed a nicer suit than he ever dreamed to own, and when Jack Webster got him an invitation to Tabitha St. Claire's latest party, Sam expensed a hired car as well.

His own car, a nondescript, mid-30s, dark blue Packard, always got him where he needed to be, but it wasn't something he could park outside Miss St. Claire's house without being assumed he was a servant, a sleazy reporter looking for a scoop, or worse.

Her house was a grand affair, with a two-story white marble foyer from which a staircase rose from either side, curving up to a central balcony (and no doubt hallways beyond). Beyond that, a great room with furniture and plants artfully placed for small group conversations, and beyond that, a vast patio with a fountain and views of Tinseltown below.

White-tuxedoed waiters circulated with trays of high-end champagne and exquisite hors d'oeuvres. A man played a piano while another crooned into a microphone, the sound mingling with the chatter of guests.

Tabitha St. Claire was in her element. She moved through the crowd as if a spotlight followed her, or perhaps it was her own radiance. She smiled, she laughed, she had a personal word for everyone.

Until her spin through the crowd reached Sam.

She wore an aqua satin gown that made her eyes look like a tropical sea, and her luxurious dark hair was caught up on one side with a jeweled clasp that sparkled in the light.

But not more than she herself shone.

Those impossibly hued eyes widened. "Well," she said in that husky voice that had seduced millions. "Hello, you. Not sure I know you."

"I know Jack," Sam said, unwilling to call Jack a friend.

"Ah," she said. That one word—not even a word, really, but an exhalation of understanding...and disappointment.

"Which is a misfortune," Sam added, "except that it allowed me entry here. Jack is..." He wouldn't lie. "Might we call him a necessary evil?"

Her demeanor changed again, then, from closed off to more open. Her smiled widened; she stepped closer, giving more intimacy to their conversation; and her long lashes dipped in the barest of winks. "I think we just might. I'll drink to that, Mister...?"

"Sam," he said. "Just call me Sam."

"Sam." She said his name like a prayer, and clinked her fine champagne flute against his.

And he, who'd hardened his heart against starlets and Hollywood and the whole sordid business, fell, hopelessly smitten.

He saw her when he could, becoming part of her social circle without being immediately obvious, getting himself invited to other parties, other places where she was known to appear. He was vague about what he did, implying family money, investments, a life of relative leisure. There was a thread of truth running through it; he'd inherited a small sum, just enough to keep him in a decent spot at the Ballington Hotel and Apartments.

Sam found his way into Tabitha's financials, saw nothing unusual. Two years ago she'd taken an extended trip to Europe, which wasn't out of the ordinary; she'd been fresh off the popularity of her latest movie and obviously wanted a break. He hadn't found any newspaper articles or newsreels of her trip, but he assumed she'd gone on a much-needed vacation rather than a publicity junket.

Discreetly, he talked to her friends, casually turning the conversation topic to Tabitha, and he listened carefully to the responses. He expected them to say she was wonderful—he was still a relative stranger, so he was unlikely to hear gossip or true feelings—but he paid attention to how they spoke of her. How their eyes moved. Their posture. The tone of their voice.

Not all of them were actors, but even if they had been, he couldn't believe every one of them could pull the wool over his eyes. But to the last one, they all projected honesty and sincerity when they praised the name of Tabitha St. Claire.

She was a devoted friend. Kind, caring, generous.

Heard you were sick? She had matzo soup delivered from Canter's Deli. Fallen on hard times? She called in favors, got you a bit part to tide you over. Despondent over a breakup? She was the shoulder you cried on, the person who brought you chocolate or gin (or both) as required.

She was the life of the party, whether for her quick wit or her thoughtful conversation.

No one had an unkind word to say, except perhaps that her work schedule kept her from seeing her friends as much as they would like.

And, of course, Sam kept a close eye on Tabitha herself, which was far from a hardship.

Her friends were all telling the truth, he believed. It was Tabitha herself who had a secret.

He could see it in her eyes. Those tropical-sea eyes held a hint of sadness, especially when she didn't think anyone was looking.

Having feelings for someone he was hired to investigate went against all of Sam's professional judgment, not to mention ethics.

It was a bad idea to go to the cinema with her, choosing a theater all the way out in Oxnard for more anonymity. A bad idea going in after the lights were down, sitting in the back with his arm around her, slipping out just before the credits started to roll.

It was a bad idea to go down to Sarinana's Tamales in Santa Ana, Tabitha's stunning chestnut hair tucked under a hat as she stood slightly behind him (lashes lowered to hide those brilliant blue eyes), letting him place the order, and then taking the food to a local park where they sat in the shade of a fragrant eucalyptus.

It was a bad idea to drive through the twisting canyon roads on a clear night, the stars glittering overhead like handfuls of blithely scattered diamonds, and sit close together on the beach, listening to the shush of the surf and breathing the warm, salty air.

It was a bad idea, when Tabitha rested her head on his shoulder and whispered, "Sam Belmont, I think I'm falling for you."

It had been a bad idea to tell her his last name.

It was the worst idea of all for him to respond, "I think the feeling's mutual, sweetheart."

Sam saw something in Tabitha's eyes when she told him she needed to go away for a few days. He saw the way she bit her lip, how she couldn't quite hold his gaze, how she clenched one fist, half behind her back, until the knuckles were pale.

She was waiting for him to ask why, and where. She was dreading the questions.

He brushed a kiss against her lips. "Of course, sweetheart," he said. "You have a good time. Call me when you get back."

She wrapped her arms around him, cheek against his shoulder, and he rested a hand on her silky hair. He felt her take a deep breath, and he closed his eyes, wanting to do the same, but not daring to breathe at all.

He already had her sister's name and address, of course. He'd gone up to Bakersfield once, checked her out. She lived in a modest home on a modest street in a dusty city known for oil fields and not much else.

So to be safe, he left before dawn in his nondescript Packard, chugging up the Tejon Pass out of Los Angeles and down into the San Joaquin Valley as the sun struggled up over the mountains. The odor of cows from the dairy farms clung in the swiftly heating air.

When he arrived, he bought a newspaper and sat at the entrance to the neighborhood, eating an egg salad sandwich he'd brought with him, one that tasted like dust. He waited. It was a normal part of his job, waiting, and he was good at it. It gave him time to think.

Unfortunately, the drive from Los Angeles had given him time to think, too, and he really didn't want to be thinking.

He didn't even want to be doing this anymore.

When she arrived, it was in a Chrysler, also navy-blue, a low-end one. It was an everyday car, not something a top actress would drive—not the silver Packard she was known for. This was a car she'd tucked at the back of her garage, and probably paid her mechanic handsomely to never reveal the details of to anyone.

She parked two blocks away from her sister's house. Sam eased his car behind her, stopping halfway down the block. One long, slender leg, then another, emerged. She wore a sedate driving suit in dove-gray, sunglasses, her signature hair under a scarf. She looked carefully in both directions before closing the car door.

Sam slipped on his own sunglasses, went around the block in a different direction, and drove through the neighborhood until he reached her sister's street. Tabitha was almost to the house. He pulled into a driveway three houses down, cut the engine, waited.

Through his open window, he heard the bang of a screen door followed by the squeal of a child. The toddler—the boy he'd seen on his previous visit—ran across the browning lawn. Tabitha's sister, Betty Simpson, followed at a slower pace, shading her eyes against the sun as she waved.

They had the same grace, shared the same hue of hair, but Betty didn't have the same energy, the same *je ne sais quois*. She was a beautiful woman, but not in the way Tabitha was.

Tabitha crouched down, and the little boy launched himself into her arms. She laughed, a full-throated, beautiful, sparkling sound Sam had heard only a few times before, and he was gratified that at least twice, he'd drawn that sound from her.

Now, watching, he understood.

The hint of sadness in her eyes. And the only thing that could chase it away.

By the time he was on the descent out of the Tejon Pass toward Los Angeles, Sam knew what he had to do.

He gripped the steering wheel until his hands hurt, clenched his jaw until it ached. The sweat trickling from his armpits and down his back wasn't just from the heat of the midday sun beating down on the car.

Professional ethics be damned.

If he never worked again, well, that would be his penance.

It was all more important than that now.

When he got to LA, he drove straight to his bank, withdrew the amount the studio had paid him thus far. He winced when he saw the amount that was left. It would be a lean few months.

But his heart had made the decision, and had made his mind up for him.

Then he went to the studio, to the pink-stuccoed bungalows in the back lot, and sat down in front of Jack Webster's photo-strewn desk. Another day, another set of broken dreams.

Sam didn't take off his jacket, no matter the heat. As much as he wanted a drink, he refused Jack's offer of that fine whiskey.

"Word is you've gotten pretty close to our Tabby," Jack said, tapping his cigarette ash into a square, green glass ashtray. He squinted slightly, his gaze shrewd. "Not too close, I hope. Might not look good for a big star like Tabby to be getting too close with..."

...with a nobody like you, Sam guessed the unspoken words. He'd known he'd have to tread carefully so he didn't make an enemy today.

Besides, once Sam came clean to Tabitha, Jack wasn't going to have anything to worry about.

"Close enough to confess I haven't found a thing on her." Sam said. Jack's eyebrows rose. "She's a stand-up gal; if she's got a secret, then knock me over with a feather."

He reached into his jacket's inner pocket, set the envelope of cash on the desk atop the photos. Jack's eyebrows inched higher.

"It's all there, minus the expenses," Sam said. "Sorry I wasn't more help."

Jack set his cigarette in the ashtray. His eyes narrowed. He leaned forward and slowly pushed the envelope back to Sam's side of the desk.

"Keep it," he said. "Drop in a bucket for us, and I can't have anyone spreading rumors that the studio doesn't pay its bills, doesn't honor its contracts." He picked up his cigarette, breathed in, released the smoke so it curled around his face like a dragon's breath. "Besides," he said. "You did the legwork. If there's nothing to find, there's nothing to find."

Sam picked up the envelope, returned it to his pocket. Jack's expression hadn't changed, and Sam knew the implication beneath his words.

Not quite a threat, but close enough.

Jack stood, and Sam followed suit. He wasn't the least surprised when Jack didn't hold out his hand.

It would have taken everything he had not to wipe his own palm on his trousers if he'd shaken the studio executive's hand anyway.

Sam addressed the envelope, sealed it, went to the Post Office.

Then he went back to his apartment at the Ballington and waited for Tabitha St. Claire to call.

She did, a few days later, inviting him to dinner.

He drove his own car; he didn't have the money to hire a nicer one even if he'd wanted to. He wore an older suit. He thought about selling the expensive suits, the pricey shoes, but decided he might as well keep them in case a future job required them.

She met him at the door with a kiss. Her white cocktail dress, splashed with colorful flowers, had a nipped-in waist and a flowing skirt that swirled when she turned, and her hair was rolled up, exposing her neck. She smiled, but it was a tentative one, and he could still see that sadness in her eyes.

He knew she'd never be complete, not here in her big Hollywood mansion, when a piece of her heart was up in Bakersfield.

She took a step backward, maybe noticing his return peck hadn't been enthusiastic, and seemed to see him for the first time. The lower-end suit. The fact that he hadn't brought flowers.

Maybe, even, the look in his own eyes.

"Sam?" Her husky voice was hesitant. "It's...good to see you."

"You look beautiful," he said. He was here to tell the truth, and that, at least, was an easy truth.

"Thank you," she said. "Come in. Before supper...there's something I need to tell you."

She led him through the foyer, into the wide living room with its conversation areas. Beyond, the French doors were open onto the vast patio, and he saw a table had been set out there. Candles, waiting to be lit. Plates, waiting to be filled with food. An assortment of tulips in a glass vase.

Beyond, the sun was setting over the Pacific in heartbreakingly beautiful streaks of red and pink and orange.

They sat next to each other on a sofa, angled toward each other, not leaning back, not getting comfortable. She had something to tell him, and he suspected he knew what it was.

But he had things to tell her, too, things that he guessed wouldn't lead to a romantic dinner on the patio.

Still, he took her hand. Despite the lingering heat of the day, her flesh was cold.

"I need to tell you something," she repeated. "Something almost no one else knows. I...it's a secret, but...I can trust you to keep a secret, can't I, Sam?"

If only she knew. "Of course," he said. He didn't say "sweetheart." He wanted to, so desperately, but the word caught in his throat.

"Three and a half years ago," she said, "I made a mistake. I thought I was in love, but I wasn't, not really. I guess...I suppose I just wanted to be. Loved. I trusted someone I shouldn't have, and... Well." She shook her head ruefully. "Well, I'm rambling, aren't I?"

The grip of her cold fingers tightened. "The thing is, Sam, I have a child. The sweetest little boy you ever did see. I named him Charlie, after my father. But Charlie, he lives in Bakersfield with my sister—everyone believes Charlie's hers, and we need it to be that way." Her words were coming out in a rush, so fast that he couldn't break in. "The studio—the studio wouldn't understand. They own me, Sam, and a child would change my reputation, and I'd lose work. I'd lose everything. I don't know what else I'd do. I love Charlie beyond anything, and this is how I pay for him to live, but he needs to be a secret, Sam. I can trust you with this secret, right? I can, can't I?"

Sam closed his eyes, tried to find some sort of composure, balance. When he opened them again, the fear in Tabitha's ocean eyes struck him like a dagger to the heart.

He squeezed her hand, but wondered if her fingers were so numb she didn't even feel it.

"You can trust me to keep your secret," he said. "But I need to tell you I have secrets of my own. Sweetheart"—it broke out, cutting him on the way—"I know about Charlie. I...I was there on Tuesday."

Her eyes widened. She drew in a deep breath, then froze, an alabaster statue. Her chin rose, ever so slightly. In another moment, he might have admired the graceful length of her neck.

Her lips parted, but she couldn't seem to form words. He used the silence to continue.

To tell her how the studio had hired him.

To tell her how he'd fallen for her.

To tell her...

"I quit," he said. "Tuesday, when I got back. I told them I'd found nothing about you, and I tried to give them back their money, but they wouldn't take it. I sent it to your sister, anonymously. Every penny. For Charlie."

She looked down, away, anywhere but at him. Her fingers loosened in his, but he didn't let go. Couldn't let go, not yet.

"No one will ever know from me," he said. "I'll take it to my grave, I will."

Finally, her gaze rose to meet his again. The sea in her eyes was stormy with emotion.

"So all of this"—she gestured vaguely with her free hand—"was a lie? A ruse? You were hired to get close to me?"

"No," he said, shaking his head. "I was hired to find out if you were hiding something, but I fell for you all on my own. That part, that's real. As real as anything."

She made a noise, a sort of cross between a huff and a sob. He let go of her hand. Her fingers slipped away, and he ached from the loss of her touch.

She stood. He did the same, drawn upward as if by unseen strings.

She faced away, out at the dying sun, then turned to him. "I love you, Sam Belmont," she said. "And if that's my mistake, well, I've learned that not all mistakes are entirely bad. I trust you'll keep quiet about Charlie. With all my heart, I do."

"But," he said. Expecting. Knowing.

"But," she said, "secrets do nothing but cause pain. The studio won't accept Charlie in my life, and the studio won't accept you, either. I can't keep you both secret. I just don't have the strength for that."

"I know," he said. "I love you, sweetheart, and that's why I'm walking away."

When she raised her hand to cup her palm against his face, her fingers trembled, and her eyes trembled with unshed tears.

"If you ever need anything..." he said.

"I know," she said. "Thank you."

He didn't feel he deserved her gratitude, but he accepted her touch. He took her hand in his, pressed a kiss on her palm, then turned and walked out of her life.

He got in his car, drove to a liquor store on Wilshire Boulevard just down the street from the Ballington, and bought a bottle of whiskey. Not the high-end kind, but not the cheapest, either.

Then he went home and spent the next few days with that bottle. Allowed himself that escape.

He expected it was the last time he'd see Tabitha St. Claire, except on a movie screen, distant and untouchable.

He was wrong.

Six months later, Tabitha St. Claire came knocking on the door of Sam's office.

His office was the front room of his space at the Ballington Hotel and Apartments. He didn't need much, so he'd turned the living room into an office, and kept his personal stuff in the bedroom, sharing a bathroom down the hall. The address gave his business a certain cachet, and he didn't have to pay two rents.

His best furniture was in the office: a sturdy wooden desk and filing cabinets, comfortable chairs, and the newest typewriter he could afford.

The door opened and there she was, swathed in a scarf and sunglasses. Best that she not be seen soliciting the services of a private detective, of course.

He was stunned to see her. He managed to get to his feet, but for once, words failed him. And then she said,

"I trusted you, Sam Belmont. How could you?"

He choked the words out. "How could I what?"

"They know," she said, and her voice quavered, and he knew

that behind those sunglasses, her aqua eyes were filled with tears. "Somehow, they know."

"They don't know," he said, catching himself before he added "sweetheart," which would have been so easy, so natural. So painful. "If they knew, it'd be in the papers."

She shook her head. "It's more devious than that. You know what they're offering me now? The role of the mother. Or the friend. Or the secretary. No more headliners. Plus, Esther and Lev Miller didn't invite me to their anniversary party." She slapped a pale hand down on his desk. "That's just the tip of it. It doesn't have to be in the papers. They know, and that's the end of my career."

"It wasn't me," he protested. "I told no one."

"Well," she spat, "*someone* did. I've kept a close eye, and I haven't seen anyone around, anyone digging. If, as you say, it wasn't you, feel free to investigate who it might have been, Mr. Belmont." Her chin went up. "If you find proof—real proof— you're welcome to let me know."

Sam never found conclusive truth. He suspected a so-called friend of hers, a jealous actress, but never gathered enough proof.

Hollywood history would detail the rest.

After a declining popularity at the box office, Tabitha St. Claire's party invitations dropped off, too. Attendance at her parties slowly declined, although some people probably still came out of curiosity.

Then she scheduled her own birthday party.

It was to be a lavish affair, the kind that Hollywood had never seen. Dramatic, over-the-top. The place to be seen.

Or not.

The RSVPs were almost non-existent.

And then she learned Joan DeForest—the actress who'd essentially taken her place, had been given the roles she would have won—was holding a party on the same night. Because at the last minute, she'd been issued an invitation.

An obvious afterthought. Out of pity.

Tabitha St. Claire put on her most stunning satin gown, the last of her glittering, sumptuous diamonds. She ensured her hair and makeup were exquisite. She arrived in a limousine.

She swept in, called everyone to her...

...and dropped dead at their feet.

Hollywood history would be more sketchy about Sam's life. Three years later, he would be shot through the heart by a man suspecting him of sleeping with the man's wife—when, in fact, he had been hired by the woman to determine whether her husband was cheating on her.

Sam Belmont, however, would not go easy into the night.

At which time he discovered, neither had Tabitha St. Claire.

Death, Sam learned, gave you more options than you might think. Well, two: stay, or go.

Most folks chose to go. There was someone waiting for them on the other side.

Sam didn't have family, hadn't been close to anyone, really. He liked his space at the Ballington; for all its seedy underbelly, he loved Hollywood.

So he watched the Ballington decline, and then have a resurrection in the 1980s, when music producers, screenwriters, and others turned the place into a bohemian, creative space. Then the bubble burst, and the historic hotel teetered on the brink of demolition, until a former Hollywood party girl on the skids, who had an affinity for old buildings, bought the place.

Nikki Ashburne didn't just have an affinity for historic properties. She had a secret.

She could see ghosts.

So she met Sam and the other ghosts who called the Ballington their home. Janie, a flapper and rumrunner, the first one he'd met after he'd died. Marla, perpetually stoned and maybe one of Jim Morrison's girlfriends. Curtis, a friend of the Coreys in the 1980s.

Sam, along with the rest of them, agreed to be a part of her ghost tour of Hollywood. But he still kept his cards close to his chest.

He kept Nikki's secret as tightly as he kept the rest.

Until the day Nikki Ashburne came to him and asked him about Tabitha St. Claire.

Tabitha, who hadn't moved on, either.

The parlor in the Ballington was stunning; Nikki had done an excellent job with the renovation. The walls were dark red above polished bead board, and there was a stunning carved fireplace along with a settee she'd rescued from an alley and had refinished. The books on the built-in shelves had been carefully sought out through months of lurking in quality used bookshops.

A crystal decanter of whisky and a set of eight matching glasses were arranged on a cherrywood sideboard covered with antique lace.

Bless her, she poured him a drink before cutting to the chase.

Nikki was short and curvy, with a curly blond bob that spoke more to the 1920s than modern day. She was, for Sam, a breath of fresh air: brash, opinionated, confident. He saw her as something of a daughter, in a way.

Now, Nikki needed information about Tabitha.

He didn't want to relive this, not again. The glass was cool and wet against his fingers. He mostly existed in a liminal state; he had to focus to be corporeal. He wanted to shimmer away. Avoid the whole situation.

But he didn't. He owed Tabitha more than that.

He'd known fairly quickly after his own death that she had lingered as well. There weren't that many ghosts in Hollywood, all things told. He knew Tabitha spent her time haunting lavish parties, reliving her heyday.

And he'd stayed away.

He started by explaining how, back in the day, the studio owned you, but Nikki cut him off with a wave of her Cosmo. "Thank you for the history lesson, but you're stalling."

"Is it that obvious?" His tone was rueful.

"Yes. Let me get you another drink."

She poured another whisky for him, and he knocked back another hefty swallow before explaining what he'd been hired to do, and how it had gone all wrong.

"I tried to find out who'd leaked the secret, but I never did," Sam said. "I think it was one of her so-called friends. After all these years, I've wondered if it was Joan DeForest. But without proof, Tabitha would never have believed me about that, either. The whole thing may have had something to do with her death; I just can't prove that, either."

"What happened to her son?" Nikki wondered aloud.

"I sent Tabitha's sister an anonymous donation," Sam said. "Everything the studio had paid me. If it hadn't been for me, maybe nobody would have found out. I don't know if someone followed me or retraced my steps. After Tabby died, I sent more money, but it was returned. They'd moved and hadn't left a forwarding address."

"They were probably benefactors of her estate, weren't they?" Nikki asked.

"No doubt," he said. "But I still felt I should do something."

"You know what?" Nikki said. "Let's find out what happened to him. You, me, and the magical power of the Internet."

He found himself smiling then, for the first time in a long time. "I'd like that," he said. "And if Tabby has to come here so you can talk to her, I'll stay out of the way, okay? You tell her that —she doesn't have to worry about seeing my face."

"That's won't be necessary," said a new voice. A sexy, husky one.

A voice that hit him hard in the pit of his stomach, harder than the bullet that had taken his life, and infinitely more painful.

Tabitha St. Claire had come to the Ballington.

Sam nearly lost his corporeality, unsure if he was trying to decide whether to stay or go.

She was as beautiful as he remembered, and it made his heart ache. Even if he didn't technically have a heart anymore.

She wore a stunning mint-green satin halter dress, a diamond choker clasped around her throat. Her long chestnut hair was carefully formed into waves, with a diamond comb tucked in, glittering in the light.

She came over to him, and he rose from his seat, whisky forgotten, everything forgotten but the memory of her brought back in front of him.

She held out her hand, and he took it. For this moment, both of them fully corporeal, no matter how hard it was to maintain.

"Don't leave," Tabitha said to him. "I heard what you said. We...have so much to talk about. After Nikki and I talk."

"I didn't tell," he said, his voice catching, so unlike him. "I need you to believe that."

"I do," she said. "No more secrets," she said.

It had always been a bad idea, but he didn't care. "No more secrets," he agreed.

TWICE TOLD TALES

LOREN L. COLEMAN

We move from two very soft fantasy love stories with just a hint of magic to a much more traditional fantasy, complete with heroic knight, virtuous maiden, and a dragon. Or so it would seem...

Loren L. Coleman has written BattleTech, MechWarrior, and Conan novels, as well as many original short stories. He's a co-owner of Catalyst Game Labs, and supervises all kinds of properties, including games, novels, and anthologies. To find out more, go to lorenlcoleman.com.

In recent years, Loren has decided to revive his writing career. In 2020, he published his first novel in a while, Three Wishes. *He used the challenge of writing a story for* Chances *to get him back into the writing fold. "Twice-Told Tales" is an auspicious start to the second half of Loren's writing life.*

The ringing clash of swords shattered the afternoon's peace, and William rode into the ambush exactly on cue.

Dragon's Glade was an overshadowed meadow of tall, thin grasses and stunted heather. A sullen, muddy brook cut it near perfectly in half, skulking past the single oak which bore carvings of twenty generations of the kingdom's offerings to Vlarr the Terrible, the great wyrm of Undermountain. On the far side of the brook the princess' escorts, two of the King's Finest, fought afoot against three times their numbers of black-garbed cultists. Standing back to back, great sweeping arcs from the knights' silvered broadswords kept their attackers at a good length. Their heavy armor turned a number of weak thrusts, though Sir Thomas' left leg showed a thin trickle of scarlet where one of his opponent's blades had pinked him.

On the near side of the clearing, Princess Clementine fought for control of her horse against another pair of attackers. Barely eighteen, only a year shy of William's age, the daughter of King

Athelstan wore full leathers instead of a lady's riding gown. Her raven-black hair was pulled back into a severe braid, allowing her anger and fear to show in the flush along her neck, her cheeks. She sawed hard against the reins but to little effect. One of Vlarr's cultists had his hand firmly into the mare's bridle, twisting down and back in an experienced hold. The other slapped at the princess' riding boot as she lashed out trying to kick in the side of his head.

William reined in hard at Clementine's side, his dappled gray pitching forward. William had almost no tack, just bit, bridle and reins, but his legs clamped against the gray's barrel in a strong grip and he leaned far back to prevent being thrown over the animal's head. Before the horse had come to a full stop he was already sliding down from its broad back, and managed to catch the second cultist with a kick in the side of his shoulder.

The man tumbled awkwardly to one side. William spun, slapped his horse's rump, and the startled beast bolted forward. The brigand bounced off the horse's shoulder and rolled hard into a clump of purple heather.

"William!" Sir Thomas shouted. "Get the princess out of here!"

That was the plan, wasn't it?

The cultist had a choice. Release control of the princess' mare, or take on William with only one hand. There was no winning answer. William clapped his hands roughly against his opponent's head, over the ears, then kicked hard up between the man's legs. That dropped the cultist easily enough. Then it was the work of a few heartbeats to grab the side of Clementine's saddle and vault himself up behind her.

Reaching around her slender waist, William seized her reins in one hand and a good grip on the forward edge of her saddle with the other. With a kick and a yell he pushed her mare into an immediate gallop, storming across the meadow to lose themselves into the thick, thick forest.

A half mile along the trails, including a couple of sharp turns to throw off any pursuit, William relaxed the mare back into an easy walk. He continued to hold the reins in his left hand. His right had found its way to the princess' waist.

Breathless, Clementine leaned back into his embrace.

"It was fortune itself that you came along when you did, my ranger."

William exhaled long and hard, releasing tension from their escape and the wild race through the woods. "I think it's easier when you slip your guards and sneak from the castle unnoticed." He frowned against the side of her face. "Though I supposed today, without Sir Thomas and Sir Stephen, I would have been tragically late."

"Father has doubled my *guard*." Her voice grew soft. Scared. "The sacrifice to Vlarr is only a few weeks away. I believe they begin to doubt my conviction."

By the dragon's beard, William would hope so. Clementine was no soft daughter of the royal family, born to privilege and the honor of marrying well to expand the kingdom's domain and wealth. She had been raised as this generation's sacrifice to the great dragon, Vlarr the Terrible; the Terrifying; the Hunger of Undermountain. Under that pressure, she had grown wild and eager for a full life that would end ceremoniously after her eighteenth birthday. It was one of many reasons she and William had grown so close so quickly, but there was still the very real problem that she was royalty and he was not much more than a local boy of good legend but common birth.

It made for a fine story, but so far the king was not impressed.

"You've already given so much to those around you," William whispered into her ear. "Inspiration. Hope. No matter what you decide, I am here for you."

"And I'm glad." She melted back into him, soft and warm and very, very alive in his arms. Then, "Take me to the Tower. Today. Now. There may not be another chance. The dragon's cult grows more bold in their attempts to stop the sacrifice and raise their dark god. Father may put me under lock and key until the Virgin's Eve. Let us be together. It's the one regret I would carry with me to my death."

"You know that is the one thing I should not—cannot!—do." William felt a flush rise along the back of his neck as his tongue slipped. It warmed his ears, his cheeks...and other regions not to be mentioned in polite company. "You must be pure of body and thought on The Eve."

Craning her head back, she kissed the edge of his chin. "My thoughts have never been pure when it comes to you."

"Well, let's hope the legend is a bit looser on those requirements."

Clementine laughed. William always marveled how she could find such moments of joy and happiness in a life lived under the pall of Vlarr's legend. She twisted around in the saddle, until they faced each other from mere inches away.

"You make me happy, my ranger. Let me bring you to Father. Let him reward you as he should have before today. My champion."

William swallowed dryly. Desire burned warmly within him, and not without cause, but he wasn't so certain the king would be as generous as his daughter described him.

"I cannot," William finally said. "I should search the forest trails for some clue to the cult's location. And there is Sir Thomas and Sir Stephen. If they won through, I will help them locate their horses. If they did not, I shall bring their bodies back for an honorable burial. It would be unseemly to accept praise or reward while their fates are unknown."

She laid a hand alongside his face. It was warm, warm.

"Always the proper champion. Very well. But you will call on my father soon. I demand it, my William."

He bent forward, and laid a chaste kiss upon her soft, soft lips.

"As my love requests, of course."

Leaving Clementine near the edge of the woods—a short, safe ride back to her father's castle—William backtracked his own trail toward Dragon's Glade. His thighs ached from the bare-backed riding and his ankle throbbed where he'd twisted it dismounting so roughly in the glade. He limped along, and despite his legend as a woodsman and apprentice ranger he checked each shadowed trail crossing for the tiny strip of cloth he'd tied the day before to mark the correct path.

It was two lefts and some moments later when he turned around a bend in the wide riding trail and came face to face with the eight cultists of Vlarr.

Each wore black tunics and the red sash which had come to be known in only the last generation as the dragon's emblem. Thin, black cotton wrapped about their heads, allowing only their eyes to show, protected them from recognition. Their swords were in hand—a good safety precaution this late in the day, on trails so close to town.

The first two men merely nodded at William as they traipsed by him. The third limped along, rubbing hard against the muscle high and inside his left thigh. His dark eyes stared an accusation.

"Would you rather I had aimed higher?" William asked.

The other man shook his head. Mumbled, "Forget it." and trudged onward.

Eight cultists. And then came Sir Thomas and Sir Stephen, leading their horses and William's.

Sir Stephen embraced William like a brother, because they were, even if William was born on the bastard side of the sheets.

"Well done," he greeted his younger sibling. "Would have fooled me."

"The village idiot on a three-day bender could fool you," Sir Thomas groused, limping past. He tipped William a sly wink. "But I think the princess bought it."

"Did she?" Stephen asked.

William shrugged with exaggeration, then smiled. "It's in the bag," he promised, but a twinge of conscience assailed him as he accepted his horse's reins and took up station following the line back to town.

It was one thing to sell a story someone had been raised their whole life to believe, he knew.

The real difficulty came later. When the story had to sell itself

---

Vlarr's "lair" under Mt. Cauldron passed though a wide, steaming vent at the base of a sheer cliff face. Holding a flaming brand, William sidestepped through a fissure, wedging himself through the sharp-edged entryway. He stepped into an ancient cavern that tunneled its way back into the bowels of the mountain, smooth and wide and very, very long. Here it was cold and dry. No "sign" of the dragon.

From the depths of the mountain came a deafening, grating roar that stood upright the small hairs on the back of his neck.

"Yeah yeah," he called out, listening to his voice echo off into the blackness. "Very funny."

According to legend, the great dragon bided its years consuming the "bones of the mountains" deep, deep underground, belching up fire and brimstone on those rare occasions he tunneled up near the surface. Every year or two the earth would shake, and sometimes the ground cracked open in a new place glowing with a red-orange intensity that sent local villages to prayers and local knights to parade about the kingdom in an effort to calm any hysteria.

Vlarr was not coming early, they promised. The pact still held.

William remembered, as a child, joining a large group of boys on a dare. Hiking within sight of the steaming fissure. Only seven of them left the cover of the woods to approach the mountainside. Half a mile, one cautious step after another with one eye on the sky at all times as if the dragon might swoop down at any second. Every hundred paces or so one of them chickened out and raced back for the trees. Only William dared to hike in close enough to throw a rock over the edge, hearing it rattle and crash down the sharp, severe drop.

That was the first time he'd heard the dragon's terrifying roar, bursting out of the fissure as if disturbed by the rock William had thrown.

He had wet himself, then run full tilt back to the woods where his "friends" were long gone. He curled into the roots of an ancient oak to recover his breathing and pray to any god listening that the pact would hold, please merciful stars let it hold.

It was a memory he could laugh at now. A little.

Fifty paces in, William stepped past the flared bell of an enormous horn. The mouth of the bell was taller than he was, sloping slowly back into a long, long funnel supported by a wooden cradle. It ended where the tunnel poured into a large underground amphitheater lit by dozens of flaming brands. William crouched down to inspect the beginning of the horn. A hinge of wrought iron metal covered in flakes of rust—easily scavenged off any gated fence in the kingdom—was mounted into the massive instrument's delicate mouth. Twist the metal pieces, and on this end there was a nerve-pinching shriek of tortured, rusted metal.

Outside, the rest of the world heard Vlarr.

"Still scaring the local boys with this little trick?" William asked.

Maer Linn, the king's administrator over one of the many local townships, sat at a heavy table of raw, unfinished oak, packing black tar-like paste down into ceramic pots. There were stools enough for a dozen men at the round worktable, but he sat alone and in a great deal of shadow, far from any of the small torches, his hands and arms and part of his face smeared with the sticky paste. When applied to flame, the pots would burn long and deep, producing a sooty, black smoke which (at the Virgin's Eve) would herald the "arrival" of Vlarr.

"Every time the little bastards stick their nose out of the woods," he said. "Every time."

"It's effective." William cradled his brand in a sconce far from the oaken table, then slumped onto a nearby stool, watched as the maer continued the dragon's work. Waiting.

Finally, Linn paused between smoke pots and glanced sidelong at William. "Well?" he asked.

William broke into a lop-sided smile. "That should be, *Well, Sir William?*" he said.

Linn grunted. "'Bout time you got the old man to pony up. Time's getting short." But he gave William a single nod, regardless "Stephen said you hit your marks just about perfect. Grady says he owes you a kick between the legs, but he'll forgive you so long as it all goes smooth on the Eve."

With Sir Stephen as the newly-named Champion, it should go well enough. So long as the princess was ready for her part.

"Yea. About that." William shifted uneasily on the stool. "I'm getting worried about Clementine. She hasn't tried to bolt—not once. Not like we thought she would."

"Like *you* thought she would." The local maer was not known for pulling punches, whether enforcing the king's will or subverting it. "I told you months ago, better to get her in a family way. It's a surer bet."

"She's not some doe-eyed school girl, Maer. She's the king's daughter. I'd have had to force her, and that's a wild card we didn't want to play. Remember?"

Maer Linn slammed down the smoke pot, cracking its shell. "I remember you going sweet on the girl! Slow played the whole heroic-damn-tale the group spent years building around you. Now we've got no time left and you haven't set the hook." He rubbed a black-tarred arm across his mouth. Spat. "I should've taken you to the whores years ago. I just thought you'd play the script better if it was all fresh and new to you as well."

A flush warmed William's face. "The script is the problem. It's gotten too complicated. First it was treasure that kept the dragon sated. Then someone added a virgin sacrifice. Now, the last four generations, it's royal blood, with a champion. Then *you* had to go and invent the cult of Vlarr to step up pressure. Whatever happened to the rule: Keep It Simple, Suckers?"

"You run the same story more than once, you have to embellish. Keeps the tale fresh and everyone focused." The maer snatched up a nearby rag and aggressively scrubbed paste from his hands, his arms. Once he'd calmed some, "Look. This has worked for twenty-one generations. The king will bejewel his doomed daughter with enough of his treasury to keep us all living large for another twenty years. Our champion is in place, and the festival is being prepared. Our only weak spot is the girl. You have to deliver!"

William nodded, but without confidence. "Clementine loves life. Just as bold as you please. But what if she refuses to be rescued?"

"She can't."

"But what if she does? If she faces this with no regrets, and we lose our leverage? She'll want to go home."

Maer Linn stared at William a moment, then turned back to his worktable and began packing a new ceramic pot full of tarry sludge.

William watched him, for a time, then nodded as he slipped from the stool and reclaimed his brand from its cradle. It was what he had been afraid of all along.

His princess wouldn't be allowed to ruin the story.

No one would.

Twilight fell as William paced the observatory atop Champion's Tower, careful of the soft, spongey wood below the eastern wall where water rot had done its damage. He wore simple breeches and a fresh-laundered tunic—his armor already removed and in a pile atop a stone bench. The observatory smelled of damp wood and old stone, and pigeon dung from the aerie on the floor above. It had a gray flagstone hearth on which he'd built a small, smokeless fire to warm the room, and he'd unshuttered the windows to air the place out while waiting for Clementine. Who was late. Again.

Princesses!

The tower sat halfway between Dragon's Glade and Vlarr's mountain; a lonely spire thrusting up from the forest like some sentinel of old. Gray stone and black wrought iron. Crenelated works that had weathered poorly over the last several generations until it looked like "the old guy has lost some teeth," or so the *cult* liked to say. King Atheltsan's great-great-grandfather built the Tower to commemorate his daughter's champion, chosen from among the King's Finest, who had "faced" Vlarr alongside the first royal sacrifice. The tower had been kept up for a single generation, but yesterday's heroes are oft forgotten and the treasury was not infinite. Plus, the knights themselves were sworn to poverty. At least in the eyes of the citizens. Such that now the tower was little better than an old landmark. A monument to the kingdom's better times.

If there had ever been any.

Above the forest canopy, William heard Clementine's arrival only by the faint echo of hooves as she rode directly into the base which would double, tonight, as a stable. There was no taking the time to close the heavily-reinforced door. Just the sound of the princess' hurried feet against the Tower's winding stone staircase.

This was it, then. The night she'd asked for and he'd finally acceded to with a strange mixture of heady anticipation and dread.

It had been easier, in the early years, in stolen moments and short rendezvous. "Chance" encounters, easily arranged and well-chaperoned at first. The shared conversations which grew between the apprentice ranger and the dragon-cursed princess, where eventually they spoke openly of oh-what-could-have-been. She had been the first to use the word "love." (Exactly on script.) And it was she who had stolen the first kiss between them. (Which wasn't.)

William stood in the center of the room staring up at the ceiling. This was where *the hook* would happen, trading his feigned honor for that of Princess Clementine's, freely given. The common boy laying with royalty. *Lying with royalty*. He should have been scared. He should have been eager with anticipation. Instead, he felt like a cad, even as Clementine rushed to his arms, already...

Crying?

Her sobs were loud and pained, coming between deep hitches in her breath as she raced up the final flight of steps. William moved toward the head of the stairs, and was met with great force as his princess rushed into the observatory and threw herself into his arms. Hair in tangled disarray. Her bodice tore along her right shoulder and the sleeve completely ripped away to hang in tatters along her side. Only a small scrap of cloth covered her breasts, which she carelessly held in place with all the modesty of a terrified woman.

"William! Thank the heavens, William!"

Her arms encircled him as she kissed his neck and face with desperate strength. A drowning woman, grasping a lifeline. Any lifeline.

Still reeling from her disheveled appearance, William had a distant awareness of both her hands on his back and her bodice falling open to reveal the womanhood now pressed against him in cringing terror. His earlier image of her, with wanton needs, now replaced with frightened vulnerability.

"Clementine! What happened? Who did this?"

"Cultists," she sobbed into his neck. "Oh, William. They found me. They chased me! They tried...they tried..." There were sounds of boots—many, heavy boots—against the tower stairs. "They have found us! This is the end!"

This was not on script.

What the maer thought he was doing, sending out a party to harass the princess on this night above all others—and then not telling *William* about it—was outrageous. And even so, the cultists had gone too far. There would be hell to pay come the morrow!

First, however, he had to defend Clementine's honor. Again. He pushed her behind him and she stumbled toward the hearth, falling to the ground but catching herself at the last moment. He stepped up to the stone table. No time to replace his armor, he ripped his sword free of its scabbard and turned to the stairs, prepared to "fight" their way free of the Tower.

Except that it wasn't "cultists" of Vlarr rushing into the observatory.

It was King Athelstan. Flanked by four of the King's Finest. All with weapons drawn.

"Father!" Clementine shouted in relief.

Of course, in relief. She had been terrorized and terrified. But William also saw the flash of confusion—then anger—in the king's eyes. Read the drop-jawed terror on Sir Thomas, and the naked rage of the other three knights. He saw himself, as they must see him now: having doffed his own armor, now standing over the king's half-naked and sobbing daughter while threatening the king himself with the blade bestowed upon *Sir* William not a week before.

Rule number two: know when you're beat.

Without hesitation William reversed his blade and stabbed it down into the flooring where it bit in and stuck. He stepped back, hands at his sides, trusting the sovereign to remember enough control to not kill an unarmed and surrendered man.

"This is not...Sire! You cannot believe...Clementine, for pity's sake, tell him!" But when he risked a glance, he saw that no help would be forthcoming.

The princess had swooned into a faint, collapsing upon the observatory's floor. She lay on her side, long, raven hair spilled down over her bared breast.

Leaving him alone, impaled on his own hook, and the script of his legend in tatters.

Being named a knight, even if not one of the King's Finest—not yet—brought certain advantages. William was not required to wait for the king's convenience in the stocks or the dungeons. He spent the week confined to his room or praying in the chapel. And when he was finally summoned, it was not in irons and fetters but free to walk upright and face his sovereign as a man if not exactly an equal.

Waiting in the king's study also gave William a spot of hope. Had the king decided to condemn him, Athelstan would have done so publicly and with the immediate option for William to demand trial by arms. Not that he should expect to prevail, so unused to armor and the long blade, unless he drew Sir Stephen or Sir Thomas by lot and they could script out a dramatic contest. No. The king's study meant a private audience and private justice. Which meant that Clementine must have recovered and spoke up for him.

Pages opened both doors at the far end of the room, and King Athelstan strode in with a determined gait. His white beard was closely trimmed and his eyes clear. He still had a strength in his shoulders, although it had been decades since his last campaign. A strong man who had seen his younger sister sacrificed to the dragon and had not hesitated to prepare his own daughter for the ultimate service to his realm.

Sir Stephen walked at his majesty's right shoulder. Another of the King's Finest, Sir Hector, his left. Neither knight looked happy. In fact, his half-brother was swallowing back extreme anger. Not good.

The two knights took up flanking positions on William, in case they needed to subdue him. Also not good.

Athelstan's gaze was stormy and his nod to William's bow was terse. Rather than take a seat, he stood behind his table and glowered at the young knight.

"My daughter's memory of the night in question is...incomplete." He ground out each word between clenched teeth. "She assures me, however, that, knowing you as she does, she finds it difficult to believe that you would...comport yourself in the way in which it appeared."

Difficult, not impossible, that the princess' friend would attack her. Not exactly how he would have written the endorsement.

"Sire. My statement remains true and unblemished. Your

daughter was attacked but not by me. I would never raise my hand against her or against you."

That was walking a line and William knew it. No man sat so long on the throne without the ability to read people. But William was new and rightfully afraid. He hoped that would cover a great deal.

"You would not raise a hand to my daughter?" Athelstan asked.

"No, Sire."

"At least, not in anger?"

Okay, now William couldn't be certain how much the princess had told her father. Taking liberties with the royal family might also be construed as an act against the throne.

"Your daughter remains pure of body in my presence," William said with absolute conviction. Fortunately, he was still able to say that. "I love her as my friend and as my sovereign's daughter. And that will be even more true after the Virgin's Eve."

"I want to believe you, Sir William. I truly do." The king shook his head, and there was doubt in his eyes for the first time. "I'd like to believe you were caught up in strange and bizarre circumstance. I even considered allowing you to prove yourself in trial by arms. But then I began to worry whom I might doubt, should you prevail. My daughter? Another of my Best? Such is the fragile line between love and terror, that I find myself in the untenable position of being *forced* to believe you but needing you to pay service for what may have happened. Therefore, I have decided. And what I have decided amounts to a sentence of certain death, sir knight."

William tried to keep his back straight and his eyes level. If he would meet his end, it would be as a man. He could not help, however, the defeated slump in his shoulders. Truly, he did deserve a sentence of death. Not for what had happened, but for what would have happened without the unscripted assault. He had betrayed the king, yes. All right. Worse, though, he had betrayed his true feelings for Clementine.

"I understand and accept your judgment, Sire."

Athelstan nodded. Once. Decisively. "Then I suggest you find the chapel and summon your courage, Sir William. Because two nights hence, you will face Vlarr as my daughter's champion. And I do not expect either of you to return."

Of course he'd...wait...What?

Black, sooty smoke blanketed Mt Cauldron; drifted about the rocky fields in low-hanging clouds.

Two thousand witnesses cowered at the edge of the woods. They would never see much, half a mile from the base of the mountain, William knew. Smoke. Some falling rocks. A gout of flame, perhaps, if Maer Linn's black powder magic was concentrated enough.

Several hundred villagers braved the field of beaten earth which had been arranged for them not an arrow's distance from the steaming fissure. Braved the field or, William saw, had been pushed forward. Most of them stood about giant bonfires, singing tribute to the great wyrm, Vlarr. Many of them gripped talismans for luck, or safety.

All of them were pretty drunk on the King's best ale.

One hundred knights marched out under command of Athelstan, approaching the dragon's lair without hesitation or (sign of) fear. Not even when the first, screeching roar bellowed forth did they lose a step. They paused only at the king's command, about as near to the Undermountain vent as William had stood on that day long, long ago, when he'd thrown the rock that had (unkowingly) begun his rise to legend. William now stood strong at Clementine's side, offering her an arm to steady her as the knights paraded by her, one by one, thanking the princess for her strength and her sacrifice. A few even offered William their prayers and belief that he would be the first to defeat the terrible wyrm.

He appreciated the gesture.

Sir Stephen was last, save the king, to pay his respects. Grief drew down his gaze as he clasped hands with his brother. Of course it did. William wore armor plated in heavy gold. His shield: pure silver polished to a mirror-like finish. And his sword, a piece of the finest steel with an edge sharp enough for shaving, was encrusted with a kingdom's ransom in diamonds and rubies. Melted down and fenced, the "Champion's tithe" would have set Stephen up for life as a traveling noble. Traveling far, far away, of course.

If the wealth carried by William was exquisite, Clementine's was nothing short of divine. Seventeen years of preparation had gone into her gown of cloth-of-gold. Sapphires and emeralds ran down each heavy pleat. Diamonds studded her belt and her gloves. She wore heavy bracelets, a heavy, gem-set necklace, and carried a scepter crowned by one of the largest, most perfect opals anyone had ever seen. She stared straight ahead, as if in a daze, waiting for her father to lean in and give her a single, brief kiss on the center of her forehead.

There, she caught his eye.

"Believe in us," William heard her whisper.

It all but undid the king, who bowed for the first and last time to another person as he bid his daughter a final goodbye.

Twelve knights detached themselves from the parade. The King's Finest. In a line, they escorted the princess and her champion to the edge of the fissure. Dark, sooty smoke drifted around them in a haze. Another rusty, grating bellow and an eruption of flame shot skyward, the backwash of heat almost certainly felt as far back as the singing crowd. Against William's face, it felt strong enough to begin melting the gold on his armor. The Finest stumbled to a ragged halt, finally losing a small measure of the bearing.

William glanced at Clementine by his side. If she lost control now, things could still end badly. But she faced the fire with stoic patience and then nodded him forward.

"After you, my love."

Rigid and weary, William shuffled to the edge of the fissure. Wearing so much wealth, it was hard to move in any other fashion. He stared down into the steaming vent, counted to five, and then stumbled back a few paces as another gout of flame erupted in his face.

Behind him there were screams and the sound of running feet. Rocks shifted and rolled down the nearby mountainside, adding the thunder of a small avalanche to the chaos. William did not need to see a "cultist" to know they were there, lighting off smoke pots and starting new rocks crashing down the side of Mt Cauldron. He trusted the script, set his shield, and stepped onto the narrow trail which would carry him to the bottom of the fissure.

Clementine followed.

The sulfurous, sweaty air nearly cooked William alive before they reached the bottom of the vent. No way would he fit through the broken-edged rock, not in the bulky armor he wore, but Maer Linn had provided with a huge boulder rolled aside to reveal their once-in-a-generation access to the ancient cavern. A single brand lit the way. Pulling Clementine with him, William ducked into the cool, dry embrace of Undermountain as, behind them, the largest flames yet exploded in the fissure and roiled upward to the raging bellow of the terrible Vlarr.

Under cover of the massive gout of flame, a hidden mechanism rolled the boulder back into place behind them. And as the echoes of the dragon's roar faded, Clementine covered her ears and shook the sound from her head.

"Sweet heavens that's loud. You will have to show me how you do that."

Uh…"If we hurry," William said, sticking to the script, "we might find a way for you to escape your fate." He nodded up the ancient cavern, away from Maer Linn's workshop, where some "concerned citizens of the realm" would find her, help spirit her away. She'd be lost to William forever. He felt his stomach drop. "I'll do my best by you, until the dragon takes me."

"The exit is that direction?" The princess turned, and looked deeper in the mountain. She grabbed the nearby brand. "So this way to Vlarr." Hiking up her gown with her free hand, she plunged forward with her father's deliberate stride.

Aren't you…you are…wait!" He ran after her in a clumsy, bow-legged gate, the plates of his armor rattling noisily. "Why aren't you—"

"Afraid?" she asked. She stopped in front of the large bell of Vlarr's horn, studied it with bright-eyed glee, and laughed a single note of merriment. Then she spun, rose on her toes, and managed to plant a hard kiss on William's mouth before continuing. "Oh, my dear sweet William. You are many things, but an accomplished liar isn't one of them. If I hadn't sold those *assaults* to my father, we'd both be in big trouble. Now hurry along!"

William barely managed to catch up and enter the cavern of Undermountain at Clementine's side. Torchlight flickered at the walls, and a large brazier near the maer's worktable added more light than William had seen before.

Half a dozen men sat on stools around the table. Maer Linn stood between them and the two bejeweled sacrifices. Arms crossed. Eyes dark and dangerous.

"Do you have any idea who we are?" Maer Linn asked.

The princess dimpled and curtsied. "You're the men behind the dragon."

She shook off the heavy bracelets and stripped away her neck-

71

lace, letting them fall into a rough pile with the gaudy scepter on top. "Those are fakes, by the way." She tugged at the heavy skirts of her gown. "Most of these are paste. We can discuss the real treasures, once we're past four hundred years of fake—if impressive—history."

Linn looked at William, who shook his head. "I didn't!" he swore. Then, back at Clementine. "I...You knew?"

"We suspected. For two...three generations now. Princesses keep diaries, you know. The evidence began to pile up. Patterns. Always a member of the King's Finest ready to brave certain death. Always a boy who rises from the local legends to take his place. Not bad. But you really should have changed your story over the years."

"Then...that night in the Champion's Tower. There was no unscripted attack. You came in there with a plan to...You already thought that I...But you..." He looked at the maer. "She..."

"She *hooked* you," Maer Linn said.

An embarrassed flush crawled over William's scalp. He breathed out a heavy sigh, relieved that the charade was finally over. "Okay. So...this works. Right? We were worried about the final act, but the princess is on board."

"Not quite," Clementine and Maer Linn said at the same time.

The princess nodded for the maer to continue.

"She's been telling a story to us for years," he said. "Which means she has her own ending in mind."

"Only what we promised my father at the end. His daughter back, and an end to the curse of Vlarr." She smiled. Turned to William and caught up his hand. "As an apprentice ranger it was never going to happen, you understand. Not even as a knight. But a Champion? A Dragon-slayer? We can work with that."

William laughed, sharp and short. He wouldn't meet her eye. "I'm no champion. Not a man who could slay a dragon. I couldn't even win the princess' heart."

Clementine stepped into him and caught William's chin in her hands, gently turned him to face her. "But you did. In every moment we stole together. Every fantasy you let me live out at your side. Our shared hopes and dreams. All those what-ifs? Tell me they weren't real." Her gaze was open, guileless, and warm. "Tell me you don't love me."

He did. Heaven help him, he had for a long, long time. "Would you believe me if I did?"

"No. Like I told you. You're a terrible liar." She kissed him. "But we'll work on that too."

Yes, William thought. They likely could.

SPRINTERS

MICHAEL D. BRITTON

We move from a traditional(ish) fantasy world to a hard science fiction setting. Michael D. Britton takes us into a contest like none we've ever seen before.

Michael has published more than 80 fiction titles, including a recent story in Fiction River: Superstitious, *as well as in upcoming issues of* Pulphouse. *He has made a living as a writer for thirty years, leading marketing departments and producing live TV broadcasts. Find out more about his writing at michaeldbritton.com.*

I was gone.

Dead.

But I dreamed a strange, software-influenced dream.

I wasn't quite clear on how I could be dreaming when my body had been disintegrated and my mind literally blown. But somehow, a dream washed through whatever part of me still existed, as my physical structure was reconstructed by the built-in technology I'd been supplied by my owners.

The dream consisted of a recursive, blinking, flashing, repeating image of the explosion that had ripped me apart, against a shadowy visual of a dark mineshaft on one of the border moons. I was operating a sonic extractor, loading handfuls of terrelium into a crate. My hands mere skeletons, my sleeves shredded blue rags. It was rather disturbing.

Which is saying something, considering I'd just been blasted to smithereens.

Soon enough, however, I would awake, good as new. Sprinters never really died—we just got...delayed.

As I floated in the sensationless void of interstellar space, the nanomedics gathered my atoms from the vicinity, then worked furiously to reconstruct me—faster than the eye could see—

swarming over and through my torn body, a coursing wave of energy and intelligence. They raced to repair the tissues and restore my life.

I felt a brief peace—relief, perhaps—realizing it was not all over, and that I'd live to see Roxy again.

We'd never had much of a chance to formally declare our love for each other, but I don't think we ever had to. It was obvious something was there. Something stronger than death.

I was thinking of her when I made my fatal mistake. I really shouldn't have tried to thread the needle—the space between the chunks in the tail of that comet had been narrower than I'd calculated. I should've left the navigation to the liveware, but I didn't want to lose Roxy. We needed to finish together, at the top of the pack, or risk never seeing each other again.

In a matter of about two minutes following the explosion, the nanomedics had brought my atoms back together and reactivated my autonomic system: brain, heart, lungs. They kept my consciousness suppressed and activated the dream sequence I was now experiencing. They also left the pain receptors in my brain disengaged while they methodically rebuilt the rest of my body at a frantic pace.

The bots reassembling my body—hundreds of millions of them—belonged to my sprintpod—my racing vessel. Each bot was composed of a level six hyperprocessor, several tiny tool-wielding appendages, and a certain amount of organic material to make them compatible with my biology. Working as a networked unit, they moved the length of my body in a microsecond, a coordinated symphony of healing, bringing me back to the way I was before the explosion hit.

But it was sixty seconds too late.

On the initial impact, my sprintpod had been torn apart by a core overload. As I came to consciousness following the body rebuild, I read the status report projected within my iris.

It wasn't good.

My ship was already spread across nearly a quarter AU of space.

I ran a mental algorithm immediately, activating the return sequence. Floating in the immense blackness of space, I watched the distant stars tumble around me. I knew I was the one spinning, but it always helped prevent nausea if I just told myself that I was the one at relative stop.

I waited.

As the return signal rode the EM Flow and reached each of the splinters and fragments of my ship, each piece—anything larger than a pinhead—reoriented itself in space and started toward my signal, each piece driven at near-light speed by a gravitational inertia-drive the size of a water molecule. Within a couple of minutes, the sprintpod was reintegrated by the same technology that had repaired my body, and I was on my way once again.

But the delay of just a few minutes would be hard to make up. I would certainly not win this one—a pity, since I'd hoped to retire with a bang. It would be perfect if Roxy, and my brother David, could make the top three for this final heat.

By now, Roxy was at least a tenth-parsec ahead of me, so I'd have to get creative to catch up.

When the sprintpod was fully reintegrated and operational, having formed its original shape all around me, I checked the nav and set a new course through the heart of the Dawn Dancer Nebula, a shortcut that most sprintpod racers considered a suicidal run.

But hey, I'd been dead before.

"I can see you."

I spoke not with my voice, but whispered the words directly from my mind. The message traveled though my teleneural patch and directly into the EM Flow. The Flow carried my coded thoughts to the intended recipient—Roxy Jones.

As my recently-rebuilt, remarkably streamlined sprintpod emerged like a laser-bolt from the red, pink and gold plumes of the Dawn Dancer Nebula, I eased forward on the virtual throttle ever so slightly and picked up even more speed. This open region on the other side of my shortcut would be a perfect place to gain the ground I'd lost.

"Only in your dreams," came the eventual reply. "I'm at least a quarter parsec ahead of you by now, love," she messaged. I could sense the playful tone of her voice, even though my ears weren't even a part of this discussion. It was one of the reasons I loved her...her heart came shining through, no matter the technology in between.

"Don't be so sure," I thought back. "Check your scan."

After a few moments, her delayed message entered my mind's receiver. "How in the name of Jupiter did you catch up? I saw you disintegrate."

I smiled. Even through the code translation, I could sense her astonishment. And I knew she was glad I'd made it back.

"I danced through a nebula," I thought to her. "Face it, Roxy. There's no stopping me."

Before I could receive her reply, my proximity alert sounded in my head, and the sprintpod's autostabilizer kicked in. The virtual controls grew suddenly sluggish and dissolved into the console as the system's liveware took over, weaving the sprintpod through a vast, uncharted band of asteroids.

My restraint harnesses automatically tightened under the torsion stresses. I could feel the snug belts across my body as the forces pulled my guts around my ribcage. Suddenly the fairly spacious cockpit felt much smaller.

I spoke aloud to my liveware. "Where'd this mess come from?"

"Uncharted."

The liveware's voice sounded like a bored teenage boy speaking through a metal tube—probably the voice of the designer.

"No kidding," I said, bracing myself as the sprintpod made a hard bank to port, followed by an equally sharp starboard maneuver. "Any theories on the origin?"

"Category seven dwarf planet 67543 is not scanning—conclusion: this asteroid field is the remains of that planet."

"Theories on what destroyed the rock?"

"Negative."

The liveware was an amazing autopilot, but not much of a strategic thinker. Or a conversationalist.

"Scan debris for foreign elements—identify any fragments that are not indigenous."

"Debris is 99.998 percent indigenous material—balance comprised primarily of tertanium alloy and trace particles of Roentgenium Y-26 isotope."

David.

"Stop."

My sprintpod came to relative stop within three seconds of my command, the sound of the engines deepening to a low, droning moan.

My brother David's sprintpod was the only one in the league with a tertanium alloy fuselage, and we all ran on RY-26 fuel cells.

And he was no longer showing up on my scan display.

The question was, if David had hit the dwarf planet, and his fuel cell had ignited and destroyed his sprintpod and the planetoid along with it, why hadn't his restoration kicked in? Could the failsafe have been knocked offline in the blast?

I hardly had time to investigate, but I couldn't exactly leave my brother's atoms to float around this debris field.

"Activate matter collector," I said.

"Specify parameters."

"Collect all carbon-based matter in a five hundred thousand kilometer radius on all axes. Commence now."

A whining hum filled the cabin as the sprintpod's onboard matter collector drew all carbon-based molecules into a container in the aft storage compartment where my spare parts and waste matter closet were located. After about three minutes, the hum stopped.

"Matter collected."

"Resume vector."

I was plastered into the back of my seat as the sprintpod shot back to half-max velocity—the best it could manage in this debris field. I was soon clear of the floating rocks and picked back up to max velocity.

"Initiate microscan of collected matter," I said. "Compare quantum level readings to database file Harrison, David."

"Microscan and cross analysis complete."

"And?"

"Collected matter matches specified file 99.63 percent."

I closed my eyes. Took a ragged breath. Swallowed hard.

My older brother. Dead.

And not coming back this time, since the restoration program programmed to his personal template had been obliterated.

Unfortunately, I had no time to mourn right now.

"Placement report."

"Five sprintpods ahead, three behind."

Great. I'd lost two positions while scooping up the remains of my brother. If I fell in the last half of the field, I'd be joining him soon. Those were the stakes.

As a sprinter, it was my lot to run race after race. My only goal was to not fall into the losing half of the field.

Winners lived to run again, and had a chance at winning their freedom after twenty heats. Losers were placed in the mining colonies where life expectancy was about six months, tops.

All for the gambling pleasure of the Elite.

I'd placed in the top half of all nineteen of my heats, since I'd first started racing nearly a year ago. If I survived this one, I'd be free.

If I fell into the lower half, I'd die in the deep, dark shafts of some border moon.

I looked at the field display, a green grid with glowing blue dots. There she was, not too far ahead of me.

Roxy and I had fallen in love not too long after we'd been captured, right before our first heat. That made this one her freedom race, too. We maintained a strong competitive façade in the race environment to keep up appearances, but off-track, there was a chemistry neither of us could deny. My deepest hope was that we'd both win our freedom this day, and have a chance at a life together.

But David's death, and my subsequent delay, might just mean I'd only ever get to dream of my red-haired beauty from the depths of the mines. I noted Roxy's decreased position, considered the mathematics of the field, and sent her a message.

"How did you fall into fifth place?"

After a few moments, "I slowed down when you hit the debris field and stopped. I was trying to figure out what you were up to. I didn't see Marshall or Hunt coming from behind. They blew past me and left me in the stellar dust."

"It's David," I messaged. "He's dead."

"His restoration failed?"

"Apparently."

In the ensuing silence, a terrible thought occurred to me. Now that Roxy had lost her third and fourth place spot, only one of us could finish in the top half of the field.

And the other would head to the death mines.

A quick look at the field showed that Roxy had no way to catch Marshall or Hunt at this point.

But I could still catch her.

The local stars rushed by, the distant ones seemed to hang immovably around me, as if I were standing still. I was soon within range of Roxy, with only three parsecs left in the race.

"Well, you've seen the field," she messaged to my mind. "It's you or me, now, love."

I didn't reply at first. Finally, I thought, "I know. I'm trying to figure out how to make this work."

"Maybe you should just be trying to figure out how to win."

"Roxy."

She didn't answer.

I checked the sprintpod's backup power reserves and shunted it all to the engine. As I slipped forward at a hundred and ten percent velocity, my mind raced with equal speed to figure a way through this dilemma.

It was like experiencing a grief cycle. My first instinct was to deny the reality of the choice I was being forced to make. I told myself that maybe if we tied, the Elite would grant us both our freedom.

Not likely. Such a thing was unprecedented, and the Elite were not known for their compassion or generosity. Most likely they'd send us both off to the mines, or make us race one-on-one to break the tie.

Escape was impossible.

Like the return signal that reassembled the sprintpods, our bodies were infused with a cell-tether-cellular-level restraint processor that disabled our ability to travel outside the general race track parameters. Any attempt to do so would instantly put us in a paralyzed coma and send us back to the finish line under liveware control.

As I came within ten kilometers of Roxy's aft thruster wake, my heart grew soft and I eased off the power, slowing to ninety-five percent max and dropping back from her sprintpod.

After a moment, I heard her in my mind. "What's the matter, love? Push your sprintpod too hard?"

I chose to not answer. Instead, I continued to tackle the logistics—to find *some* way to beat this game.

Perhaps there was a way I could disable (or even destroy, if necessary) one of the leaders—make room in the top half of the field for both of us.

The sprintpod was equipped with a proton vaporizer—not a weapon—a tool for clearing distant obstacles on the circuit. If I could get within range of Marshall or Hunt, I could maybe knock out one of their engine clusters with a quick jolt from the PV. Even if I could make it look like it was a malfunction, I'd be docked three wins for violating the rules, thus having to win three more races to gain my freedom—but that was a small price to pay, and a chance worth taking.

There wasn't much time left for deliberation, so I made a determined effort to catch the other racers and do the deed.

I pushed my sprintpod to the max, then used my power-shunting method to get it up to a hundred and ten percent again. At that rate, I shot past Roxy like she was standing still.

She didn't send me a message. She was probably wondering what I was doing. Or maybe thinking I was a horrible coward.

I checked the field display, and I was approaching Hunt, but not fast enough. I wouldn't be in range in time to change the standings. I needed more power. For more power, I'd need more—

Matter.

"Convert matter sample *Harrison, David* to add to fuel reserve. Shunt additional power created to engines."

"Complying."

David would be glad to know I was making use of his atoms.

My velocity increased to one hundred fifteen percent.

Still not enough.

I quickly dropped back, and Roxy shot past me, back into fifth place.

As we neared the final half-parsec stretch of the race—a straight run between two huge nebulae, the answer struck me like a laser.

When a sprinter won his freedom, he was granted one material possession with which to start his new life. Most chose their sprintpod, as it could be sold in the trading colonies for parts and converted into useful items such as food, clothing, passage on a freighter, or even a piece of land on a planet in a safe star system.

If I won, I could claim Roxy's sprintpod, then find out which mining moon they took Roxy to, and when she died, I could salvage her body and use the sprintpod's restoration technology, programmed to her personal template, to bring her back to life after she was discarded by the Energy Consortium. As long as I could get to her body within three days of her death, I could whisk her away, restore her, and we'd be free together.

Otherwise it would be too late—she'd be irretrievable beyond that time frame.

With new determination, I sent my sprintpod rushing headlong down the nebular corridor, quickly gaining on Roxy.

I pulled alongside her—I was so close I could see her through her starboard panel.

She looked over at me.

I thrust forward, ready to put my plan into action, but just as I started to creep ahead, I thought I saw her face change. I thought I saw a tear in her eye.

My heart leapt. What if my plan didn't work? What if I couldn't find out what moon she was sent to? What if I couldn't get to her body within three days of her death? And most of all, how could I consign her to that pain and misery for even a moment?

No.

I couldn't go through with it—the risk was too great, the price too high.

There was no time to discuss it with her—the seventh place sprinter was bearing down on us fast. I pulled back on the throttle and dropped to eighty percent.

Roxy disappeared in front of me like a flash.

Too bad the last time I'd see her face, it had that look of pain.

I breathed a long, heavy sigh. I'd done the right thing. I'd rather she lived—rather she was free.

I watched the field display as, one by one, the leaders crossed the finish line. Looking out the front of my sprintpod, I saw the distant flash of light at the end of the nebular corridor as Roxy passed into safety and freedom, and the finish line force field was snapped into place behind her.

Our connection through the Flow was severed. It was over.

Terrelium mines, here I come.

———

I waited to be processed at the finish line force field with the rest of the losing half of the field.

This was a new experience for me.

I'd heard rumors about it. After you're in the huge race hangar and disengaged from the sprintpod interface, mech-orgs three times the size of a man pull you from the sprintpod, strip you out of your flight suit, brand you with a new category tag and reprogram your cell-tether, then cram you into a slave freighter bound for the outer systems.

As it turned out, it wasn't that bad. The mech-orgs were only twice the size of a man.

But absent ruth and wrath, they were as rough as advertised. When the one assigned to me—a green-fleshed brute that announced itself as *Thale 86*—grabbed my arm to extract me from the sprintpod, it nearly ripped my arm out of the socket.

"Watch it!" I shouted. These guys were not programmed to treat us with the same respect we sprinters were accustomed to. We may have been slaves, but as sprinters, it was important that we not be damaged in any way. Now we were just fodder for the mines—expendable bodies to be tossed around and used up.

Thale 86 did not respond. It just sliced off my flight suit with a precision laser embedded in its index finger, shooting it right down the middle of my chest and down one leg without me feeling anything more than a tickle. Then it clenched its hand around my neck from the back and steered me toward a corridor that led directly to the slave freighter.

They didn't waste any time.

An announcement over the Flow indicated we were headed for Moon 171. Didn't mean much to me—one mining moon was like any other. I felt the engines kick in. With no windows, I could only assume we were on our way to our doom.

The freighter's gray walls were accented by gray, short-pile carpeting on the floor, and gray support beams running the length of the gray ceiling. A dismal transport to our dismal destination.

A ship of the damned.

Some smaller mech-orgs came through a door into the main chamber and handed out work suits—full-body outfits of dark blue Zeflar fabric—flexible, durable, and sure to outlive me to be used for another thousand slaves of my build. Like all the men and women in this large room, I slipped into my suit with eyes cast downward in sorrow and shame. The fit was snug.

As I sat and waited for our inevitable arrival, I counted about eighty of us on the flight—the losers of over a dozen of today's races. Nobody looked at anyone else—no one made conversation. They were all too busy contemplating their coming deaths.

I was too busy thinking of Roxy. And my brother, now that I had a moment to think about it.

About three meters to my left I spotted one of the guys from my heat. He was about my height, with a blond buzz-cut and hazel eyes that stared vacantly ahead.

"Is that you, Jordan?"

His eyes slowly turned to stare at me. "Jorgenson." He stared some more. "I saw on my field display—what you did. Why?"

I swallowed hard, cast my eyes down. "I uh, one of my engine clusters fizzed. My sprintpod's liveware didn't have time to make the repair before it was all over."

"That didn't show on my screen," he said, his voice deep and hollow sounding, as if he were incapable of speaking up.

I just shrugged, rubbed at the stubble forming on my chin. "You think there's any way out of this?"

He snorted gently. "No." A beat. His eyebrows flicked upward. "This is the beginning of the end. They say it's easier if you just accept it."

"How's that coming for you?" I asked.

He repeated his little snorting sound. "Workin' on it, man."

The transport shuddered gently.

"We've slipped to Planck velocity," I said.

"Yeah," said Jorgenson. "We should be in the moon belt in a few hours. Say goodbye to your life."

More like, say goodbye to Roxy.

To my heart.

Not only did we get along like we'd known each other forever, but our sprinting skills were well-matched, so that we had both made it through nineteen wins, and it had looked, at least for a time, like we'd be graduating to freedom hand in hand.

Roxy kept me on my toes, forced me to exceed my own self-expectations. Made me feel alive. Made me really look forward to the freedom we were working toward.

But this was *not* what I had in mind. I'd planned to go out quite gloriously—which is part of why I'd tried that crazy maneuver that got me killed in the second half of that last race.

I had *not* planned to wind up a mine slave.

I looked around at the ship's gray walls, the sleeping or catatonic ex-sprinters on their way to a short life of hard labor, and at the four towering mech-orgs standing as sentinels at each end of the chamber with their boxy heads, bovine eyeballs, and stretched-out, cloned flesh over their muscular, robotic bodies.

And I started to second guess my decision to lose the race.

The entrance to Mineshaft K-947-beta looked like the mouth of a long-dead dragon—rugged dark-gray and black rocks forming jagged teeth of stalactites across the giant roof. We filed into its rocky throat in single file under a black sky pin-pricked with tiny diamonds of distant starlight.

The mech-orgs didn't poke, prod or shove us—which somehow made them even more menacing, and made me feel like a lamb going to the slaughter. The beastly guards just stood there with their boxy heads, emotionless faces, and powerful musculature, looking like they had only two settings: docile and kill.

Right before being swallowed up by the great hole in the mountainside, I felt panic rise in my gut. Was this the last time I would see the outside? I looked up at the stars—the place I'd spent so much time as a sprinter, trading wins with my beloved—and almost—*almost* tried to run.

But before the message got from the animal-instinct part of my mind to my muscles, a bald-headed woman just three paces ahead of me broke loose and desperately dashed for freedom.

It was a pitiful sight—as she reached the ten-meter radius from the entrance, her slave cell-tether paralyzed her and she fell on her face in the gravel, skidding to a halt with a grunt.

Two giant mech-orgs approached her—clearly in no hurry, since she wasn't going anywhere. As she moaned helplessly, locked in the constraining grasp of the cell-tether, the mech-orgs raised their shoulder cannons in unison, and blasted her at close range without ceremony. The energy beams converged on her midsection and disintegrated her, rather slowly—one wave of white-hot energy moving toward her head, the other toward her toes. Within a few seconds, she was a small pile of black powder emanating a wisp of smoke like an escaping soul.

The mech-orgs holstered their shoulder cannons, then turned to the harried slave line as if to say, "Any questions?"

We all just turned back toward our fate, and trudged on with our heads hanging down and our arms limp at our sides.

Defeated.

Like the prisoners in ancient stories, I kept a count of the days, as best as I could calculate, on the wall beside my bunk. I used the blood that came from my knuckles and fingers each day to mark the tallies.

While working, I cautiously allowed myself to think about Roxy. I had been worried that thinking of her would somehow break me. But I found that focusing on her helped me forget about my reality.

I also thought about freedom. I recalled the woman who'd attempted to escape that first night. Thoughts of escape seemed hopeless. Every scenario I could think of ended with me getting blasted to powder. Sometimes that seemed like the only way out of here—carried out dead.

I discussed some of my escape ideas with Jorgenson, since he sometimes worked nearby. He always shot them down. He was hopeless. Resigned.

"You need to quit with the talk of getting out of here," he'd say. "It's not going to happen. Why not make it easier on yourself and just give it up?"

"I can't. Experience has taught me not to. When I first started sprinting, I was clueless. I'd been picked by the Elite in some 'random' selection process following my capture. When they first strapped me into a sprintpod, there were plenty of people who expected me to either put myself inside an asteroid at ninety percent, or just finish last and wind up here on day one. But I believed in an alternative. They told me I could win my freedom after a twenty wins. So I determined to make that a reality. Were the odds against me? Of course. But I didn't care. I took the chances in each heat that were required for a win."

"And now here you are, a free man," said Jorgenson sarcastically, gesturing around with his hand at the darkened cave that served as our dorm room.

"You're missing the point," I said. "This is just a hiccup on the road to my freedom—another challenge to overcome."

"Riiight. Like the way you overcame the challenge in that last heat—by throwing it."

"I don't know what you're talking about," I said.

"Oh, come on," he said. "It was so obvious you let Roxy Jones win."

"Which just further proves my point that I am in charge of

my own destiny," I said, conceding his accusation while bolstering my own argument.

"Try telling that to the mech-orgs," said Jorgenson.

I turned over in my bunk and faced the wall, where I could just make out my tallies.

Sixty three.

"I'll get out of here," I mumbled. "Or die trying."

Three days later I saw a chance to prove my words.

I noticed Thale 86 had a problem with its right eye—some kind of cataract or something. Mech-orgs had the eyes of cattle because although the Elite could clone flesh a-plenty, they had trouble with the complex optical organ. They just couldn't make cloned human eyes work. So, the mech-orgs got beef cattle eyes, which would otherwise have gone to waste in the meat production facilities. They looked weird enough with their stretched skin and their boxy heads, but the cow eyes made them look particularly creepy, like hornless minotaurs.

With Thale 86 having a blind spot, I decided to take advantage.

At the end of the shift, I took my time clearing up my area. The only ones left in the small cavern in which I was working were Thale 86, another mech-org, Jorgenson, and me.

"Move," said Thale 86.

"All right, I'm coming," I said. Then I dropped my sonic extractor. "Oh, sorry." I bent to pick it up as Thale 86 stepped toward me. I ducked low to the floor and turned to his right, then quickly jumped up behind him and grabbed his shoulder cannon before he could turn his head to track me.

Despite my hopes, the cannon didn't detach.

But I had my finger on the trigger, and I fired.

It hit the wall.

The other mech-org turned and fired, just as Thale 86 spun around with me hanging on its back.

The blast struck Thale 86 square in the chest.

It froze in place, forming a shield for me as I continued to piggyback it and fire its cannon at the other mech-org. I hit it, and it froze. I jumped down and moved toward the doorway out of the cavern.

Jorgenson leapt in front of me and blocked my path.

"What are you doing?" I asked, panting. "Don't you want to be free?"

"Oh yes, I do. That's why you're not going anywhere."

"Are you crazy? We can get out of here right now."

"No."

With that, he decked me with a right hook that came out of nowhere, crashing into my chin.

"What is the *matter* with you?" I yelled, scrambling back to my feet and squaring off with the large man.

"I'm securing my freedom."

"By staying here?"

"Exactly."

"I don't understand," I said.

"I'm under contract, you idiot."

"For *what*?"

He stared at me coldly. "Nine heats. I had nine more heats to go—and freedom never felt farther away. I just didn't believe I could win them all. Not with you and Roxy Jones out there, filling up two of the top spots every time. I'd been barely placing in the top half my last four races. So when one of the Elite approached me with an offer, I couldn't refuse."

"Offer?"

"They took me out of the sprintpods—put me here. I'm on a six-month deal. I work for the mech-orgs. They're programmed to not injure me or harm me in any way. I'm here to help with security, as a spy and an enforcer. I talk people out of escaping, infiltrate escape conspiracies, quell breakout rebellions. And I—"

I charged him, enraged. "Traitor!"

He lunged at me at the same time, and tackled me to the ground, pinning me.

"I guess they feed you pretty well, too," I grunted, noting his strength, and noticing for the first time that his face was ruddier than the rest of us pale, frail, non-collaborating rock chippers.

"Why couldn't you just leave well enough alone?" he said through gritted teeth. "You couldn't just let it be and die here peacefully, could you?"

"You make me sick," I spat. Summoning my strength, I pushed him off me and tried to stand.

He'd somehow managed to get to his feet faster than me, and kicked me in the ribs. I heard a crack-pop sound and fell to the floor in agony.

He kicked me again.

Repeatedly.

He punctuated each devastating blow with a word.

"I *kick* just *kick* want *kick* to *kick* be *kick* free!"

I could feel my insides turning to jelly under the force of his work boot. I saw stars. I vomited.

And then he lifted my sonic extractor from the floor, came and stood over me where I lay helpless. "I'm sorry," he said. "You'd do the same thing in my shoes."

As I thought, *no I wouldn't!* he brought the heavy tool down on my skull with all his might.

Blackness.

I was gone.

Dead.

I was gone.

Dead.

But I dreamed a strange, software-influenced dream.

I'd felt this sensation before. It seemed that my body was being repaired by sprintpod technology.

My dream consisted of a recursive, blinking, flashing, repeating image of Jorgenson smashing in my skull, against a shadowy visual of my Roxy accepting her freedom race winnings. She stood before an Elite race organizer. The Elite waved an instrument across her forehead, deactivating her constraining cell-codes. He asked her what she wanted as her one material takeaway. Without hesitation, she pointed to my old sprintpod.

The one programmed for my personal restoration template.

The nanomedics swarmed over and through my crushed body, a coursing wave of energy and intelligence. They raced to repair tissue, using preset triage criteria as well as making logic-based decisions as they went.

First, they reactivated my autonomic system: brain, heart, lungs. They kept my consciousness suppressed and activated the dream sequence I was now experiencing. They also left the pain receptors in my brain disengaged while they methodically rebuilt the rest of my body at a frantic pace.

The whole process took less than two minutes.

I opened my eyes to find myself cradled in Roxy's arms.

"I beat you," she said, smiling down at me.

"Not as bad as Jorgenson did," I said.

She leaned down and kissed my forehead.

"How did you find me?" I asked.

"Your body was tossed into a waste heap on that mining moon. David helped me track you down—we got to you two days after you were killed."

"My brother? He's dead."

"Clearly not," said David, stepping into the sprintpod's cockpit from the aft area.

"But I collected your atoms," I said, confused.

"It was a setup," said David. "The Elite wanted to make that race the biggest betting opportunity in history. So they staged my death. The ruse was intended to pit two freedom racers against each other—to make you choose between death and love. It made major headlines in the entertainment world."

"And you took part in this deception?" I said, getting angry.

"I still needed three straight wins. They offered me my freedom. They also threatened to dock me ten race wins if I didn't cooperate."

I frowned. But then I started to smile as I contemplated the fact that my brother, my love and I were all alive—and all free people.

"Well," said Roxy. "How do you feel, dear?"

"As good as new."

"And you're only a couple months late for your freedom," said David.

"Well, sprinters never really die," I said. "We just get...delayed."

ON THIN ICE

DAPHNE CROWE

One of four pseudonymous writing Crowes, Daphne resides in Nobtucket —a quintessential, if mythical, Cape Cod town. This is Daphne's first appearance in Fiction River *anthologies but is also one of over a dozen Crowe stories to appear in* Fiction River. *Crowe stories have also appeared in* Pulphouse, *Daw Books and in Level Best Books'* Best New England Crime *anthologies, as well as in* Alfred Hitchcock's Mystery Magazine, *the upcoming anthology* Secrets *and the anthology* Yearning to Breathe Free, *whose proceeds go to support The Refugee and Immigrant Center for Education and Legal Services (RAICES). Daphne maintains a cyber presence at daphnecrow.com and nobtucket.com.*

Based on a true story—writer speak for a grain of truth embellished to a fare-thee-well— "On Thin Ice" combines a fortuitous encounter with Daphne's love of all things French, the adventure of racing cars on frozen lakes, and just desserts for obnoxious showoffs.

Catch your breath now, because you won't have a chance to breathe again for pages.

I'm done with men. Done looking for Mister Right. Done having to shed Mr. Wrong. Put a fork in my love life and call it done.

Done. Done. Done.

At the top of my list of New Year's resolutions for the year 1972: *Carpe Diem*—seize the day. New year. New me—Anne-Marie Malveaux—single female looking for adventure all on her own. When life gives you lemons, trade them in for something better.

Which is why I'm freezing my butt off driving a ragtop plastic jeep around the foothills of Putnam County, New York looking for Nine Pin Pond Road. I have directions from the guy who gave me a great deal—or so he claimed—on the demo model Citroën Méhari on the floor of the gazillionth car dealership I visited looking for a replacement for the car my last Mr. Wrong wrapped around a telephone pole.

Somehow he walked away. My ten-year-old Pontiac got towed to the land of mangled metal. He's suing for whiplash, lost wages, and pain and suffering.

I'm 99.44% sorry he didn't die.

My old insurance company dumped me. The new one's rates are through the roof. They'd dump me, too, if they knew I was about to take the car they're insuring out on a frozen lake to race around a bunch of orange traffic cones for a small pewter prize—if I win, place or show. Registration opens at 9:30. It's already nine and I have no idea where I am.

I must be nuts.

The road bumps over frost heaves, in and out of potholes, passes through second-growth woods—bare trunks and branches of oaks and maples and who knows what else—I'm no botanist. Here and there a giant granite boulder pokes out of the ground. I catch glimpses of clustered single-story summer cabins boarded up for the winter. The engine whines, but the front-wheel drive helps *La Machinette—Machin* for short—yeah, I name my cars, so shoot me—as the road climbs.

I keep telling myself this is a dumb idea. What chance do I have testing my suburban driving skills on ice when I can't navigate my way through scrubby woods? If I do come across a gingerbread house though, I'll know not to eat the trim.

An arrow-shaped sign nailed to a gnarled oak tree points to Lakeside Lodge up an unpaved track, little more than two ruts and a hump in the middle. On a small rotted board below it, scribbled in what looks like faded crayon: Nine Pin Pond Road. I downshift *Machin* into second and turn up the road.

The track opens into a large dirt parking lot packed with an eclectic assortment of cars—domestic and foreign, Rust-Oleum red beaters and shiny new models. I recognize some of the hood ornaments and model names from my search through every car dealership within twenty miles of home.

A string of Saabs, a couple of Mini Coopers and the kind of Citroën they smuggled all that dope inside of in *The French Connection*, form a single file line along the edge of the lot, nosed toward a short road leading to the lakeside beach. Drivers sit inside the first three Saabs in line. The driver of the Mini Cooper, a petite brunette in tight green ski pants and a form-fitting white cable knit sweater, leans against her car talking to a full-bearded redhead.

I pull up in front of the rambling wood structure, parking in a slot with a sign marked

Icekhana Registration
10 Minute Parking

swing open the black canvas and clear plastic door and step into the cold sunshine.

"Hey," a male voice shouts, "You're not going to race that thing, are you?"

Tug Granderson spots the bright red Méhari as soon as it emerges from the woods surrounding Lakeside Lodge's parking lot. He only half listens to Janice Summers yammering in his ear as he watches the plastic jeep cruise the lot. The driver—a twenty-something honey blonde with shoulder length straight hair—hunches inside a loden green duffel coat with, no doubt, those wooden root beer barrel buttons all the preppies love so much. She looks lost.

"Larry Esposito's a jerk." Janice taps Tug on the shoulder. "Are you listening?"

"Huh?"

Janice yanks Tug's beard. That gets his attention.

"I said, Larry Esposito's a—"

"I heard you. He's always been a jerk. So what?"

"So, if you had any shred of feeling left for me, you'd punch him right in his big fat nose."

"Why? What, specifically, has he done now?"

He doesn't really care. Janice's problems are no longer his problems, although she doesn't seem to have gotten the message, no matter how many times he tells her it's over between them. Women! Can't live with 'em, can't get rid of 'em. If he were a jerk like Larry Esposito, he'd brush her off and break her heart without a second thought. Why does Janice have to make it so hard to be a nice guy about the breakup?

The blonde pulls the Méhari into the spot reserved for icekhana registration. Tug takes a step in that direction.

"Hey!" Janice says, "Where do you think you're going? I'm talking to you."

Tug keeps his eyes fixed on the blonde head emerging from the Méhari's open door.

"Be right back," he says over his shoulder to Janice.

He raises one hand toward the blonde.

"Hey! You're not going to race that thing, are you?"

I turn toward the sound of the voice.

The bearded redhead marches toward me in long easy strides like a TV western sheriff on a mission.

I pull wayward strands of hair out of my duffel coat, wait for him to approach close enough so I don't have to shout.

"I was considering it."

More than considering. I'm damned well going to take my chances. I didn't drive all the way into the hinterlands to watch.

The redhead stops in front of me. He looks clean. His beard is neatly trimmed. No dirt discolors his fingernails. There's a knife edge pressed into his khaki pants and the lamb's fleece of his leather jacket is creamy white. His boots are old but polished. Yet, a faint odor of oil and grease wafts off him.

His mouth is set in a hard line. Yet, his eyes—grey with hints of green and gold—are soft and kind.

"Why?" I ask.

He points at *Machin*. "It's a Citroën."

He points at the green clamshell Citroën DS convertible waiting in the line to the lakeshore. "Citroëns have a good reputation around here."

Again he points to *Machin*. "You'd better be good, is all."

"I intend to be."

The words are out of my mouth before my brain has a chance to engage.

"Then you'd better get inside and register."

He looks at his watch.

"They're about to start the first run, beginning with Class A—front-wheel drive, front engine. Once you're registered, you can line up behind me."

Again he points to the Citroën DS.

He turns and starts walking toward his car. Over his shoulder he throws, "Good luck," and a smile so bright it rivals the sun.

The difference in temperature between outside and inside Lakeside Lodge sends me into an immediate sweat. I peel off my duffel coat and carry it over my arm.

The lodge is much bigger inside than the one-story, wood

shingle exterior facing the parking lot suggests. A large, airy dining room extends out into a glass enclosed porch that overlooks the lake. There must be a hundred fifty to two hundred people milling around in small groups, sitting at Formica topped restaurant tables sipping something warm or standing at the porch windows watching officials refining the placement of traffic cones on the lake's smooth ice surface.

Racing club officials sit at the registration table placed inside the front doors. A club official—a dignified older man whose deep-set brown eyes and Roman nose somehow look familiar— holds out his hand as I approach. "Driver's license and registration."

I pull out my wallet and hand over the documents.

"New Jersey," he says looking at my license. "My son works in New Jersey. Maybe you know him."

Like that's likely, but something about this man niggles at me. He does look familiar. "Probably not. New Jersey's a small place with a big population."

"Larry." He hands back my documents. "Larry Esposito— Esposito's Foreign Cars in Teaneck."

I resist slapping my forehead. Of course, this is what the guy who sold me *Machin* is going to look like in thirty odd years.

A warm, smooth voice sneaks up behind me. "Anne-Marie. You decided to come after all."

I turn into an unwanted embrace.

"I need to pay the entry fee," I say, wiggling out of his octopus arms and roaming hands.

"No need. Don't take her money, Dad." He leans in for an over the shoulder hug. "I always pay for my customers."

I manage to elude him with a shrug.

His voice loses some of its treacly warmth. "First time anyway."

A cold blast of outside air seeps inside with a redhead and brilliant smile poking through the front door.

"Are you registered yet?"

His eyes fix on Larry. On me. The smile fades. The twinkle dims.

"Tug," Larry says. "I see you've met Anne-Marie."

"We haven't been introduced," the redhead says. He walks in and extends his hand to me.

"Anne-Marie Malveaux," Larry says, "Meet Theophilus Ulysses Granderson."

"Tug," the redhead says. "Everybody" he glares at Larry, "calls me Tug."

"Pleased to meet you, Tug." I put a special emphasis on Tug.

Our fingers touch in a spark of blue electricity.

"Static electricity," we say together.

"Pinkies," we say and laugh while locking pinkies. A pleasant tingle runs through my arm. We keep laughing.

"Hadn't you better get to your car," Larry says to Tug. "Wouldn't want my arch rival to miss a run. I want to win King of the Ice fair and square this year."

"That's why I'm here. Anne-Marie needs to get her car in line. The Mini Cooper's next on the ice. I've got to run."

He tips a finger to his forehead in a kind of salute and disappears out the door.

"Are we done here?" I ask Mr. Esposito, Sr.

He nods. "You're number 101." He hands me a cardboard sign with 101 printed in bold black letters. "Put this under your windshield wiper. You'll hear it called over the loudspeaker."

He pats my hand as I take the card. It feels every bit as creepy as the hug from his son. "Good luck, young lady."

"I'll need it."

Outside I hurry into my coat and gloves and pull *Machin* in line behind Tug's Citroën DS. He's got the top down. He's leaning against the driver's door watching the Mini Cooper roll down the pathway to the beach.

I hold up my 101 card prior to slipping it under the windshield wiper.

Tug smiles, but the brilliance is gone.

"Now what do I do?"

"Never raced before?" he asks.

I shake my head.

"Not gymkhana or rally?"

I keep shaking my head. Maybe if I shake it long enough my brains will fall out. I feel totally stupid and out of place and I can't get far enough away from the Esposito's *père* and *fils*.

Tug points to a Saab weaving its way through the traffic cones on the ice.

"Follow the path laid out between the pairs of orange and red pylons, like skiing through gates in a slalom. See how that Saab is doing it?"

"It looks pretty easy."

A tinge of the brilliance returns to his smile.

"Looks are deceiving. The ice is fresh. No snow, so no traction, or damned little. You have much experience driving on ice or snow?"

My head keeps shaking. "Not much. I've driven on snowy roads at all ahead creep speed in my Pontiac."

"Front-wheel drive is different. Driving on black ice, like today, you won't go much more than 10 or 20 mph. But it's the equivalent of driving at high speed on a dry, paved racetrack. The trick is in the cornering. That's where the driving skill comes in, where the wheels lose traction and you end up fishtailing or going in a straight line when you're trying to turn."

We watch the Saab's rear end wiggle and waggle in the turns

until the car finally breaks free and pinwheels through two sets of pylons before going completely off course. It slides to a stop before the driver turns it around and eases it back onto the course.

Tug shakes his head in disgust. "He's going to have a terrible time and lose a bunch more for knocking over those pylons—five second penalty for every pylon moved. And they'll have to reset them before the next car can start."

"Is that how it works? I was wondering why there's only one car on the ice at a time."

"There's a timer set up at the start and the finish. It records down to the hundredth of a second. They add the penalty seconds to the recorded time."

The Saab accelerates on the straightaway just before the finish line, then skids to a slower speed before bumping up onto the sandy beach.

"Bad luck, Howie," Tug shouts and waves to the Saab driver as he passes us on the way to a spot in the parking lot.

"I'll get it next run," Howie shouts back.

"He's an optimist," Tug stage whispers to me. "Worst driver in Class A. He'd be as well off in a Class D Front Engine, Rear-Wheel Drive. At least everyone in that class expects to fishtail off course and rack up lots of penalty points."

"I thought front-wheel drive, front engine cars handled better on ice. It's one of the reasons I bought *Machin*."

"*Machin* is it?" A devilish twinkle lights up the gold in his eyes.

I blush. "I name my cars."

He laughs. It sounds smooth and sweet like honey. "Me, too."

He slaps the top of the front leather seat of his convertible. "*Machin* meet *Monique*."

"*Machinette* — little machine. *Machin* for short. It means whatchamacallit or thingamabob in French."

I'm hoping he'll explain Monique. Maybe it's the name of the woman I saw him talking to.

"I just like the name Monique," he says. "No cool story."

A little bit of brilliance moves from his eyes to my heart. Somebody thinks my naming scheme is cool.

"Maybe you can give me some tips on how to keep from spinning out? I mean, we aren't in direct competition. I'm in the ladies division."

"And you need to hold up the good name of Citroën." The full brilliance returns to his smile. "On paper, there's not much to it. In front-wheel drive you let off the gas, don't brake, and steer into a skid when the rear wheels break free. If the front end loses traction, give it some gas and steer it where you want it to go. It's more feel than anything else. You'll get the hang of it."

I'm not feeling as confident as he seems to think I should.

"Anything else? Like some magic fairy dust I can sprinkle on *Machin* to keep her on the straight and narrow?"

"Can't use chains or studs. Against the rules. But," he winks, "there is one trick. First, let some air out of your tires. That way more rubber meets the surface and it gives better traction on black ice."

"You said first. What's second?"

"Can you keep a secret?"

"Between the only two Citroën owners here? Sure."

He points to the small patch of sandy beach where the cars wait before going onto the ice.

"When you're waiting there, back up and move forward while turning the steering wheel lock to lock. That way you'll load the microgrooves in your Michelin X tires with sand. It'll improve your traction at the start. Every little bit helps."

"Thanks. I'll need all the help I can get."

"Then let me help you let some air out of your tires. They're going to be another couple of minutes resetting those pylons."

He pulls a dime out of his pocket and hands it to me.

The touch of his fingers sends a jolt through me as strong as I imagine the shock from an electric eel—only much more pleasant.

"Static electricity," he says, but the look on his face says he had as strong a reaction as I did.

"Right," I say.

I'm careful to avoid touching him while he shows me how to press the dime against the stem in the tire valve to let out some air.

The loudspeaker calls Number Three.

"That's me," Tug says. "You'll do fine."

He gives me that little finger to the forehead salute and jumps into his convertible. I'm left at the top of the road, the last of Class A, until the loudspeaker calls One Oh One.

The Mini Cooper bumps up off the ice onto land as Tug's Citroën glides off the beach and approaches the timers at the start line. As soon as the loudspeaker announces *Tug Granderson Number Three in a Citroên DS 21 Pallas* Monique accelerates through the timer.

Her wheels don't spin. Her rear end never fishtails. She never touches a pylon, much less moves one. In less than a minute, she's barreling down the final straightaway. I barely have time to load sand into *Machin's* tires before Tug has Monique passing through the finish line. We wave to each other as we pass at the ice's edge.

The loudspeaker announces the time for Janice Summers Number Nineteen in an Austin Mini Cooper at one minute fifty three seconds flat. I fix my mind on beating that time.

The loudspeaker announces Anne-Marie Malveaux in a Citroën Méhari.

And I'm off.

I accelerate slowly, letting off on the gas when I feel the tires losing traction. Hunched over the wheel, hands clutching it in a death grip, I will *Machin* to keep between the pylons, will the rear end to follow the path of the front.

I never shift out of second gear until I hit the final straightaway. When I pass the finish line, the speedometer reads 17 mph.

I downshift and tap the brake until the speedometer reads 5 mph and I bump up onto the beach.

Adrenaline courses through my body. I'm on the top of the world. I didn't spin out, go off course or touch a pylon. All I need now is my time.

Inside the Lakeside Lodge people are milling about, eating, drinking, watching the cars on the ice and listening to the loudspeaker give a running commentary on each driver and car. My heart sinks as I realize he must have commented on *Machin* and on me. I didn't hear a thing I was so busy trying to navigate between the pylons.

A warm, moist hand lands on my shoulder.

"Nice run, Anne-Marie."

It's Larry.

"My father and some friends have a table," he points to a window-side table on the enclosed porch, prime race watching real estate. Why don't you come join us."

"I have to go powder my nose," I lie. I don't even own any face powder. I force a smile onto my lips.

"We'll be here when you get back," Larry shouts after me.

I follow a sign to the rest rooms for Setters and Pointers with silhouettes of the appropriate dog species on the doors. Maybe the lodge hosts dog shows in season.

I hang out in the three stall rest room, washing my hands while I debate with myself in the mirror and delay my return to the main room until I can think of a good way to avoid the Espositos. The woman in the Mini Cooper comes in and enters a stall. I'm still there when she comes out to wash her hands.

"You did great," she says.

"I did?"

"Didn't you hear your time?"

I rattle my brains with another shake of the head.

"One minute thirty-three and twenty-five one hundredths seconds. And not a single penalty." She shakes water off her hands before grabbing a paper towel. "You keep that up and you'll trophy for sure."

"Tug gave me some pointers," I say.

"Tug's good that way."

"You know him well then?" I'm fishing.

She lets out a staccato, bitter laugh. "I knew him better before we broke up."

"You're not...?" I'm not sure how to characterize what they might have been to each other.

"In a relationship?" She tosses her paper towel in the overflowing trash basket. "I wish. He's a great guy. He deserves to find someone more compatible with him than I am. I was living in his margins. We drove each other crazy."

She looks me in the eye. "How well do you know Larry Esposito?"

The name itself makes me feel slimy. I shudder.

"That well," she says.

"No. I just met him. I bought my car from him."

She throws back her head and laughs out loud. "I shoulda known."

"Known what?"

"That that bastard couldn't attract someone like you."

"I take it you don't care much for him."

"You could say that. Listen." She holds my forearm in a tight grip. "Esposito's telling everyone that he brought you here. He'll try to get his claws into you, buy you dinner, ply you with drinks. This place is a lodge. They have rooms in the wings. If you get my drift."

I got it all right.

"And," she lets go of my arm, "Tug has a thing for you."

"He does?"

She nods. "I still know him well enough to know when he's smitten. He's a one girl guy. When he finds the right one, it'll be for keeps. If you feel the same, don't let him slip away."

I find Tug in a corner of the main dining room sitting by himself at a chipped Formica table tapping the end of a pencil on a pad of paper covered in calculations.

"Mind if I join you?"

He looks up from his paper.

"Where did you come from? I wanted to congratulate you, but you'd disappeared."

I pull out a café chair and sit.

"I was in the ladies room, hiding from Larry Esposito."

Tug scowls.

"I bought *Machin* from him. He told me about the icekhanas here. That's all. Anything else he's saying is pure fiction."

The scowl leaves Tug's face. He smiles. The sun comes out.

I place my hand over his on the table. It tingles.

"You feel that?"

"Yeah," he says.

"You ever feel that before?"

He shakes his head.

"Me neither. But I don't want to lose it. Do you?"

The sun and the moon and all the stars light up his face.

"Do you believe in love at first sight?" he asks.

"I didn't used to."

The loudspeaker interrupts our spell.

Calling all Class A entries for your second run.

Outside we line our cars up and hit the ice. I shave three seconds off my first run. Tug is first in Class A and by some arcane indexing system only Einstein could understand, he's tied with Larry Esposito, who drives a Class E BMW, for King of the Ice.

At the end of our third and final run, by the same arcane indexing system used for King of the Ice, I'm in third place in the Ladies Division. King of the Ice depends on the results of Larry's final run.

Tug, Janice and I sit at his table in the corner working on a pepperoni pizza and Michelob on tap.

"Did you hear anything strange while you were on the ice?" Tug asks us.

"My engine whining," I say. "I get better time maxed out in first than shifting up through the turns."

Tug pulls on his beard. Lines form on his forehead.

"What?" Janice says.

"Nothing."

"I know that look, Tug Granderson. Something's eating you."

He stops stroking his beard.

"You're right. You always could read me like a book," he says to Janice, but he smiles at me. "I drive with the top down so I can hear how the tires react to the ice. I could swear I heard crackling as I went around this last time."

"You mean, like the ice isn't as strong as they think?" I ask.

Tug shrugs. "It's probably nothing. But…"

"Maybe you should tell the club officials. The heavier cars will be on the ice soon. If the ice isn't safe…." I swallow a piece of pepperoni. It goes down hard.

"I already did." Tug taps his pencil against his pad. "I told old man Esposito. He said I was only trying to prevent his son from beating me for King of the Ice."

"Serve him right if he falls in," Janice says.

A wicked smile crosses Tug's face. "Poetic justice."

As always Larry's third run in his Class E BMW is the last run of the day. He does his usual spin out after he crosses the finish line and sits on the ice near the beach waiting to hear his time.

We three watch through the windows in the lodge. Most of the other drivers, with no hope of winning or changing their status, don't hang around to watch Larry grandstand.

"Why can't he drive off and come into the lodge like the rest of us?" I ask.

"Ego," Janice says.

"Maybe he doesn't want to hear bad news where everyone can see him." Tug holds up his pad of paper. "By my calculations, he needed a way better run than that to beat me for King of the Ice."

"You have his time?" Janice asks.

"Not down to the hundredth of a second." Tug taps his Timex. "But he's off by at least ten seconds or I'll eat my hat."

"Oh. My. God." A woman gasps and leans her forehead against the porch window. "Oh. My. God."

I squint in the growing dusk. I rub my eyes.

"Are you seeing what I'm seeing?" I ask.

Janice is giggling.

Tug raises his arms above his head like the winning prize-fighter after the final bell.

"I guess so," I say.

Down on the lake, where the ice meets the shore, Larry Esposito and his father stand shoulder to shoulder watching Larry's BMW sink front end first through a hole in the ice.

"Couldn't happen to a nicer person," Tug says.

I join in Janice's giggles,

Tug puts his arm around my waist. I lean my head on his shoulder.

When I wasn't looking, I found my nicer person.

TRAIL RUN

KATIE PRESSA

Katie Pressa's latest for Fiction River *isn't quite about a race, but it does feature running—which seems to be a theme in this volume.*

Readers know Katie for her romantic suspense novels and, indeed, her previous story in Fiction River, *"Night Moves," appeared in our romantic suspense* Special Edition: Summer Sizzles. *Her most recent novel,* Shotgun Wedding, *appeared in 2019. Find out more at katiepressa.com*

About this story, she writes, "In 2020, white America learned the phrase 'running while Black' and thought that's a new problem. It's not, and it's one of Gabrielle's worries as she approaches a running group in Northern Michigan, looking for companionship as she runs in an unfamiliar city."

I

June, 2015

From the rise back in the trees—and God, there were a million trees—Gabrielle stared at the gathered runners in the parking lot. As she expected, most were men, although there was a scattering of women throughout, identifiable mostly through their brown or blond ponytails. Most everyone wore compression tights and long-sleeve racing shirts, and all had expensive shoes.

And, as she expected, they were all white.

She let out a breath, and remembered the promise she had made to herself. She would meet people. She would meet *runners.* Houghton was known for its trails, although she didn't want to think about them in the winter. Michigan Tech was the snowiest university in the entire lower Forty-Eight, something she had thought about every single day since she arrived.

She had no idea how she was going to survive the winter. She barely survived winter in Chicago, and at least that was a *city*. This was the end of nowhere, and it was her own fault that she had landed here.

She could turn around and leave. She hadn't parked her car in the lot. She'd parked in her usual spot on campus, half a mile from here. She was thinking that the walk would warm her up.

And yeah, maybe she was thinking that she could escape without anyone seeing her.

Gabrielle wiped her hands on her compression pants. Even though it was July, she had to have covering over her legs and arms. She'd learned that on her very first run on the Tech Trails. Branches grew into the single person trails, and scratched at her arms and her legs—and once the branches drew blood, well then, the bugs followed.

She had never been to a place filled with as many bugs as the Upper Peninsula. Gnats, no-see-ums, mosquitoes, gigantic flies, and other winged creatures she didn't even recognize had attacked her that day—and on her runs afterward.

Bug spray only half worked, so she'd tried to run through the city itself. She didn't like the stares. The U.P. wasn't known for its diversity, although Houghton—because of the university—was better than most communities. But the people of color up here weren't usually Black, either. They were Asian or Asian American, who had come for the engineering school. There was also a smattering of Native Americans, who were mostly locals.

She'd only been in Houghton a month, but she had not had any real problems anywhere in the U.P. No one tried to hurt her, and the cops didn't stop her because of her skin color (yet).

But she had been acutely aware as she made her way along the city sidewalks and neighborhoods that she was Running While Black, and people stared at her.

Plus, she got the stupid absentminded but good intentioned blurts, as she called them. Some white person, startled that they were faced with someone they considered Other, would say stupid shit, like *I had no idea Black people ran.*

Gabrielle rolled her eyes just remembered the times she had gotten that here or some variation on it. And she would probably get it when she joined the runners. Not to mention the added variation. She was a Black *woman* who ran, and usually a male-dominated group like this one would see her as particularly strange.

That thought nearly made her turn around again. That was the problem, coming to mostly white communities like this one. They were tiring. Not that the people were unkind (although some were), but that they were *ignorant.* And they didn't think they were. They thought they were open-minded and tolerant and understood that people of different races not only existed but could co-exist with them.

Still didn't stop the stupid though. And the problem with the stupid here, as opposed to Chicago, for example, was that she didn't have her own community to go home to and bitch about it all.

So...either she could turn around and spend the next eleven months on her own, talking only to professors, librarians, and the occasional barista, or she could suck it up and see if she could find a running partner for the dark winter mornings that loomed ahead.

Right now, cold and snowy seemed very far away. It was barely seven a.m., and while the temperature didn't seem high—70-something—the humidity was already stifling. There had been bad thunderstorms the night before, and they had left the ground soft and the air thick with moisture. Not to mention, she could hear bugs making some kind of communal buzzing noise, almost as a warning to her.

Then she straightened her shoulders. She had spent a month running on her own, every single day. It wouldn't hurt to spend one morning with a local running club. At least they would have running in common.

At least she would have something to laugh about with her friend Charise over the phone later tonight.

Gabrielle's fingers tightened around her water bottle. It was still stiff from all the ice she'd put in it at the apartment this morning. Then her left hand brushed the pocket with her phone, making sure the phone was zipped in place. Her left ear felt naked without the single headphone she usually kept there during a run.

But she was going to talk to people, or maybe just suffer in silence.

She checked her watch. Ten minutes until the meeting started. She didn't think they'd start running at the start of the meeting, but she had no real idea. She had only been to a few running club meetings in Chicago, and then she'd bailed. Running clubs in Chicago usually weren't about the location. They were either about what happened afterward (an evening at a pub) or they were about protection (women running together in dangerous parts of the city).

This club had no socializing planned afterward—and this early, she couldn't quite imagine what that would be anyway. And there wasn't a women-only group in all of the Keweenaw Peninsula, at least that she could find. Although, to be fair, she had ruled out most of the smaller towns, because small towns made her nervous.

Not that Houghton was big. Maybe 30,000, if you counted the outlying areas. And the university when it was in session. She'd lived in neighborhoods that were larger.

Now or never. No one had noticed her yet. They were milling and talking and several of them were stretching the old-fashioned way, grabbing a foot with one hand and pulling, which would probably do more damage than good.

Not that it was any of her business. Not that she would say anything when she got there.

That decided her. She would say hello, use her first name only, answer questions politely, and see if this group could introduce her to some hidden trails or something she might have missed on her own.

She started down the rise, making sure she walked with confidence—even though she didn't feel any.

2

Zach leaned against the hood of his Forester, and tried not to feel defeated. The drive over here had been harder than he thought it would be. Even though he had only damaged his left shoulder, the pain slid all the way across to his right. The unfamiliar movements of driving—even an SUV as automated as the Forester—had aggravated the injury.

And opening the driver's side door had just been embarrassing.

Not that anyone seemed to have noticed. As usual, the runners kept looking at the trailhead, not at the cars behind them. The runners were shifting from foot to foot or jogging in place or, in a few cases, doing short runs across the dry grass.

This summer was warmer than normal, and Zach felt that too. Or maybe he was already hot because he had used the contraption the physical therapist had given him when she couldn't talk him out of running. The contraption—which was what it felt like —pressed his arm in place, and wrapped around his torso, almost like a straightjacket.

The physical therapist said it would make sure he didn't jar the injury as he ran, but he'd tried it on his own two days ago, and it left him feeling off-balance—and short of breath. Or maybe that was the fitness he'd lost with the enforced rest.

He'd been walking everywhere, and he could go to the pool now, if he didn't strain his arm too much. But neither of those things were running, and until he had stupidly lost his balance on a ladder in his own office, and tried to save himself one-handed, ripping everything, he had had a six-year-long daily running streak going.

He had been training for the Two Hearted Trail Run. He'd done the marathon before, but this year, he'd planned on the 50K, and he had really been looking forward to it. The Two Hearted Trail Run went through the U.P. forest that inspired Hemingway to write the Big Two-Hearted River, *not* that Zach was a Hemingway fan. He wasn't. The man had been the definition of toxic masculinity. But the area was beautiful, remote, and breathtaking. Zach had actually stopped in the middle of his marathon to watch the sun ripple across Lake Superior, and he hadn't regretted the extra minutes at all.

But it was not meant to be. He'd nearly pulled a bookshelf on top of himself the week before the 50K and he'd been angrier about that than anything else. It had taken him almost four weeks to control his emotions enough to rejoin the weekly running group. They'd encouraged him to come walk, but he didn't want to. Someone would have felt obligated to walk with him, and he hated being someone's charity case.

So he had stayed away.

He used his right hand to adjust all the Velcro straps on his contraption, then reached inside the SUV, narrowly missing hitting his injured shoulder on the window slope. He'd hit the shoulder once—just once—after the injury and the surgery, and that one time would stay with him for the rest of his life. That hit had hurt worse than the initial injury itself.

He grabbed his water bottle out of the cup holder, then

pushed himself back up. July in Northern Michigan could be hot. Today's high was supposed to be 86, which didn't sound like much to people who lived in the rest of the state, but up here that kind of temperature plus the humidity equaled extreme misery.

He'd be glad when winter returned.

He gingerly pushed himself out of the SUV, double-checking his shoulder clearance as he did so, then stood up straight. He put the bottle on the roof of the Forester, and just happened to catch a movement out of the corner of his eye.

A woman was walking down the slight incline on one of the trails. He didn't recognize her. She was dressed like a runner, but he'd never seen clothing that bright before. Her compression pants were the usual black, but she wore bright orange shoes and a matching bright orange long-sleeved tech shirt.

The orange set off her dark skin. An orange sweatband held her hair away from her face. She looked determined, her face turned directly toward the group.

Apparently, she wasn't running on her own. Apparently, she had come to join the runners.

Zach sprinted toward the group, feeling the imbalance in his form as he did so. He needed to beat her there. The runners were a motley combination of scientists, mathematicians, engineers and trail runners. None of those groups were known for their social skills. And at least half of them hadn't mastered Midwestern politeness, despite being raised somewhere nearby.

Zach had been born and raised here too, but he'd been socialized in what he privately called the Real World. He'd gotten the largest academic scholarship given in his community, and it allowed him to pick the school of his choice. He chose Stanford for their excellent history department and, delusionally, their well-known track and field organization. Delusionally, because he thought he could walk onto one of the best track-and-field organizations in the country and qualify. He never did. He didn't even come close. But he did have the advantage of training with the best on off-hours, early mornings, and summer vacations.

He'd brought all of that training, and his knowledge of the world outside of the U.P. back here when his father got ill. What Zach hadn't realized until he showed up to spell his mother was that she was in the middle stages of dementia. His parents had just hidden it from him.

He'd stayed then, helping them both, until his father passed away last year. His mother followed within days which, Zach liked to think, showed she was more aware of what was going on than it seemed. When she had been 100% herself, she had loved Zach's father beyond reason, and often said she couldn't imagine life without him.

She didn't have to, since they were together now, in whatever afterlife they both believed in.

Thought of them made him sadder than he wanted to be. He crossed the grass, careful to avoid the visible dips, and reached the group a few minutes before the new runner did.

She didn't seem to notice him. Instead, she stopped by Barb Geisinger, the oldest woman in the group. Barb ran the diner near campus, so maybe the woman had seen her before.

Zach was barely close enough to hear.

"This the running group?" the woman asked.

Barb nodded, then said something in her Yooper accent that made Zach wince. "Yah. We accept everyone here."

She had never said that before, and probably wouldn't have said it now, if the woman's appearance hadn't startled her.

"Well, good, then," the woman said with a smile that didn't quite reach her eyes. "Is this everyone or are there, like, groups?"

She meant training groups for different distances. Zach had encountered that in California, and had hoped to implement it when he came here, but of course, he couldn't.

"This is it," Ronnie Hareld said. He was the closest thing to worldly among the runners, besides Zach himself. Ronnie was working on a master's in Cybersecurity, but he had come at it after getting a bachelor's in Theater and Entertainment Engineering. He had encountered almost all the personality types Michigan Tech had to offer.

The woman looked at the trail as if she had never seen it before.

Ronnie extended his hand and introduced himself, first name only, the way they all did here. Zach liked to think of this club as a kind of Runner's Anonymous. They could reveal more about who they were if they chose to.

The woman took his hand, without a lot of enthusiasm, it seemed to Zach, and said, "I'm Gabrielle," then went back to looking at the trail again.

It seemed like she already regretted coming. He had no idea what she had expected in the middle of the U.P. There weren't a lot of runners, and there certainly wasn't much diversity.

To his credit, Ronnie actually caught her discomfort and decided not to add to it. He let her wait, like the rest of them.

Then Tag Drummond, who had stepped in as group leader when Zach got injured, raised his hands over his head and clapped.

"Okay," he said. "We're taking the 5K Nationals training route today, so expect a lot of looping, and watch the signs."

The woman turned to Ronnie. "5K Nationals?"

"Nordic skiing," Ronnie said. "We take advantage in the summer, because they hate it when we run on their trails in the winter."

She nodded the way people did when they didn't entirely understand, and then hung back on the edge of the group to keep an eye on what everyone else did.

Zach decided not to approach her. She seemed nervous enough, although she hid it well. He moved to the front of the group, shared some small talk about his shoulder, and laughed over his contraption, even though it was really digging into his ribcage.

The 5K course was not one of his favorites. When he led the group, he took the time to build a new course at various lengths, so that they changed up which trails they went on and what direction they'd go. Sometimes he even led the group out of the university area, and deeper into the wilds of the U.P. Sometimes they even appreciated it.

But maybe Tag had decided to remain closer to campus for Zach. Everyone knew this was his first day back running, and they figured he would need some support.

He wanted to pretend the injury hadn't even happened. Maybe, just maybe, if he was smart and trained properly, he would be ready to run the marathon at the Mount Bohemia Trail Running Festival in October.

He knew that was pushing it, but he could always fall back to the half. He wasn't going to consider anything shorter.

"...about thirty minutes from now," Tag was saying, "my girlfriend and her friends will show up with some snacks and beverages for us. I'm going to do a headcount now, so we know when everyone gets done..."

And whether or not they had to have someone walk the trail to see if someone got stuck or lost or injured.

They'd only had to do that once since the group started, but that once had been scary enough. Barb's husband Mitch had passed out on one of the side trails, and it'd been hell getting the EMTs to find him. That had been the beginning of the end for him. He had cancer anyway, but he'd been fighting it until then.

Tag went to the trailhead. Technically that was not where the Nordic 5K training trail began, but no one complained. They would have to walk from the parking lot anyway, so rather than do that, they'd run it. That was what they always did.

Which meant the Nordic training route really wasn't 5K. It was closer to 5.5K, but Zach had never told the group that, and no one apparently had double checked him—or if they had, they hadn't cared.

He hung toward the back. He wasn't going to run at his usual pace. When they reached the single part of the trail, he would probably hold up the whole group. Better to bring up the rear.

Besides, that way, no one would see him attempt to run with only one arm functioning.

He let out a breath. He was more nervous than he thought.

Part of him wondered if he had come back too early. And the rest of him dismissed the thought.

If he had, he could always walk.

He didn't want the group to see that either.

Then he grinned at himself. He wasn't thinking entirely about the group. Some of his desire to stay out of their view came from his own internal sense of self-worth.

He didn't want to walk. He didn't like to think about his new gait.

And he really wished he could run at the usual pace.

So it was less about them, and a lot more about him.

Maybe it was time he acknowledged that, before he set one sneakered foot on the course.

3

Because she had no idea what speed this group trained at, Gabrielle had no idea where she should stand—the middle of the pack or the very end. She was a recreational runner, not a serious one, or so she usually told her friends.

The second half wasn't really true. She *was* a serious runner. She just wasn't competitive. She didn't care about her times. She didn't try to get a personal record every race. Some years, she didn't even race at all.

But she ran five days a week and hadn't missed for over two years. If something got in the way of her run, she would get very cranky.

She wasn't involved with anyone, though, so the only person who had to deal with her crankiness was herself.

She moved to the middle of the pack, mostly because being all the way back irritated her. She usually got behind someone who walked or moved so slowly that they might as well have been walking.

And she had seen the guy wrapped up like a mummy near the very back. He had a runner's build, but that thing around him to hold his arm in place was kinda scary. If he hadn't used it before, he would be off balance, and if he was off balance, he would veer all over the course.

She'd taken these trails enough to know that in some parts there wasn't any room to comfortably go around someone like that. She'd be irritated, not because she was trying to beat some imaginary record, only important to her, but because she didn't like walking when she planned on running.

There was no timer, no buzzer, no air horn to start this group forward. Just the scraggly older guy who had greeted them all, waving his arm and yelling, "We're off!"

Two runners in the front—Ronnie the friendly guy, and another young man of indeterminate age, wearing glasses so thick that Gabrielle wondered how he could see. They were attached around his head with some cord or rubber thing, so apparently he was nearly blind when they fell off—took off at a gallop.

Two of the women followed at a good clip, and then a few more headed out. Gabrielle ran with them, until she couldn't any more. It seemed, in this small self-selected group, she was one of the faster runners.

The trail was difficult though. It was truly a trail—a pounded flat dirt area, with grass growing through. She hadn't understood until that Tag guy had said this was a Nordic training ground why the trails were like this. They weren't designed for runners; they were designed for what she had grown up thinking of as cross-country skiing. Nordic skiing, according to the very serious folk up here on the U.P.

Right now, though, only part of the area was flat dirt. The rest was churned up mud. Apparently other runners had been there before this group, and left their mark on the soft ground.

The bugs were thick, just like she expected, and either her bug spray didn't work well or the bugs were so bad that this assault was an improvement. Behind her, she heard some good-natured conversation, and someone laughing, saying "You really can't keep a good man down, now can you, Zach?"

She didn't hear the reply. She was working too hard on this course, mostly trying to keep pace with the leaders. The course was hilly, which she should have expected—Nordic, after all—and there were a lot of ruts and tree roots on the path. There were side trails that veered off, some that had big signs that said *Keep Out! Wrong Way!* Which, she had learned the hard way on previous runs, meant that they were one-way trails that fit only one person, and there was nowhere to go if someone showed up going the other way.

Still, she managed to settle into a rhythm, at least here in the wider part of the run, and it actually felt good.

It also felt nice to have other runners around her, even if the conversation so far consisted of "On your left!" and "Watch out for that root!" She was actually grinning, something she figured out when a bug dive-bombed its way into her teeth.

She slowed, choking a little. The bug had gone too deep to spit out—not that she would have spit in front of people she didn't know. Instead, she moved to the side and opened her water bottle, swallowing the cold, clean water like a lifeline.

She also felt the stupid bug go down her throat, and hoped to hell the bug was dead, and not something that stung. She whispered quietly to herself, "Protein," just like her coach in high school used to say when kids got a lungful of gnats in the crap-ass course near their even crappier West Side school.

Footsteps echoed on the path, and she went a little deeper into the trees so that whoever was coming wouldn't trip. It was the mummy guy. Despite his contraption, he had great form and a really smooth stride. She envied that. She looked like a chunky child who had never run before every time she went out, no matter how hard she practiced.

He was surprisingly good-looking. He had blondish-brown hair in need of a cut, so it streamed behind him. He had angular cheekbones and a strong chin. He was grinning. His blue eyes sparkled with sheer joy.

She usually didn't find white guys with perfect bone structure good-looking. They usually made her catch her breath and wait until they had left the area she was in. She had had the most trouble in her life with two groups of white men—the really good-looking (entitled) ones who thought she was a maid or some other employee, or the older ugly ones (who were probably wearing the face they earned after fifty) who called her all kinds of names.

She rarely encountered the second kind on runs, but the first kind were thick on the ground here, particularly the farther north she went. She'd been following the Underground Railroad path to Sault Ste Marie for her dissertation, and she had learned fairly quickly that most former Southern slaves went *through* these parts. They didn't actually settle here.

The research was fascinating, but the trips she had to take to find primary materials made her more nervous than she cared to admit.

The mummy guy passed her, and his grin widened. "C'mon!" he said. "You'll miss all the good snacks."

She had to listen hard to hear that last part, he went by so fast. No one was close behind him, although she could hear other runners crashing along the trail, just out of sight.

She did not want to get caught up with them, so she capped her water and sprinted after Mummy Guy. He was already long gone—or so she thought.

Because when she rounded the next corner, she could see him just ahead. A large tree branch had fallen along the course—probably during that violent thunderstorm the night before—and the runners ahead of Mummy Guy leapt over it.

"Oh, shit," she whispered to herself. He was into the run. He wasn't thinking about his arms or his balance.

He was going to jump it too—she just knew it.

She didn't dare yell at him, because if she yelled at him, he would turn back toward her and either trip on the branch or lose his balance from the movement of turning.

She hoped she was wrong about what he was going to do. She hoped she had misjudged him or (honestly) was just applying what *she* would have done in his shoes.

But nope, she wasn't wrong.

He leapt over the branch and for one brief shining moment she thought he was going to make it. Then his left foot got tangled in some smaller branches—apparently he hadn't jumped as high as he thought he had—and he moved his right arm laterally to balance himself. The mummy suit contraption thing undulated as if a snake had jumped inside—he probably was trying to extend his left arm too—and he tripped forward, the way good runners did, one foot after another, moving faster and faster until something caught him again, and he pinwheeled down an embankment she hadn't even realized was there.

The fall was almost silent—which told her he'd done this before, because seasoned runners fell. Athletes fell. Newbies fell and splatted and screamed all the way down.

Leaves floated up, almost like something out of the Road-runner cartoons. She half-smiled. Mummy Guy probably wouldn't have appreciated being compared to Wile E. Coyote.

She reached the branch about a minute later. There was no evidence that a man had fallen here, and she wouldn't have believed it if she hadn't seen it with her own eyes.

The branch was larger than she expected—not something she would ever have jumped.

She carefully went around it, the edge of the branch reaching for her compression pants. She would have been scratched all to hell if she was wearing shorts.

She got to the other side, and saw that part of the path had crumbled away, probably in the same storm that brought down the branch. She leaned over the edge, but she didn't see him—for a moment anyway.

Then she did, sprawled awkwardly on his stomach, using his good arm to find purchase, trying to pull himself up, and failing because of the angle.

"Hey, you okay?" she called, but he didn't answer her. He had to have heard her, because she could hear him cursing softly as he kept trying to push himself into a sitting position and failing.

She looked back down the trail, but didn't see the runners she had heard earlier. Maybe she heard an echo from the runners who had been ahead of her, instead of the ones behind her.

It didn't matter. What Mummy Guy couldn't see was that he was still on precarious ground. The area where he had landed had no real base beneath it, because the water that had taken out the hillside above had undercut the place he was resting several feet below him.

She started down the dry side of the hill, but needed both hands. So she reached up and put her water bottle on the trail. That way, when the organizers started searching for the missing runners, they would think to look down here.

She kept one hand braced on the hillside, and the other out for balance, ironically mimicking the motion Mummy Guy had tried to use when he lost his balance jumping over that branch. The ground was mushy and wet, and came apart in her fingers, threatening another cascade of dirt down the side of the hill.

There had been localized heavy rain during those storms. One of the cells had let loose over her apartment, flooding the backyard. The street two blocks away remained dry.

Mummy Guy was trying to move his knees forward, still unable to get purchase. She wondered if he was injured anywhere else.

She didn't try to talk to him anymore. She just had to get down to him. Then she would worry about climbing back up.

4

Zach couldn't lean properly, so every time he got his free hand underneath himself, he toppled over, which didn't help his mood. Every time he toppled, he jarred his uninjured shoulder, but that jar echoed through his entire back and side and *injured* shoulder, making him see stars. He was sliding deeper into the muck, unable to figure out a way to get his knees beneath him, so that he would stop falling.

Just great. This was all just great. He had been stupid, and what made it worse was that he realized he had been stupid in the middle of the stupid, as he was in mid-air over that damn branch, before his left foot caught on something. Even if his foot hadn't caught, he probably would have fallen, because he felt off-balance in midair.

He had lost track of his injury. He was feeling so good as he ran—the first time he had felt good in weeks—that he forgot he was hurt. Not even the bouncing hurt, because his arm was properly wrapped—for running. Not for falling. He would have caught himself with his hand without the damn contraption. It would have hurt. It might even have ripped something in his shoulder. But at least he only would have been hurt once.

Now he had no idea what the extent of his injury was. Or reinjury. Or new injury. His left ankle was aching and he kept trying to will that pain away. He didn't need another injury on top of this one.

"Hey." The voice was female and gentle. "I want to help, but you'll have to tell me where I can touch you. I don't want to hurt you worse."

He couldn't turn around to see who the voice belonged to but the voice didn't have a Yooper accent. The accent was classic Midwestern—Broadcast Midwestern, one of his colleagues called it.

Zach knew all the women in the group, and they all had Yooper accents or some variation on the upper Midwestern dees and does. This woman didn't, which meant it was the newcomer.

Of course, she would be the one to see him. What a great introduction to the running group—having to rescue the idiot who started the whole thing.

"When I push up," he said, "if you could just brace my torso, I think I'll be able to get my legs underneath me."

"Okay," she said. Then hands lightly touched his waist. "Here? Or somewhere else?"

"Let's see if that works," he said.

Her grip grew stronger—much stronger than he expected—

and he slid his right hand underneath his chest. With her help, he was able to stay upward long enough to slide his legs forward and out, so that he was actually sitting down, instead of lying face down in the mud.

Mud coated the front of his contraption, his tights, and his brand-new shoes. It probably coated his face too. He would have said that he had never been so embarrassed in his life, but that wasn't true. This was just one humiliation on top of millions that he had suffered due to clumsiness.

But this was the first time he'd ever face-planted and had to be rescued by a beautiful woman.

"I think I'm okay," he said, hoping she'd leave and go on with her run.

"I don't think so." She was crouched beside him, her shoes sinking into the mud. She swept one hand behind her. "You fell quite a ways, and I had trouble getting down. I have no idea how we're going to get up this."

He looked. She was right. The hillside was raw mud, made worse by fall.

"And this area is unstable," she said. "Looks like water ran underneath us, so you're on some kind of overhang."

Anywhere else in the Midwest, that might not have been an issue. But they were near Lake Superior, where the glaciers had carved serious hillsides into the land. The Nordic training track started at 1,000 feet and he had no idea how high the elevation ended up being, but that didn't really matter. What mattered was this hill was impossible to climb.

"Fortunately," he said to her, "there are a million trails here. If we can go down the hill, we'll encounter another one. Everything loops against everything else. If we are where I think we are, we might even run into the rest of the group."

She grinned. The grin lit up her entire face. "A cheater's course, eh?"

"If this were a race, yeah. All you have to do is cut through the woods to shave minutes off your time."

"Well," she said, "you're going to have to show me this shortcut."

"And I'm afraid I'll need your help to stand up," he said.

"That's why I'm here," she said. "I'm going to follow your lead on how to help you, though. I have no idea what is injured and what isn't."

Yeah, me either, he nearly said, but then realized she was talking about the contraption, not the new injuries.

"I had surgery on my left shoulder a few weeks ago, and I figured if I strapped it up well enough, I could run." He made himself smile, hoping it looked self-deprecating. "Obviously, I was wrong."

"You weren't wrong," she said. "You ran beautifully. You just don't jump very well."

He let out an involuntary laugh. "You saw that."

"It was—well, whatever the opposite of poetry in motion is."

"Yeah," he said. "I couldn't figure out how to stop myself, and then the ground crumbled, and here I am. Mud Man."

She extended her right hand. "Hello, Mud Man. I'm Gabrielle."

"Mud Man is my superhero name," he said. "I would prefer it if you don't spread it around. Call me Zach."

"It's rather hard, Zach, to keep your secret identity secret when your costume gives you away." She ran a finger around her face. "I have some wipes in my pocket. You want them?"

He shook his head. "I don't want to waste them. I have a hunch I'll fall again before this is over."

"I'm going to do my best to prevent that," she said.

He ran his right hand over his face. She was right: he was solid mud. He felt the mud slide when he ran his hand over it, but his hand was muddy too. He had probably made things worse.

"Better?" he asked.

Her eyes twinkled. "When we get back to civilization, Mud Man, we'll have a discussion about your costume choices. I think you might want a new designer."

He laughed again, surprised that he could, given the ache in the left side of his body. He slid his feet forward, and braced them in the muck.

"We're going to want to go right," he said. "I'm going to do my best to stand. If you could support me the way you did last time, I would appreciate it."

"No problem," she said, as if she did this every day. She was still crouched, but her position looked stable enough. She put her hands on his waist, which made him feel a lot more secure.

Surprisingly.

He leaned a little toward the right, using his right hand for leverage. He managed to get upright, but nearly fell sideways. Gabrielle steadied him. She stood with him, then slid her arm around his waist, and braced his right side, careful not to hurt the already inflamed left.

"The path is that way." He pointed through the trees. "Looks like we'll have to cross that little wash the water made."

He was worried about that. The wash looked deep and muddy, with water pooled at the bottom, and he couldn't jump it.

"It's narrower about a yard up. I suggest we go there," she said, and half pulled half led him to what must have been a rivulet in last night's torrent. The water must have split in two different directions, uniting near the area where he fell.

Gabrielle led him over that narrow area, and then waited beside him as he got his balance again. They crossed the second narrow area, lukewarm mud seeping into his shoes.

Their next step, though, was solid ground. She held him firmly, keeping him braced. He felt like an old man heading down the slight incline, partly because his shoes were mud-covered and partly because he hurt in places he hadn't even realized he could hurt. He had really done (another) number on himself.

"Almost there," he said. He could see the clearing ahead. They would still have a walk ahead of them, but it wasn't as far it would have been if they had somehow managed to get back up the hill.

He was glad of that. He wasn't sure how much father he could go. The adrenaline was draining from his system, and the aches were starting to take over. He needed to sit down, and soon.

5

Zach was shaking, and Gabrielle would wager he didn't even know it. He was probably in shock from the fall, and the sooner she got him back to the university, the better. From there, they could determine if anything was broken, if he needed his surgeon, or if he needed the E.R.

Until then, it was her job to keep him distracted, but she had no real idea how to do it.

"How did you hurt your shoulder?" she asked, and then winced. She didn't want him focusing on the injury. She wanted him to move forward.

"Bookshelves," he said through gritted teeth.

"Bookshelves attacked you?" Humor had worked a few minutes ago; she hoped it would work now.

"More or less. The ladder was the real culprit." He picked his way across two large roots, moving like he was in pain.

"Ladders usually are," she said. "Your bookshelves or a friend's?"

"Mine," he said.

"Sounds like they need to be replaced before they strike again," she said.

"Only if they continue conspiring with the ladder," he said.

"Did the bookshelves fall down?" she asked.

"Just some books," he said. "And me. And that ladder."

"I'll bet your family was worried," she said.

"They may be," he said. "I haven't told them yet."

That surprised her. "What?"

"I live alone."

"Oh," she said. "I just figured you had family here. A partner, kids, maybe."

"Not yet," he said. He sounded distracted. And then he smiled. "There it is!"

A few yards ahead of them was a dirt trail, one of the single-file ones.

Oh, well. If she and Zach were going the wrong way on the trail, someone else would have to move. Or help them.

"I'm all turned around," she said. "Which direction is the university?"

He nodded toward the right. "Almost straight ahead of us."

Okay, then, she wasn't as turned around as she thought. It felt odd, though, being on this nature trail in the middle of the city. She could hear birds chirping, and some horseflies buzzed near one of the mud puddles. But she couldn't hear the other runners, which she thought strange.

Maybe they had already returned. She had lost track of the time as she helped him, and right now, she wasn't in the position to look at her watch.

"Sorry about screwing up your run," he said.

"That's the least of my worries," she said.

"Well, it's not a great introduction to the group." He was limping more than he had a few minutes ago. "It's a good group. Eclectic, though. More engineers than liberal arts majors. Most running groups aren't like that."

Sideways information. She hated that. She was glad he couldn't see her face. He assumed she wasn't an engineer, so he explained how engineers operated. It annoyed her. She *wasn't* an engineer or even had much science in her background, but that didn't mean she couldn't do it, based on how she looked.

"Are you connected to the university?" he asked. "Or do you work for one of the corporations?"

There were more corporations in Houghton than she had expected, many with tech backgrounds, although some of the old stalwarts, like Ford, remained.

"University," she said, not wanting to be annoyed at him. He was injured. He probably wasn't thinking about the assumptions he was making. "I'm here for a year to do research for my Ph.D."

"So you *are* one of the engineering types," he said. "I thought so."

Her cheeks heated. She had it exactly backward. He had assumed she *was* a science nerd. She had misjudged him.

"I didn't say that," she said.

"You don't have to," he said. "Tech doesn't have a lot of advanced degree programs, and the only Ph.Ds. it offers are in science and engineering. So, if you're not an engineer, then you're some kind of scientist."

He said that without judgment, although he was looking down. But that might have been because he was trying to negotiate the narrow path.

"Well," she said, "sorry to disappoint, but I'm actually going to be on loan to the history department in the fall."

He turned to look at her, a frown creasing his face. The frown was prodigious, and she wasn't sure why, exactly.

"*You're* the specialist in Michigan history?" he asked.

She nearly said, *Don't I look like a specialist in Michigan history?* But she caught herself—why did she always have to catch herself? Why couldn't other people catch themselves?—and said, "Yes."

Because to say anything else was to justify her presence here and she wasn't going to do that.

"God," he said, "I'm such an idiot. Of course you are. Gabrielle Carter."

Her last name startled her. She hadn't given him her last name.

"I was on the committee that finalized your appointment," he said. "I'm Zachary Visscher."

"Oh," she said, not sure what he wanted from her.

"I should have connected the name, but I didn't. We weren't expecting you until August. Does University Housing know you're here?"

"Yes," she said. "They had a lovely apartment for me right near campus. They're probably the only ones who know I'm here."

Except the librarians and researchers at the libraries and research centers in town. She'd already visited them, and got assistance negotiating the various collections. At least two of the librarians were as excited about her project as she was.

"Wow," he said. "I wish we'd known. We usually have a welcoming committee and a meet-and-greet and I like to make sure our visiting professors have welcome baskets—"

"Welcome baskets?"

He shrugged and then winced. "The area has a lot to offer. So I usually put together something with my staff that includes coupons to various businesses, some produce from the Farmer's Market, cheese, some Borealis Broo—"

"Borealis brew?" she asked.

"Yeah," he said. "It's a KBC IPA. You clearly haven't found Keweenaw Brewing Company yet."

"Sounds like I've missed a number of things," she said.

"Well, we'll get you your basket," he said. "Or I will. And it'll be extra big, because I owe you."

"You don't," she said. "Anyone would have helped."

"Yeah, except I got your outfit covered in mud, ruined your

first run with the group, and gave you a bad impression of every-thing," he said.

She laughed. "What are you? Houghton's Welcome Wagon?"

"God," he said, "that's a phrase I haven't heard in forever. Maybe not even used in conversation ever."

"My mother used to say it," she said. *In a derogatory manner. About snotty white people.* But she didn't need to add that, because he didn't need to hear it because he was being nice.

"Well, wow." He stumbled forward, and she pulled him a little tighter against her, just to make sure he didn't fall again.

He smiled at her, but his eyes were glassy with pain.

"I'm, um," he said. "I'm a professor in the history department, which means I also teach American Studies and a whole variety of other courses."

Because the liberal arts weren't as important here. She had been warned about that when she applied for the temporary posi-tion. Her advisor downstate had put in a good word for her, though—or maybe several good words.

And maybe, just maybe, she was a diversity hire. It looked like the university was starting to expand its awareness, which would either be good or awkward. She wasn't sure which, and she was prepared for both.

Or maybe she wasn't. She had assumed that Zach would be thinking of her in a way he didn't seem to be at all. Maybe she had come here a bit too defensive.

Or maybe he *was* an aberration.

"What are you researching?" he asked into her silence.

"Oh," she said, caught off-guard. She was supposed to be asking him questions, not the other way around. "The Under-ground Railroad went through the U.P., although the history books say that's unofficial. I'm not so sure. There's a history of former slaves up here who stayed, including some in the Keweenaw Peninsula."

"Gaines Rock," he said, citing an outcropping named for a former slave named William Washington Gaines who made quite a name for himself in the U.P.

"Among others," she said. "I think there's a lot more to be discovered. No trains ran up here, which kept slavers out, and some historians assumed that's why some Black families stayed in the U.P. I know that a lot of Black families crossed into Canada at Sault Ste Marie. But they had to get there to the Soo, and there's too many folk who settled here from Georgia and Virginia and other places south. You usually find a small percentage of Black settlers in every community the Railroad went through—or rather, every *Northern* community."

He let out a deep breath. "You're going to be doing some real hardcore investigation."

"I've already started," she said. "There are just too many questions that no previous historian has even tried to answer. Black history gets lost, and I want to find it."

She half expected a *Good for you!* from him, which would have been horribly dismissive, but that's what she'd heard from other history professors, particularly white ones, who heard about her research.

"It sounds fascinating," he said. "If there's anything I can do to help, I will. I know some of the tricks in the Van Pelt and Opie's records, and I can help you navigate them."

His offer surprised her. She had already found that the university's research library was a goldmine, but a goldmine that was difficult to negotiate.

"This area is rich in untapped history," he was saying. "A lot of people escaped up here and tried to hide from their pasts. It's a real vagabond part of the country. It's a harsh place to live, and that brought a certain type of person—individualists who could handle the loneliness of the winters, mostly. They didn't leave a lot of records."

"We don't know that," she said. "I'm finding a lot more than I expected."

Of course, she had to dig for them. But that was why she was here. She actually loved digging in old records.

The path curved, and then tilted up a few yards. She thought she saw some buildings up ahead, but she wasn't sure.

He was really dragging. Each step seemed like work. They crested the small rise, and the path widened. She recognized it now. The path joined the trailhead. The signs were just ahead, half-hidden by trees and morning shadows.

He let out a small sigh, as if seeing the trailhead made him even more tired. She braced him and kept him moving, hoping she wasn't hurting his already damaged back.

They walked into a clearing. A single folding table was set up just off the path, and white people she didn't recognize stood behind it, pulling bottles of Gatorade out of coolers stored beneath the table. There were some baked snacks and some salty items and, it looked like, a pile of fruit.

"Hey!" the scraggy old guy who had started the run yelled. "It's Zach!"

The entire small crowd cheered.

Zach straightened. "This is Gabrielle," he said, sounding like he had a lot more energy than she knew he did. "She rescued me. Unlike you people!"

"We are looking for you," the scraggly old guy said. "I'll call off the teams."

He went away from the group, his cell phone out. Barb, the woman who had introduced herself earlier, walked toward them, holding Gabrielle's water bottle.

"This is yours, I trust?" Barb said.

"Yes, thank you for rescuing it," Gabrielle said.

"Thank you for rescuing Zach," Barb said, then peered at him. "You need to sit down," she said to him.

"He needs to go to the emergency room," Gabrielle said. "He took a hell of a fall."

"I'm..heh." He let out a small laugh. "I was going to say 'I'm fine,' but I'd be lying."

"I'll take him," said the man, Ronnie, who had introduced himself to her before the run.

"I don't mind," she said. "My car is already going to get muddy."

She swept a hand down her body, and as she did so, she realized she wasn't as mud-covered as she thought.

"My truck is made of mud," Ronnie said. "I off-road as much as I can."

He reached out a hand, and helped Zach forward. Zach didn't fight him. Maybe Zach was beyond fighting him.

Gabrielle felt almost bereft letting go of him. She wanted to see this through, but she had no real right to.

Then she reached into the zippered pocket of her pants. Tucked into her phone's case were some business cards. She pulled one out and extended it.

"Call me," she said. "Let me know how this goes."

"Sure thing," Ronnie said, and reached for the card, but Zach grabbed it first, then nearly fell over.

Both Ronnie and Gabrielle caught him, and Zach let out an involuntary moan.

"I think he jarred everything," Gabrielle said to Ronnie. "He'll need some kind of scan, but he did manage to walk out, and get onto his feet, so I'm thinking he's just bruised. He wouldn't have been able to walk that easily if he had broken something."

"Got it," Ronnie said.

"I'm right here," Zach said. "I can speak for myself."

Ronnie's gaze met Gabrielle's over the top of Zach's head. Ronnie raised his eyebrows as if he couldn't quite believe that.

Zach stuck Gabrielle's business card in his pocket. She pulled out one more and handed it to Ronnie.

Ronnie nodded, then winked. He helped Zach turn around.

"Um," Barb said, in that way some women had, when they should have sounded uncertain, but they really used vague words as a command. "Maybe Zach should wait here. You can drive the truck to the trailhead."

"Is that allowed?" Gabrielle asked.

"Do we care?" Barb said, with all that confidence that some people had about breaking rules because they'd never had any consequences. "Just do it, Ronnie."

He nodded, then guided Zach back to Gabrielle. She put her arm around him, holding him up like before.

No one had brought chairs. But at least Zach wasn't walking anymore.

And if Barb could give orders, Gabrielle could too.

"Could you get him some Gatorade, and maybe a banana?" she asked.

"Oh, yeah, sure." Barb said, and peeled off.

"I'm not helpless," Zach said, but he was still shaking and he was wobbly.

"That's clear," Gabrielle said. "But better to have someone drive you and act as a second ear for the doctor."

"They're going to tell me not to run," he said.

"Yes, they are," she said.

He frowned again, another prodigious frown, and this one was more foreboding than the last one. "I don't want to give up running."

"You're not," she said. "You're going to take a break to heal."

"Would you?"

She wouldn't want to. "It would break my streak," she said. "But yeah. If it meant I would heal, yes, I would."

He let out a gusty sigh. "I hate logic."

"Me, too," she said, and laughed. Other people were watching them out of the corners of their eyes. Maybe they thought he had invited her.

Let them. She didn't care.

"I took your card," he said, "because I want to buy you dinner."

She turned and looked at him. That handsome face was caked with mud, but his bright blue eyes didn't look nearly as glassy as they had before. They looked sharp and alive and intelligent.

"You don't owe me anything for doing this," she said. "You'd have done the same."

He shook his head, and nearly lost his balance again. Her grip on him tightened.

"I want to take you to dinner," he said, slowly, as if each word was critical, "because I want to get to know you better. You and I have a lot in common. Running, teaching, history..."

She blinked at him, startled. He was right: they did have a lot in common—at least superficially. And a dinner would allow them to figure out if their shared interests were worth building a friendship over.

Or more.

"This would be a date?" she asked.

"Yeah," he said, and maybe hearing the hesitation in her voice, added, "There's nothing to worry about. I'm not your immediate supervisor."

He hadn't realized her hesitation came from a different place. She had never dated a white man before.

"A date," she repeated.

She was intrigued. She was more than intrigued, really. She liked him, and clearly, he liked her.

"How about this," she said. "How about I call to see how you are, and then we set up a dinner somewhere."

"Nope," he said. "Give me three days to recover enough to not embarrass myself, and then I'll take you to Joey's."

"The seafood place on the water?" she asked.

"Best fish and chips in Michigan," he said. "If you like that kind of thing."

She smiled. "I do."

"I'll meet you at eight," he said.

"You won't remember." Barb was standing slightly behind Gabrielle, holding the Gatorade. Gabrielle hadn't even heard her approach. "You're in shock and in pain."

She was right; he probably wouldn't remember.

"So," Barb said. "I'll remind ya. Because this here lady, she's gone above and beyond for you, and deserves kindness." Then Barb winked at Gabrielle, and added, "Doncha know."

Gabrielle laughed. She'd never heard anyone deliberately use that phrase in conversation before.

"I do know," Zach said. "I'll be there. At eight."

A truck zoomed over the grass on the trailhead. Ronnie had been right—his truck was made of mud. Gabrielle couldn't even tell what kind of truck it was.

It stopped right next to them, passenger side next to Zach. Barb walked over and pulled the door open.

The truck was huge. Zach would have to step into it. Gabrielle kept him braced as he tried, his only free hand on the side of the truck. She took most of his weight as he leveraged himself inside.

He groaned involuntarily, and then smiled at her.

"I'm usually not this much work," he said.

"Good," she said with a smile. "But promise me something."

His smile faded. "Anything," he said.

"No more fights with ladders," she said.

"Or branches," he said. "I'll rest, just like the doctor ordered."

"Orders," Barb said.

"Order*ed*," Zach said, nodding at Gabrielle. "I listen to sensible people."

Her smile widened. "I already have you fooled," she said. "I'm not sensible."

He pulled the door closed. "I can't wait until our dinner," he said. "You give me something to look forward to."

The truck shuddered as Ronnie put it in reverse, and then it drove off. Barb was still holding the Gatorade.

"You want it?" she asked.

Gabrielle watched the truck disappear across the track toward the university.

She took the Gatorade from Barb, and tilted it toward her in a mock toast. "Thanks."

"He's a good man," Barb said. "I think you'll have fun."

And then she walked back to the table.

Gabrielle looked over her shoulder. The truck was gone. The run was over. But this morning had been the kind of change she had hoped for.

She met some people. She met some *runners*. She'd learned a few things about herself. And she ended up a little different.

As much as she enjoyed her work, every day had been the same since she had come to the U.P. She had come here to make friends, and maybe she was at the start of that.

But she also had a date, which she hadn't expected. With a man who shared her interests, something that was hard to find.

And those two things combined to give her something she hadn't had in months, maybe years. Something to look forward to.

Just like Zach had said.

GUN RUNNING ON VACATION

STEFON MEARS

Okay, it's a stretch. "Gun Running on Vacation" shares the word "running" with Katie Pressa's story, but that's about it—oh, well. That and romance, of course. But the kind of running in this story is obviously very different from the previous story.

Stefon writes about anything and everything, but he's best known for his Rise of Magic series. Stefon publishes a lot of fantasy, but my favorites are his mystery short stories, including some that just appeared in our second Holiday Spectacular. His short fiction has also appeared in our Year of the Cat series as well as in seven volumes of Fiction River *so far, as well as other publications that aren't produced by WMG Publishing. Find out more at stefonmears.com*

Stefon got the inspiration for this story when he went on a trip with his oldest friend. He writes, "The Sea of Cortes down in Baja Mexico is a beautiful place. But on the drive down there from California, you pass by a number of places where the chapparal is littered with the bones of old houses. Their frames and walls remain, but their windows, roofs, doors, all gone. The contrast of that struck me when I went down there on vacation.... I found myself thinking about Americans traveling abroad, coming to a place of such contrasts – and getting stuck. Maybe a man whose best friend wasn't the stand-up guy that my best friend is. I started thinking about the worst way this could go, and still have a slim chance of ending well, and then I had to get to the keyboard."

We're glad he did.

I

Jon

It all started with a colossal fuck-up. And I was looking at him.

Derek. My best friend for ages, and partner in crime for the past decade. Might as well have been brothers. We were close enough, and we looked the part. Both tall, lean, blonde and mean.

Well, Derek was the mean one. He had the O.C. pedigree. I had the head for money. Yeah, I could handle myself, but Derek's bad-boy streak made me look strictly G-rated. By all rights, he should have had a facial scar or an eyepatch. Some kind of warning not to push too hard.

Didn't look mean right now. Had that hangdog, I-know-I-fucked-up look I'd seen way too many times over the years. Shoulders slumped, head hanging forward, lips pulled in tight.

And this fuck-up, this was the worst of all.

Of course, part of the reason for that is that I was hearing the worst possible news in the most beautiful place on earth. A beach just outside a little town called ... well, let's just say it's called San Fernando. It's down in Baja, on the Sea of Cortez, and you can probably figure out its real name if you try hard enough. But you won't hear it from me. Not after the way things went down.

The April sun was blazing that day, at least to two boys from the Pacific Northwest. Barely noon, and so hot already that I could feel my sunblock melting down my face. So bright my sunglasses needed sunglasses.

But the place was worth it. Explained why people liked the beach so much. Lots of toasty sand, and blue-green water—not the vicious, dark blue of the Pacific or the Sound, both of which were what I knew best. Here it was more green and inviting.

And so warm. Nothing like the icy deathtrap of ocean water up around Washington and Oregon. The water here was like wading into a warm, welcoming, armpit-deep hug that gently rocked me.

And it seemed we could wade forever. We'd wandered out into the water while talking—before we got to Derek's news—and even a good hundred yards from the shoreline, the water still wasn't touching our shoulders.

Even smelled salty and clean here, which surprised me. Didn't have the kind of decay odor I usually associated with my infrequent youthful trips to the shore.

Not to mention the peaceful beauty of the chaparral and desert behind us, or the exquisite beauty of some of the other tourists, both American and Mexican, frolicking back by the water line.

All this. And Derek had to go spoil it.

"You lost *all* our money?" It was the third time I'd asked the question. I still didn't want to believe it. Wanted to think this was some stupid joke. *Ha, ha. Just a little vacation humor.* Poor taste, but better than the alternative.

But no matter how many times I asked the question, Derek's answer didn't change.

Slow intake of breath, nostrils flaring. Grimace. Nod.

"No, you son of a bitch," I said, loud enough that Derek winced.

I had to stop and check to make sure we were alone out here. Seagulls squawking overhead. Laughter back at the shore where the smart, reasonable vacationers were having fun on the crowded beach. Fishing boat motoring by a few hundred yards farther out.

Right here, just the two of us.

I lowered my voice anyway.

"No, you son of a bitch. Don't you just nod at me. You say the words."

"Yes, Jon," Derek said, eyes still downcast. "I lost all our money."

"Let me get this straight," I said, then needed a shaky breath to hold my temper. My knuckles were aching to do something unconstructive. "Not only did you go find a poker game last night, which we have both agreed you're not supposed to do. You *suck* at poker."

I gave Derek a chance to deny that, if he had the guts. But he didn't. Maybe that meant he'd finally learned his lesson? Either that, or he had a plan. And I was angry enough to assume the latter.

"Not only did you do that, instead of a rendezvous like you *claimed* you had," I continued, "but you took *not only* your walking around money. *Not only* your share of the vacation money. But *all our goddamn money?*"

Derek started to nod. Checked it. Said, "That's right, Jon. The buy-in was—"

I held up a warning finger and cut off that excuse right away, then shoved that hand back into the sea to keep from doing anything else with it.

Ten thousand dollars should have been more than enough for a freaking vacation. And this idiot...

I clenched and unclenched my fists under the water. Took a slow breath.

"So you're saying the sixty-odd bucks I've got in my wallet is all we have until we get back to the States?"

Derek nodded.

I shook my head.

"That's not going to cover enough gas and food to get to San Diego, Derek." San Diego was the closest city where we had cash stashed in a safe deposit box. And right then, it might as well have been in outer Mongolia. "Not to mention what we'll have left on the hotel bill over and above our deposit."

That part was my fault. I liked late night room service garlic fries. But compared to what he'd done...

Another slow breath. My heart was pounding with the kind of driving tempo my fists were requesting.

My fists would have to wait. At least until I heard his plan.

"So?" I said.

Derek looked up at me. Eyes narrowed.

"Let's hear it. There's no way you take the heat without

bitching, even when you're entirely in the wrong. Not without waiting until I lose enough steam that you can tell me your solution. Out with it. And you better hope it's good enough that I don't drown you right the fuck here, which we both know I should do."

Derek could take me in a fight. We both knew it. That he chose not to point this out only told me I really wasn't going to like this plan.

I didn't. Oh, I let him finish before I started in on him, but this...

"Derek," I said, once he laid out the particulars, "do you remember the little agreement we made back when we started working together?"

"Yeah, we—"

"We were very clear on who we are, and what we do. We steal cash from the outfit boys before they can stash their ill-gotten gains in overseas accounts. And what do we *not* do?"

Fire in Derek's eyes now, but I was fine with that. I was sick of being the only angry man in this conversation. He shot back what I wanted to hear, but he did it in his most sarcastic tones.

"We don't move drugs. We don't move guns. We only touch cash."

"And what is this brilliant solution of yours?"

"Necessary!" Now it was Derek's turn to check his volume. "Look, you smarmy bastard. I fucked up and I know it. But we can't pull our usual moves here. We can't exactly spend months studying the ins and outs of the local rackets, can we? Not to mention that we don't speak enough Spanish to do it right. Not down here. But that gun shipment is *tonight*. We get paid *tonight*. It's a one-time thing."

The finger he held up to emphasize his last words at least suited his tone.

"A one-time thing set up by the guy you lost our money to?

And you think you can trust this? How do we know the job isn't the only thing being set up tonight?"

"You have an alternative suggestion?"

"Yeah. Let's steal our money back. Or at least enough to get us back to the States. Sounds like this guy's O.C., or whatever the equivalent is down here. At least he's a good target, and then we skip across the border A.S.A.P."

"Oh, this coming from Mr. Cautious? Mr. Study Twice, Rob Once?"

"Well, we're kind of pressed for time, aren't we?" I tapped my chin. "And let me think. Whose fault is that again?"

"Look," he said, trying for something like a calm, if angry, tone, "this guy, he's Hector Fucking Cruz. If he just wanted us dead, he'd kill us. He's a major player down here."

"Why do you know that?"

"Doesn't matter," he said over my disagreement. "Anyway, I already said we'd do it. And he has our names."

"Fuck you," I said, shaking my head. Derek gave my real name to some gun runner? And I was supposed to just *accept* it? "Maybe I'll just call Uncle Sal and have him wire me enough to get home."

Derek caught the singular pronoun there. He also knew the only way Uncle Sal would send me money is if I came home without Derek. Probably wouldn't even wire me money, just a single, nonrefundable plane ticket or something.

Uncle Sal didn't know what Derek and I did for a living, but he suspected it wasn't on the up-and-up, and he blamed Derek for that. Hell, he blamed Derek for my dropping out of business school, too. For a lot of things.

And Derek, he didn't have anyone willing to wire him money. Not after that trouble at the docks a few years back.

Derek held up his hands like I'd pulled a gun on him.

"Whoa," he said. "Look. It's a good gig. A transfer between branches of a drug cartel. So regular their security is lax. We slip in, lift one particular crate. The delivery boys won't know it's special, so they won't miss it until delivery is complete. Might even be days before they discover it's missing. Anyway, we drop that crate off, get paid same night and we're home free."

I just stared at him. Didn't have to say why.

Derek shrugged, but had the grace to look guilty. "He had my name already. I couldn't not give him yours."

"Why did you give him your..." We both had fake I.D.s. Top of the line. There was no reason to give anyone our real names. Not unless...

Slow breaths. Just keep clenching and unclenching those fists. Anything to keep from using them.

"You didn't just lose our money, did you." Not a question. My tone was flat with certainty. "You let him front you when you ran low."

"Another five grand worth."

I shook my head. Started to turn back toward shore. Ready to let him dig himself out of this one. Maybe he gave my name, but if I never showed up for the crime, it was just hearsay.

But Derek dropped the big one.

"You owe me."

Now Derek and me, we'd covered each other's asses many times over the years. So for him to say those words, we both knew what he meant.

Derek was the reason my father was no longer around to beat me. As of back when we were both fifteen. First guy Derek ever killed. First body I ever helped hide.

"Fine," I said, and sighed as I turned back to look at him. My best friend. My brother in all but blood.

My next words tasted bitter. I had to say them though. Derek was still gambling more than he could afford, and with the wrong people. Now he was handing out our *names*...

"I'll do this. But then I'm out."

2

Maria

I stretched my arms, languorous, feeling like a cat in a sunbeam. Trying to milk the last of that setting sun.

The sun wasn't more than a fat, red-orange sliver now, over the mountains in the distance, and the crowds were off seeking their dinners. Only a few remained out here, anywhere near me. A couple sharing a towel that wasn't big enough for two. Two kids with a rubber ball and the happiest collie on earth. Playing and splashing as the tide came in. Their laughter as constant as the break of the waves.

This morning was racing ATVs across the chaparral. But I'd spent most of this afternoon—my final day on assignment down here in Mexico, and the only day I got any playtime—here on the beach. Stretched out on the big red towel that matched my bikini.

Felt weird, having the sun set behind me while I stared out across the water. I grew up around Malibu where the sand was more white-brown than the yellow-brown down here, and where the sun set over the ocean.

I wasn't at the ocean though. I was on the wrong coast of Baja for that. This was the Sea of Cortez. Little too green for my tastes, but it felt warm enough whenever I felt like getting a dip instead of baking my skin an even darker shade than my Salvadorian heritage blessed me with.

Went through enough suntan lotion today that the coconut aroma even flavored the fish tacos I'd snacked on a few hours ago.

The thought of fish tacos made my belly rumble. I checked my phone. No messages, and I still had time before I had to report for tonight's op.

With a sigh I slipped my feet back into my flip-flops and stood. Shrugged into my white floral cover up, that hung to my knees and put at least a little netting between my bikini and onlooking eyes. Enough for beachfront decency, anyway.

I shook the sand out of my towel, slipped my bag over one shoulder, and sauntered back toward the asphalt a few hundred feet away.

The street bordering the beach was filled with parked cars, even now. Only a dozen or so cruising for a parking spot. I wrinkled my nose and pretended I couldn't smell their gas, but already my sense of my idyllic afternoon was shattered.

Not more than a few hundred feet from where I'd been stretched out, and here was humanity. For better or worse. Mexican and American pop music pushed its way out of the sprinkling of restaurants, both the open-air Mom and Pop places and the indoor, sit-down types. And mixed in among the restaurants, sidewalks and storefronts crammed with enough *tourista* crap to power a smaller country's GDP.

The stores were mostly empty right now, but the restaurants looked too full.

I sighed. If I had to wait anyway, I might as well wander up the street a ways and see if I could find one that looked like locals patronized it, instead of just the tourists.

Not twenty paces along the sidewalk—beach side, so I didn't have to deal with eager salespeople—and already the old game kicked in.

Spot the Dealer.

One of the things I learned in the DEA is that pretty much anytime you get enough people together, there'll be at least one drug dealer present. Became a game with my class of trainees. We'd go to malls, shopping centers, sporting events, nightclubs and so on. We'd watch the crowd, place our bets, then one of us would "try to cop."

Not actually trying to buy. Just asking the right question to establish it was possible. "Are you holding?" or whatever the local variant was. And every locale had its own variant. In this particular beach town, the question was either *"Fumar?"* or *"Oler?"* depending on whether you wanted pot or coke. Either worked for meth, apparently. And I forgot to ask about the opiates. Reminded myself to do that before heading back home.

I spotted three potentials as I strolled along. Two guys, one girl. All dressed nondescript. Baggy jeans and plain T's. Hair slicked down, could be any color from dark blonde to black, in this lighting.

All three lingered on the street, paying the right kind of attention. Noting who was passing them. Assessing, but assessing like salesmen, not robbers. Is this my target audience? Does this person seek what I'm selling?

Except, of course, they didn't have any visible product to sell.

Wrong game to play right then. Spoiled my mood. After a long, fun day, I was tensing up again. My jaw clenched, shoulders tightening. I didn't have time for this. I wasn't down here for street rips. I was down here on the exchange program, sharing information and training with the Federal Police.

Took a deep breath and rolled my shoulders. Tried to recapture that languorous feeling, but the sun was nearly gone. I was seeing as much by yellow streetlights as by what remained of the day. And I couldn't smell my coconut lotion for the gas and oil smells of the street. My stomach continued to complain that it wanted one more round of fish tacos.

I had to look away from the crowds. Try to reset myself.

That was when I spotted him.

I'd have noticed him even if he weren't gorgeous. No way to miss a guy who sits on a bench that way. With his butt on the back of the bench, and his feet on the seat. Arms resting on his thighs like his shoulders wanted to slump and he wouldn't let them.

And those thighs were as lean and tight as the rest of him.

Growing up around the beaches of Malibu, I've always had a thing for surfers. This guy, he wasn't a surfer. Too pale for that, and his blonde hair didn't get enough sun to get the right shade.

But Lord, he had the body. Slender and *tight*.

He even dressed right. Checkerboard jams instead of something too tight and showy, and brown boat shoes over bare feet.

Normally I'd've just enjoyed the sight in passing, and gone on about my way. Especially since I had an op tonight. But it was my last night in Mexico, and I hadn't had any time to flirt all week. Even after an afternoon alone on the beach, in my best bikini. Must have gotten too good at the casual keep-away vibe.

If I came back without a story about the boy I met in Mexico, my team would never let me hear the end of it.

So I slowed up as I approached.

"You look like you just lost your best friend."

He looked over at me, his gray eyes distant. Didn't even give me the subtle check-out, which meant one of three things: 1) he was a gentleman, 2) he was wrestling with something serious, or 3) he liked his women chesty, which I was not.

"Might've," he said with a shrug. "Not sure yet."

I ruled out option one right away. This was a bad boy. Now I could claim I just had the right kind of eye to spot bad boys a million miles away, but really, the kind of scar he had along the left side of his ribs only comes from a knife.

Option three, well, if that was the case he'd shoot me down soon enough. And so what? Wasn't like I wanted to sleep with the guy, or like I'd lose any Zs over a hottie who couldn't appreciate my trim build.

So I decided to assume option two. I joined him on the bench, sitting just the way he did.

"Tell Juanita all about it," I said. Wasn't supposed to use my real name on the street down here. Just in case.

"Believe me," he said. "You don't want to hear this."

"Long story?"

"Very."

"So tell me over fish tacos." I tugged on his elbow. "I'll even buy, if you tell me your name."

"Jon," he said, blinking and frowning like the answer came out before he thought about it.

"Well, Jon," I said with a smile. "I'll buy, you talk."

Maybe it was my smile. Maybe it was the teasing tone. Maybe it was the offer to buy. Whatever it was, it was like someone got home and turned on the lights. His eyes really looked at me now —staying to my face, but in that way that I knew meant he'd checked me out with peripheral vision—and his smile was worth seeing.

We found a little place, tucked back in from the street. Ordered fish tacos, and a Dos Equis for him and a bottled water for me. *Almost* changed my mind on the possible gentleman front, because he ordered the beer without thinking and apologized. Didn't want to order beer on my dime, if I was drinking water.

But decent manners alone do not a gentleman make. He scanned the little restaurant, eyes lingering on the same things mine did.

The big guy in the corner, eating alone. A local. Nose broken at least twice. Ears boxed. Definitely the kind who liked to fight. Like maybe if anyone joked about such a big guy at such a little round table.

The fact that the tables near him were empty seemed to confirm that he was trouble. Locals were eating here, and knew not to crowd him.

Two exits, and the front door was the only good one, if there was trouble. Back exit was through the kitchen. Tight hallway. Even one person in the kitchen coming out at the wrong time could close it off.

Two plainclothes police at a table by the counter. Keeping an eye on the guy in the corner.

Jon frowned when he spotted the cops. Covered it quickly, but still. Bad boy confirmation.

Other than that, the place was nice enough. Well swept floor, not too many flies. Three kinds of hot sauce on the table. Decent paper napkins, not like those kind you need six of just to get grease off your fingers.

Brown stucco walls, decorated in broken piñatas. Colorful, but sad, in a way.

No music in here. Fútbol on decent flat-screen television, set high on the side wall. Broadcasters so excited, it must have been the playoffs or something.

We were the only ones not watching the game. Even the cops took turns watching the game and the big guy.

"So, why might you have lost your best friend?" I asked after we had our drinks.

A flash of pain in those storm gray eyes, but then he assessed me again. Odd. His eyes frowned like he spotted me for an officer of some kind. He sipped his beer, and it looked like he was buying time.

He looked away and shrugged. Took a deep breath.

When he looked back, I only saw the pain. Figured maybe playing the old game again had made me paranoid.

"Work," he said. "Without going into the gory details, we're freelancers. And he's started taking work that's outside our focused area of expertise. Work I don't want to do. He says it's a one-time thing, but I don't buy it."

"Well," I said with a lopsided smile. "That was vague. If I'm buying you dinner, I want a *story*."

He furrowed his brow in the cutest way. Then I caught him glancing at my shoulders and throat before he spoke again.

"This story's too long for fish tacos."

"Then tell me how you got that scar?"

"This?" he said with a smile. Familiar territory. A story he's told a thousand times, and he's ready to tell it again. Might even perk him up, if that first smile was any indication.

"That," I said with a nod. And I reached out and ran my finger across all six inches of scar, which made him smile even wider.

"Well," he said, drawing the word out. "This was about five years ago. I—"

My phone chirped a text message. Didn't have to see it to know what it was. I threw enough pesos for dinner and a decent tip on the table as I stood.

"Wait," he said, and I memorized the way he reached for me. The raise of his eyebrows. The troubled look in his eyes at the thought of me getting away.

That moment alone was worth the cost of dinner. But it did make leaving harder.

"Sorry," I said with a sigh. "Work calls. Maybe we'll run into each other again sometime."

And I hustled out the door before I was tempted to kiss him goodbye.

3
Jon

Even the night seemed to be saying this was a bad idea. Coyotes howling in the distance like they were laughing at us. Night sky flashing now and again with lighting from the storm out over the sea.

Got a bitter laugh out of me, the first time I noticed it. It was a clear sky above us. More stars out here, in the middle of nowhere, than I'd ever seen before in my city-boy life. And still it was a dark and stormy night.

We really were out in the middle of nowhere. Part of Baja is littered with, well, litter, but also abandoned, half-finished houses. Little structures of brick, lacking only the frames and glass for the windows, the doors for the doorways, and, oh, yes, the roofs for their houses and garages.

Derek said the exchange was due to take place in one of those abandoned places.

Our part of the plan was simple.

We drove our car out and parked about two miles away, just off the road. Little piece of paper on it swearing it was out of gas and we were going to be back as soon as we could get a gas can. Figured that would sound enough like a stupid tourist trick to fool anyone who bothered checking on it.

If they even spotted the car in the first place. Only a half-moon above us, and a dark car a few hundred feet off the road was pretty easy to lose among all the big bushes of the desert around here.

From there we took a small cart with great big, off-roading wheels, and pushed it parallel to the road in the right direction.

Plan was simple. First crew arrives. Arranges the boxes. Retreats outside to smoke. Derek's "contact" assured us that this was standard procedure. They waited outside so they could see anyone approaching, but they'd been doing this so long they only watched the road side. They'd never see us approaching from the back.

The crew supposed to pick up the crates would show up about half an hour later. Enough time to make sure everything was ready, and maybe a little extra to make the first crew sweat.

Politics and power games were everywhere.

All we had to do was slip in during that half hour, find the right crate, get it onto the cart, and get gone.

Derek called it simple. Dared to smile as he said it.

I thought it sounded like a clusterfuck waiting to happen.

Might even have been an excuse to give those drug boys a chance to play Shoot the American.

Didn't bother saying any of that. No point.

Thus, I picked my way across the rocky, dirty desert by night. Even a handful of miles from the sea, the ground was crusted with salt here and there. Especially by the roads, but even out here.

I made Derek push the stupid cart, but I had to help him here and there anyway. Get it over rocks and steer around the jutting bushes that were nothing but a collection of branches full of thorns. Didn't look like they ever had leaves, much less any kind of blossom. Wouldn't even want to call them a cactus.

The night was warm enough. We were dressed like what we were: thieves. Black cargo pants. Black, long-sleeved shirts of a thin brand of cotton to slick away sweat. Black gloves of the same material. Black sneakers and socks. Black caps pulled down tight. Black greasepaint on our faces and necks.

Each of us had a 9mm on his belt. No more than a dozen bullets each, but that didn't matter. Not really. If we needed more than a dozen bullets, we were toast. These guys were likely to have AKs.

I hated the smell of greasepaint. Even the dry odors of the desert would have been preferable. But no way I was going with a full facemask. Not in this heat. Could get sweat in my eyes at the wrong time.

Death sentence.

But then, the whole gig was feeling like a death sentence.

Took us the better part of an hour to get into position, hiding behind a big rock, maybe a hundred yards behind the right house. Damn near got blinded when I spotted the first Jeeps' headlights. So bright they could have signaled ships in a storm.

I had to turn away to avoid spoiling my night vision. Derek did too. We flattened against the rock and waited until we heard the Jeeps running roughshod over the desert dirt and rocks. Waited until we heard engines cut.

Worked in our favor though. These guys would need time for their eyes to adjust, and while they did I took a count.

Six Jeeps.

"Six?" I hissed at Derek. "There were supposed to be three."

Derek sucked in his lips. Shook his head. "Something's wrong."

"Better believe it," I said. "Both crews are here now. Let's bug out."

"No," he said. "We need to do this."

"Like hell."

Derek put his hand on his pistol.

I blinked at him. Felt like I didn't even know the man in front of me.

"We're doing this, Jon. It won't be so bad. You'll see. Maybe the numbers are bigger, but they'll follow the same procedure. All we have to do is wait."

The sounds of Spanish. Rapid fire. Not like anyone was angry, far as I could tell. Just the normal speed they spoke. Maybe they were cokeheads or something. Couldn't follow any of it.

We crept up on top of the big rock for a better view.

"Derek," I said, pointing at the layout of the twenty men in fatigues, all with AKs. Even the ones moving crates had assault rifles strapped to their backs. "That's two crews. One off-loading, one watching. And counting."

"No," Derek said.

"We need to—"

Suddenly the area flooded with light. Voices through bull-horns. I recognized *armas* as weapons, so it had to be the call to throw down weapons and surrender.

Either the *Federales*, or the army. Coming in from two sides. Whichever they were, this was more than I signed on for.

"Now's our chance," I said. "We slip away into the night before they notice us."

"No," Derek said with his ready-for-action smile. "This is perfect. While the cartel and the *Federales* are busy with each other, we snag the crate and skip."

"Are you insane?"

"It's perfect," he said again. "We just need to get them shooting."

Derek raised his pistol. Aimed at one of the good guys. I smacked the top of his arm just before he fired. Bullet slammed into the back of the abandoned house.

Shot did its job anyway. Guns blazed on autofire. Shouts through a bullhorn.

And back here on the rock, Derek and me, facing off. Murder in Derek's eyes.

I threw my pistol away.

"Fuck this," I said. "I'm gone. Shoot me in cold blood, if that's who you are now. If we go after that crate I'm dead anyway."

For the first time in my life, I turned away from Derek.

And that's when I found out the good guys were coming in from *three* sides.

4
Maria

Dawn was breaking by the time we'd gotten through most of the processing, after the Clusterfuck in the Desert. Not the official designation of the op, but it might as well have been.

Five dead on the cartel side, six more wounded. None dead on our side, yet, but only because the Federal Police had medical standing by. Just in case. Eight of ours in the infirmary. One might not wake up.

I was still supposed to go home today. As of right now, just after six in the morning. Carmelo, my handler, said the official word had to wait until all the interviews and paperwork were done, but as long as my superiors back home were willing to make me available, if necessary, chances were I'd make my flight.

I wanted to stay. Wanted to see this through to the end. Seemed like the least I could do. But it wasn't my call to make.

One call I could make, though, was whether or not I conducted any interviews. Part of the exchange program, after all, was to compare interview procedures. Plus, two of the guys we'd snagged were Americans. Might say different things to me than they would to the locals.

My paperwork was done, so I went to see about those interviews.

First guy didn't give me much. Said his name was Jason Gibson. Matched his passport, but I had my doubts. Career criminal type, from the way he sat on his hard plastic chair, to his immediate requests for specific types of junk food and soft drinks.

Had the balls to claim he was out in the middle of the night hunting for Mayan artifacts. Dressed in all black, down to the greasepaint, to avoid drawing attention, because he didn't want to have to turn anything in to the Mexican government. Carried a gun to "keep coyotes away."

Big nothing from that interview. The locals might get something if they sweated him for a few days, but not before.

The other American though...

An interview room is an interview room. They're all about the same, with a few minor variations in color and material. This place was no exception. Blank white walls, with a big one-way mirror. Camera up in the corner. Mics recording everything.

Steel table, painted brown, with a loop for cuffs. Hard plastic chairs. Red. One on one side, two on the other.

And always the smell of bleach and stale cigarette smoke.

I strolled in and plopped onto one of the two hard plastic chairs on my side. Dressed in my dark brown suit and tie, my hair tied back behind me.

My face deadpan as I stared across the table at the man I'd bought dinner for. Now cuffed to the table. Dressed all in black, even if his greasepaint had been washed away. His shoulders sagged when he saw me. His eyes looked sad as he realized who I was.

"So," I said, letting him hear the anger in my voice. Not fair, maybe. I'd known he was a bad boy. But still. "You're name's not Jon after all. It's Peter Stark."

"No," he said, voice as sad as his eyes, which were now studying the table. He shook his head slowly. "I told you the truth this afternoon. My name is Jon. Jon Rollins. My Washington driver's license number is WVVX66768212. Run it through the system. You'll see my face."

"You confirmed your other identity to agents earlier," I said.

"That was habit. A habit I need to break anyway. And besides." He looked up at me now. "I don't want to lie to you. Not to you."

Those words, or maybe the simple honesty of his tone, sent a shiver through me that I covered by shifting in my seat. Forced my brow down. My lips flat.

"Sure," I said. "Since you're in the mood to be all truthful, why not tell me what you were doing tonight?"

"My friend lost a good deal of money playing poker with Hector Cruz. More than we had with us. To cover his losses, my friend took a job for tonight, without asking me. We were supposed to steal a particular crate. Turn it in tonight. Get paid, and clear out."

I knew the name Hector Cruz. Major arms dealer, with connections all up and down the Americas. I also knew that one of the crates recovered tonight had a new, experimental variety of explosive rounds.

I further noticed that this story filled in some of the details of the vague version Jon told me over dinner. I wasn't sure how I felt about that.

"Is that what you and your friend do? Rob arms shipments?"

"No," he said. He drew a deep breath. Let it out slowly. "What we do, we've never been arrested for. Hell, no one has ever even informed the police about our jobs."

"Then there's no reason not to tell me."

His eyes flicked to the cameras, then the one-way mirror. Back to me.

"If word of this gets out, we'll be murdered. Both him and me." His voice was simple. Matter of fact.

"Have you committed any of these crimes in Mexico?"

"Nope. We weren't supposed to work down here at all. Just a vacation."

"One sec." I slipped back out of the room. Spoke softly to Carmelo, who was watching. "Any chance we can kill the recorders in there?"

"None." Then he shrugged. "But if he's not providing evidence to any crimes you or we care about, something could happen to the recordings..."

I nodded. It would have to do. Went back into the room. Took my seat.

"I think we can keep this quiet."

"Then I'll trust you," he said. And I didn't like the way his words gave me a warm feeling. But I let him keep talking. "We'd move into a city. We'd study the local rackets. Take six months, maybe a year or more if we needed. We'd figure out who was running things. From there, how the money moved. From there, what kind of cycles the big boys followed, when it came to hiding money overseas."

He shrugged. "From there, it was a simple matter of figuring out the weak spot in the chain. We'd hit the weak spot, clear five or six figures in cash and split town. Hit a new town, and do the same thing. Always slow and careful. Never rushing."

I whistled. Jon, Peter, whatever his name was was right. If word of this got out, they were dead within a week.

Also, assuming all this was true, arresting him wouldn't do any good. The victims would deny the crimes—they'd never want us figuring out how they moved their money...

I smiled. Saw a potential upside to all this. Maybe more than one.

"So," I said. "Where does this partnership of yours stand?"

"I'm done." He shook his head slowly. "My friend has changed. Maybe he's been changing for a while now, and I just didn't realize it. But I'm done." He sighed. "If I have a choice, I'll go back to business school, or maybe—"

He broke off. Looked at me. Saw the same upside I did.

"Look," he said. "My friend, he knows crime better than I ever will. But me, I know money. I was always the one who figured out how the money was moving and where it was going. If you guys can give us a pass for tonight, I would be more than happy to work with you guys in the D.E.A. as a consultant about money laundering and hiding. Maybe even become an agent, if you'd have me."

I almost asked how he knew I was with the D.E.A., but I did have an ID tag hanging on my hip.

"Your friend discharged a firearm," I said, maybe a little louder than I had to, to cover the way my heart was beating faster right then. "Maybe at the police. Can't be sure. Not sure they'll let him walk for that."

They'd already decided to give Jason a slap on the wrist and send him back across the border. We'd already determined that Jon and his friend weren't part of the cartels. Just two Americans doing something stupid. And the way Carmelo put it, if they arrested every American who did something stupid, they'd lose ninety percent of their tourist trade.

I looked into Jon's eyes, and remembered what he said about not lying to me. And I realized I didn't want to lie to him either.

I shook my head. "They're going to let you both go anyway. Give you a slap on the wrist and send you back across the border."

Jon's eyes widened, and he nodded. Then he got this determined look.

"My offer still stands."

"Why?"

"Yesterday," he said through a sigh, "yesterday I thought I knew what my life was. Told myself I was performing a public service. Keeping American money out of foreign accounts and going into American businesses. Not a good guy, but not a bad guy either. Not really."

He hung his head forward. Started to say something, then stopped and started again.

"My friend, he showed me what we are. Just criminals, pulling jobs." He glanced up at me, and back down. "But maybe I could be more than that."

"Maybe you can," I said. I stood. Started for the door.

"Thank you, Juanita," he said.

I smiled at him. "My name is Maria."

BURNED-OUT SOULS

MICHAEL WARREN LUCAS

If the characters in Stefon Mears' "Gun Running on Vacation" seem unsavory, wait until you meet the protagonists in Michael Warren Lucas's "Burned-Out Souls." When I started reading the story, I had no idea how he would make this romantic. And yet, somehow, he did.

Michael has written more than 30 books, ranging from murder mysteries, technical tomes on Internet engineering, SF, and thrillers. He's best known for his crime and mystery novels, like git commit murder. *See all of Lucas' books at https://mwl.io. And find his short fiction in* Fiction River: Superstitious, *and both years of our annual Holiday Spectacular.*

I

The thick, humid air of a summer in a Florida swamp smelled so strongly of plants and tropical flowers, seasoned with a hint of rotting mulch, that it reminded me of unhappier times. Times when I thought I had a future in the military, serving my country and all that patriotic crap. Times when I thought I'd find someone to care about, marry her and raise kids and maybe feel like a normal human being.

Being dead inside was better.

Being dead inside meant I could lurk in trees and study a multi-million-dollar house in the middle of a mucky bug-mobbed Florida swamp and count how many people I needed to murder without getting all teary-eyed.

Yes, there's other ways to rob a house. But hiring a man called Stabbity Joe as part of your team pretty much eliminates the whole "plausible deniability" thing. I'm not called Tranquilizer Terrance. You get what it says on the label.

And the woman we were robbing, one Jackie Aspen, was a corporate jackass who'd robbed her own employer.

We're just highly paid repo men.

With knives. And guns.

Miss Aspen had all the outside lights on, those yellow things that supposedly didn't attract bugs. The average bug density out here was about fifty bajillion per cubic inch, though, so the whole property looked swarmed. Buggy buzzing filled my ears.

The good news was, I didn't need the night vision binoculars to study our target. The regular ones did fine. The plastic eyepieces felt damned hot in my eye sockets, but at least regular binoculars are lighter. I was already uncomfortable enough with my legs wrapped around a cypress and didn't need heavy night-vision goggles hanging off my forehead and crushing my sinuses. The climbing belt supported most of my weight, but if I didn't anchor myself I'd go sliding straight down into the water.

Even if I didn't discover that an alligator had been lurking beneath me, my temporary partner would never let me forget it.

The stilt house sat on a peninsula barely attached to the rest of the land, raised a few critical yards above the slurry they called "ground level" in central Florida. Every wall was tinted glass, every corner painted bright reflective white, the roof a giant solar panel.

Elegant. But the windows were thick enough to resist anything smaller than a mortar. That elegant white trim was blast-resistant steel. And the building's core had a couple of those great big Tesla batteries. Killing main power wouldn't do anything but stop the air-conditioning and warn them we're coming.

The place shrieked money.

Nobody was close enough to hear. It was over a mile to the nearest neighbor. The driveway was half a mile long.

Cut the phone line? All cellular. Same for the Internet.

Blow the stilts? Military-grade steel. We'd need a half-hour to wire up the charges.

And the four mercenaries toting their big manly guns around circling the shoreline would object.

Miss Aspen didn't know we were coming, but she'd be an idiot not to guess.

The auction *was* the next day, after all.

We'd been hired blind; the broker didn't tell us who we were working for, and again, I didn't care. Aspen's employer had invested billions of dollars in this antibiotic, and expected to reap trillions. I didn't understand why blocking folic acid production in bacteria was so revolutionary. All I cared about was, Miss Aspen had copied all the data to a briefcase full of hard drives.

Miss Aspen had a second briefcase full of chemical samples.

The client wanted them both.

Our instructions said the client wanted her to serve as an example of what happens when you rob the company.

A horrible, horrible example.

That was where yours truly comes in.

Her photo didn't look like someone who deserved that. But, really, who did?

Were we working for Miss Aspen's ex-employer? Maybe. Or maybe we were working for an org that didn't want any of their employees getting their own ideas.

Bugs buzzed around me, loud enough to make normal conversation impossible. My nasty-smelling bug repellant was half a step down from DDT and probably twice as cancerous, but the gnats still battered at my cheeks and tried to clog my nostrils.

Once we finished, I'd find the most luxurious hotel room I could. Clean myself. Enjoy the payoff. Indulge all my body's appetites.

My partner pro tem Scott Dawson said "I count four mercs on the ground, two inside on the main floor. Can't count the upper floor through those curtains." He was only a few yards away, up a separate tree, but the bugs out here buzzed so loud I couldn't hear him without the earpiece.

"Agreed," I mutter back.

I'd kayak toward the property. Just before the mercs hit the alarm, Dawson would drop them and launch his little helicopter drones. I'd penetrate the house and handle the two guards inside and any extraneous civilians. The drones would deliver the grenades to the driveway. When the four men out at the road heard the chaos and raced up in their Jeep, too bad for them.

Anyone in the place except Miss Aspen? Drop them quick.

That'd give me a good fifteen minutes with Miss Aspen before law enforcement got too close. They'd pass quickly for me.

Not so much for her.

The thought triggered a flicker of feeling; not of caring, but a sensation that I *should* care. That I should feel bad for what I was going to do.

I ignored it.

It went away.

Being dead inside had its advantages.

If I didn't return, Dawson would blow the hell out of the building. It'd send a different message, yes. We'd lose a touch more than half our fee, but Dawson wouldn't have to split it with me, so he'd be okay.

The door leading to the upper floor's outdoor balcony slid open.

A dead woman stepped out.

Everything I'd murdered within myself shrieked back to agonizing life.

2

This business with the knives started by accident, in a Third

World hellhole with air too thick to breathe, too thin to drink, and too stink-ass to sell as skunk bait. I spent six straight months greasy with bug killer. The officers tried to keep us busy, but one night a couple of lunkheads started throwing knives at the wall.

I watched, silently smug, waiting for the inevitable moment when someone would slice off a finger and win a valuable medical discharge. It'd be good for a laugh, wouldn't it? And I'd already read all these Patterson novels. After a couple weeks of lunkheads hitting every part of the wall except their makeshift target, though, I rolled my eyes too hard. My bunkmate, waiting for his turn to miss the inside barracks wall, noticed.

It was either throw a knife or catch a punch.

So I threw.

I didn't even walk up to the line. Just relaxed, looked at the target, let out a breath, and gave this silly cross-body toss from the far side of the barracks.

I hit the target dead-center.

Absolute, pure luck.

More luck: the knife stuck.

I sometimes wonder how my life would have been different if I'd said *Holy shit, I hit it*. Instead, as the other soldiers stared at the knife, at each other, and at me, I'd coolly nodded. "Gentlemen."

And went back to my bunk and my book.

I didn't dare laugh until I went out to piss.

Nobody asked me to throw again. A couple days later, they quit trying to lose fingers.

But the story got around: Joe Stabinowicz was a menace with a knife.

I have no idea who came up with the nickname Stabbity Joe.

But hitting that target felt...good.

So on those infrequent occasions when I had a little time and a little more privacy, I practiced. I turned out to be pretty good with knives. Guns, APCs, all those toys the service wanted me to be good with, nothing quite gave me that sense of clarity and precision as figuring out exactly how to use *this* particular knife in that *specific* way.

Eventually, the service and I disagreed on who should be in charge of my life. We parted ways, with prejudice.

Without charges, but with changes.

They'd taken a dumb-ass suburban teenager and abraded off all the civilization. They'd taught me not to mind killing. I don't like it, sure—it's messy. Especially with a knife.

It's not like I had any other job skills, though.

And isn't that the definition of a job? Getting paid for something you'd just as soon not do, but happen to be good at? A skilled man who gets in good with odd-job corporate mercenary brokers can make a good living. Knives are a specialty skill, yes. But when you need a knife fighter, nothing else suffices.

Life isn't all blood and guts, though. Freelancing had introduced me to Kit.

We'd shared half of a MRE in a burned-out building between Buraan and Bargaal. That's in Somalia. I'd bitten my hand to keep myself from belly-laughing at her desperation-driven jokes while those kids with knock-off AK-47s were trying to find us, and failed to hide my tears at her bravery. Certain we were going to die before dawn, we'd made love under smoke-veiled stars. Somehow, we'd escaped that ruined city alive.

That one night hadn't changed my life.

It had changed my soul.

I hadn't minded killing people. But Kit's voice, her way of looking at things, even the way she smelled after a day of crawling for our lives through a city blitzed into a burned-out wreck, made me feel more alive than I ever had. Through her, I had the weird feeling that other people...mattered.

She carried empathy.

I'd caught it.

She made me want to be a better person.

And Kit, somehow, wanted me to stay with her.

Between beats of my heart, I discarded my career.

The world had other jobs for someone who didn't truly care about people. Used car sales. Real estate. Politics. I had lots of options. And Kit gave me this queasy feeling that maybe I could *learn* to care again. Maybe the service hadn't scraped off all my humanity.

I was horrified to learn how desperately I wanted that.

I'd escorted her safely back to her charity relief camp and hauled myself back to the coast to deliver the bag of flash drives that caused this whole mess. One last task before I returned to her.

An hour after I left, an explosion wiped out the whole relief team.

Letting someone taste that connection, that empathy, that completion of soul, and then ripping it away is one of the cruelest things you can do. It's even crueler than what happened to the three monsters who set that bomb.

Keeping them alive for a week didn't satisfy me. Nothing could.

But you can't stay in pain forever. Over the last five years, it's burned away.

Any compassion I had left burned away with it.

I kept freelancing because, why not? When I die, the Alfred Dow Somali Relief Fund gets a big chunk of change. Until that terminal date, I got to live a life a whole bunch of men envied. Fancy hotels where they called me sir. Well-dressed women who wanted stumpy, scarred-up me to undress them. Fast cars, international travel, intrigue and death and a black glory known only to those who order deniable blood on secret websites.

I clawed enough pleasure from every day to bother to keep myself alive.

Kit never even told me her last name, but she showed me the man I could be. And left me the man I am.

Seeing Kit on that Florida rooftop deck hit my burned-out soul like a monsoon on the Sahara.

3

My heart thumped up my throat until it wedged there.

I couldn't breathe.

My legs, already locked around the coarse tree trunk supporting me, clamped tightly enough that the rough bark clawed into my thighs. My upper body went limp. If the climbing belt hadn't been supporting me, I would have flopped backward and plunged headfirst into the swamp muck. I should have dropped the binoculars. They felt fused to my face, though.

The night, the countless bugs, my partner, the mission, all went away.

It couldn't be her.

But I hadn't seen her body.

I'd seen pieces of bodies, yes. Badly scorched and seared pieces.

I'd called out for her. I'd joined the locals searching the ruined camp. By the time I returned the locals had switched from searching to salvaging, but once they realized I didn't care about any of the loot they let me get on with the search.

There was only one road in and out of that camp. I'd been on it.

She hadn't passed me the other way.

She was dead.

The woman on that rooftop deck couldn't be Kit.

My whole body shook, but my binoculars were utterly focused.

I knew that nose. The curve of that chin. One eye a little higher than the other.

Not possible.

If you live long enough, you'll meet the man who could be the twin of your father, or your best friend from high school. Or that weird moment when you come around a corner and see your reflection escaped from the mirror.

That's all this was.

This woman surrounded by a phalanx of bug zappers was Kit's impossible twin. That's all.

I fought to shake the feelings off. Tried to shift them toward rage. How dare Aspen do this to me? How *dare* she make me feel? The thoughts couldn't penetrate my shock, though.

My gaze couldn't leave the woman.

Suddenly, I hated her. Whoever she was. Kit already haunted my dreams. My nightmares. She shadowed any night I spent with another woman. I'd plant a knife in this woman's throat and one in her heart just for reminding me of what I'd lost.

The woman let out a breath and started to inhale.

Her right hand rose.

I went rigid.

She eased her index finger into that little divot above her lips and her middle finger to her nose as if dividing her breath, and inhaled.

My anger shattered into an impossible blend of certainty and confusion.

That gesture was burned into my shriveled heart. Every time Kit had needed to still herself, she'd done exactly that.

She couldn't be alive...but.

But.

Confusion paralyzed me. The bugs buzzing in my ears seemed

a mile away. The tree trunk between my legs? Impossibly distant. My legs weren't part of me anymore. Dawson's voice, shouted from the far side of the country or maybe the Moon.

Something clawed at the inside of my throat.

My body took over. I jackknifed in the climbing belt, coughing and choking, and something awful crunched between my teeth. A bug? I'd been so stunned I'd left my mouth hanging open, and one of those flying cockroaches wanted a taste of my extra minty Pepsodent. My ribs ached from not breathing and my mouth tasted of squashed crunchy insect and my heart was somehow still exploding inside my chest.

A bug between the teeth did what I couldn't do for myself, though. It forced my mind to reset.

Maybe the woman was Kit's twin sister.

Out of nine billion people, someone will look and act like Kit.

Perhaps the resemblance would dissolve up close.

The only way I could know which...was to get up close.

And I *had* to know.

I had to know this wasn't Kit.

My cough barely died when Dawson said in my earpiece, "Must have been one hell of a bug."

"Yeah," I wheeze.

"Have you ever even *been* to Florida before?"

"Har de har har." Sarcasm doesn't carry well over a throat mike. "Is it time?"

"I'm just waiting for you to finish your snack," Dawson said.

Our contract was clear: no survivors. I spat out shards of insect shell like fragments of my heart.

She couldn't be Kit.

But whoever she was, I'd make it quick.

For Kit.

4

My shallow-bottomed kayak slipped smoothly through the mucky water of the swamp channel. I dipped the paddle slowly and drew it lightly. The constant hum of the millions of insects would swallow slight noises, and the closer I could get to the house before the fun began the better my chances.

All other things being equal, I'd rather not get shot.

My profession depended on speed. I'd left the clunky night vision headset back with Dawson. Wearing it weighed me down and limited my field of vision. Clunking around my neck, it complicated fighting. And I'd known more than one freelancer killed by strangulation on his own gear. I had a radio, a handgun most pros would dismiss as a toy, and a whole mess of knives.

Bugs battered my face and ears despite my greasy repellent. Heavy branches blocked out the night sky. If it wasn't for the illuminated house on its stilts and the massive trees around me, I might have been paddling through a black void.

The mercenaries guarding the house kept the teammate in front of them in sight as they circled the shore. They were young, though. The sort of kids who do two years in Infantry and think it makes them men to be reckoned with. All kinds of agencies will rent out a six-pack of Macho Idiots with a side of illegally modified AR-15s. You have to know the wrong people to hire bodyguards tough enough to stand against my type. Their camouflage long pants and shirts had to be sweltering in this heat.

As I approached I cut my paddle strokes down to two or three a minute. Move slow and silent, until you move fast and deadly. The kid coming up on this side of the house had the build of a dedicated bodybuilder. His skin gleamed through his open collar.

"Confirm no body armor," I muttered into my throat mike.

"Acknowledged," Dawson said in my ear.

Between paddle strokes, I tried to relax and breathe. This was the quiet before the avalanche. Once the action began it wouldn't stop.

I fought the urge to double-check my gear. I could feel the bandolier of throwing knives over my shoulder, and the other knives buckled at my waist. More knives at my ankles, and one in my collar. Soft-soled shoes. Plus the handgun at the small of my back.

Yes, I carry a gun, a little .32 automatic. I'm not an idiot. I keep my rep by stabbing anyone who can ruin it.

The deck is empty.

Whoever Kit's twin is, she's gone back inside. Even that army of bug zappers on the house's rooftop deck can't keep this infestation away.

Finding out who she was shouldn't slow me down more than a minute.

If everything went really badly, all I really needed was for her to speak. If she didn't have a British accent, it wasn't her.

I'd put her down quick. Nobody should suffer for picking the wrong friend, even if they died for it.

It'd be over, for both of us.

Another stroke of the paddle.

The kid playing mercenary moved with that slow, careful pace that said he had a whole bunch of walking to do tonight and that he didn't see any need to wear himself out before he was done. He'd done some sort of guard duty, then. And he had his rifle properly slung.

I coasted for a moment, then nudged the kayak forward.

The kid's face turned toward me.

He didn't see me. I was too deep in the darkness.

He looked like an alert animal. Not a predator. Maybe a meerkat. Something small and tasty.

I wanted to get closer before the shooting started. I tried to breathe more quietly and let the kayak glide to a halt in the nearly stagnant water.

He studied the darkness before shaking his head and taking another step.

Good.

He got most of the way around the house, letting another kid rotate into view behind him, before the sound of my paddle stirring water stopped him again. The kid's ears almost perked.

I rested the paddle across my knees.

This second alert in a minute had him spooked. I watched him juggle embarrassment against survival.

Don't worry, kid. Live another two minutes.

Instead, he reached for his shoulder mic.

Dawson was pretty good with a rifle. Not Marine sniper good, but with a stable tree to nest in, a good scope and a flash suppressor you'd never see him.

The kid dropped.

Two gunshots echoed through the night.

I paddled maniacally.

The other kid in view just stood there, his bug-catcher hanging open.

Two more gunshots, and he wasn't standing any more.

Around a couple more trees and I'd have a clear run at the house.

Another kid came running up between the stilts, shouting "Joe! Joe!"

Don't worry kid. Stabbity Joe is on his way.

That kid whirled with a bullet in the shoulder as two more gunshots split the night. Dawson followed up with two more, though. Another tombstone seed, planted.

That left one guard on the ground.

I rounded the last tree and dug deep with the paddle. The kayak shot forward.

Light flashed between the stilts. Something screeched past my ear.

I drew the paddle more fiercely and tried to pull my ears down between my buttocks.

Dawson's rifle barked twice, then twice again.

The last guard's rifle flashed in the darkness, but not at me.

Just short of the steep shore I skidded the kayak to the side, bringing the side up against the ragged chunks of torn-up concrete roadbed that reinforced the peninsula, and half-launched half-rolled up onto the land. One hand looped the kayak's line around a protruding lump of cement.

Dawson's gunfire split the buggy buzz. Twice.

The last guard screamed.

Dawson planted two more. The screaming stopped.

"Changing," Dawson said in my ear.

I clamped my hands over my ears, closed my eyes, turned away from the house, and crouched.

I didn't know who the Kit look-alike is. Or why she was there.

But I really hoped she didn't die before she answered my questions.

Before I could kill her.

5

People think of rocket launchers as monsters designed to take out tanks. They exist, yes. But rockets come in a whole bunch of different sizes.

Including some just right for blowing a door off its hinges.

Even with my ears covered, the sound rattled my skull. I could see the flash of light with my head turned away and eyes squeezed shut, as if it had traveled through my thick skull to reach my retinas. Before the echo died I rose, uncovered my head, and grabbed two knives from the bandolier.

You won't find these knives at Wal-Mart. This old lady in Tucson makes them for me out of recycled aeronautical steel. They're cut to fit my hands, perfectly balanced for the way I throw, and sharper than scalpels.

Holding them felt like coming home.

Dawson had put the rocket at the top of the door, shredding the upper half of it and knocking the bottom half wide open. Even at this distance, the smoke burned my sinuses.

I scrabbled forward, trampling the grass and charging up the clattering steel stairs to the door. The haze dissipated slowly in the still air, so I sucked a deep breath before launching myself into the cloud and through the door.

The rocket had inflicted a quarter million in furniture damage alone. I glimpsed cracked stone tabletops and shredded sybaritic leather couches, a busted-up television by IMAX and bar by Dionysus—

Past the sunken couch, a black man in camo staggering to his feet, fumbling at his rifle.

I rotated my hips and twisted my right wrist, all in one synchronized motion.

I knew the blade would miss before it left my hand.

Even in the haze and heat I realized my body wasn't right. My heart should have pounded, but instead it jackhammered against my ribs. My throat felt too tight, my head pressurized, and despite holding my breath the stink of vaporized door seemed to burn in my lungs.

The mere sight of Kit's doppelganger had totally jacked me up.

No time for yelling at myself, though.

No time to cool myself down, either.

Recovering from the first throw let me launch my second knife.

The first blade sailed past the mercenary.

A heartbeat later, six inches of black steel buzzsawed across the man's neck.

If I was on my game, the blade would have planted in his voice box—but no matter, he geysered blood and went down.

I'd already drawn two more knives.

I bolted forward before the man's body hit the ground, escaping the eye-burning noxious cloud so I could suck in something other than vaporized door, trying to loosen my shoulders so I could hit a target on the first throw.

Something moved to my right.

I jerked myself sideways.

The triple burst of gunfire stunned my ears, but the rounds punched the air behind me.

I spun on one foot, bringing the knife to bear, building momentum before I even saw—there, in the doorway, throw, throw!

But I didn't release.

My eyes needed a split second to register a young white guy, teeth in the classic Rambo clench.

It wasn't Kit.

Kit's look-alike, that is.

Not her.

My body was spinning so I finished the pivot, whirling in place and letting fly, recovering to rock back and launch the second blade, my empty hand already tugging another from the bandolier.

I didn't need it.

Rambo Junior had one of my blades in his chest and another through the side of his mouth. Nasty.

I've done worse.

But for some reason, I was shaking.

No, I knew the reason why my muscles quivered like a frightened bunny rabbit. My mind wasn't where it needed to be.

I'd delayed throwing until I knew it wasn't Kit.

That familiar-looking woman was going to get me killed.

I'd get her to speak. Ask her name.

My brain would clear.

I could kill this foolish, illogical *hope* burning in my bones.

I would rather be dead inside than feel anything as horrible as hope.

"Main floor clear," I muttered into my throat mic.

"Good work," Dawson answered.

I felt a flash of gratitude that the guy hadn't seen my hesitation.

Shattered glass from the busted-up table crunched underfoot as I raced around to the bottom of the broad stairway leading to the upper floor. Stairways are a choke point, but at least this one rose to the end of a hallway rather than into open space. The smoke from the door was thinning and spreading, burning my throat with every breath. I tried to loosen my shoulders, ready to throw both knives.

Yes, I'd rather throw knives up a flight of stairs than use a handgun. I have a better chance of hitting.

The only real solution to charging a staircase? Speed.

Bolting around the corner, I saw her at the top of the stairs.

With a heavy handgun in both hands.

Aimed straight down at me.

I could have thrown right then.

I could have killed her dead.

But that face. It haunted my dreams. Dreams I loathed and welcomed.

I knew those shoulders.

The way she stood.

She didn't shoot, either.

Instead she said "It *is* you."

Not just her body. Her mannerisms.

But her *voice*. Her inflection.

That British accent.

I froze. Knife in my hand.

She pulled the trigger.

6

I stood there like a carnival target, ready for any ten-year-old with a BB gun to pop me off.

Fortunately, she was already turning to run when she pulled the trigger.

Bullets sprayed, but all hit off to my left.

I'd only thought my brain was broken before. Kit had to be dead. All those hollow days since strobed through my shattered mind. The locals told me nobody survived—

Revelation cleared my brain like lightning.

Kit had been lying since the beginning.

She'd known about the bomb that destroyed her camp.

Those freedom fighters that had planted the device? They'd been guilty, sure. but they hadn't known where their orders came from.

She'd used me.

Used me to get to the camp, so she could blow it up.

My confused heartbreak came back together into a wholly different emotion: rage.

The one person I'd cared about since childhood had been a lie.

All that loss?

I'd mourned over something that had never existed.

With a few words—not even pretty words, just talking about how to survive and where to hide and wondering if the water pouring from that busted-off pipe was drinkable—with a few words, she'd convinced me to abandon my life.

I was just as much a sucker as any other guy.

Kit had betrayed my despair. And yes, it had been despair. I'd wallowed in despair until my soul had drowned.

Any secret hope I might have nurtured of feeling that way again?

Her appearance had scoured it out of me.

Once she died, once I recovered? Once I drank and screwed and ate and drank and screamed for a week, a month, a year?

I'd be peacefully dead inside again.

The way I had to be.

Part of me shrieked that Kit had been honest. That if I gave her a chance she'd explain, and it would all make sense. But I've been a freelancer for too long to believe that.

I needed an explanation, though.

I needed to know how she could destroy me that way. How many other people she'd destroyed the same way.

That meant I had to talk to her, just for a minute.

With a knife to her throat.

But my throat mike would pick up every word I said, and carry it to Dawson.

I trusted Dawson to carry out his part of the mission. I trusted him to carry me out on his back if I got hurt. But there's no way I would trust Dawson, or anyone, with anything so intimate as the short sharp conversation Kit and I were going to have.

I whispered "Going up, going silent."

"Acknowledge," Dawson said in my earpiece.

My fingers found the wire connecting the transmitter taped to my chest to my throat mike. I deftly tugged it out of its socket.

I'm a professional. The opposition on one gig might be your ally on the next. You can't take losing personally. You can't do the victory dance in front of the other guy.

What Kit had done to me, though?

How much more personal can you get than slicing out someone's heart?

Time to return the favor.

7

When I was halfway up the wide mahogany stairs, the lights went out.

Perfect blackness swallowed everything.

I froze, knife in each hand.

Had Kit killed the power? She knew the house better than I did. Architect's blueprints don't compare to spending time in a place.

Or, I reminded myself, maybe Miss Aspen. The person who started all this, remember?

No way to tell, yet. I forced myself to stay in place while my eyes adjusted. Late at night, miles away from anyone out in this desolate swamp, light didn't even come in through the glass exterior walls. I couldn't even see the handrail an arm's reach away. The only way I knew which way the stairs ran was because I was facing up.

I'd gambled on leaving the night vision headset.

And I'd lost.

The loudest sound was my heart thudding in my ears.

The coppery stink of blood seeped through the explosive haze into my nose.

If Kit had night vision goggles, I was dead.

"You still with us, Stabbity Joe?" Dawson whispered in my

earpiece.

He'd heard the gunfire. If I didn't answer soon, the clock would start ticking. Dawson was a professional. If he thought I'd gone down, well, there's no killing like overkill.

At the top of the stairs, dim lights faded on. Not enough to read by, but enough to show me the outline of the stairs. I forced myself to release an imprisoned breath. From the angle, the lights had to be close to the floor. Probably emergency lights. If I lived out in these boonies, I wouldn't want pitch blackness around the stairs.

Kit knew I was coming.

Feet to the far left of the treads, I bolted up the stairs.

The stairs opened onto a door-lined hallway. A pale white LED detachable emergency light hung from each power outlet. According to our intelligence, Miss Aspen used the room at the end of the hall, opposite the stairs, as an office.

Ears struggling to strain sound from the silence, I padded quickly down the hall. The soft soles of my shoes absorbed my steps.

The master bedroom door was pushed to, but not latched.

Kit might be behind this door.

The thought flooded me in a horrid toxic stew of hope and pain and despair and longing, so thick and strong that I had to stop for a breath to regain my poise. I couldn't throw a knife or even pull a trigger with trembling fingers.

Never again.

If anyone ever made me feel again, I'd cut their throat.

All I had to do was survive the next ten minutes. Or less, if Dawson started to worry.

But if I opened her office door, I'd almost certainly catch a gut full of lead.

Kit's was the other side of that door. Ready to shoot me.

Think. I'd studied the blueprints.

I drew a deep breath and crept to the first door on the right. It was closed. I tucked the knife in my left hand back into my bandolier. Very, very quietly, I tested the knob.

It turned.

Hardly daring breathe, ignoring the sweat running down my forehead and the knot in my gut, I twisted the knob until it stopped.

I made myself take a deep breath.

When I saw anyone, I would throw a knife. No hesitation.

None.

I flung the door open and hurtled myself through. Light spilled into the dark bedroom, silhouetting the low boxy shape of an orgy-sized bed and a looming dresser.

But I'd remembered the blueprints right. This bedroom had a second door, connected to the office.

A heavyset dark shape lurked in that doorway.

I want to say that I threw right away.

But my treacherous mind took in the crouching shape. The way light glinted off the long metal-and-plastic shape at its shoulder. He was poised to mow down anyone who came in the office door.

Something in me whispered that Kit had a handgun, not an AR-15.

The crouching man snarled an obscenity and tried to whirl his rifle toward me.

I launched a knife at his gut.

The rifle went off.

Three rapid bangs shattered the quiet.

I launched the second knife just as something slashed through my shoulder.

I couldn't die then. Not without answers.

The pain hit.

8

When people are still trying to kill you, you can't stop to inspect your wounds.

My right shoulder burned. So did the bicep.

But my fingers could still clench. Good enough for now.

Put any other shooters down. Drop Miss Aspen.

Thirty vital seconds with Kit.

Then tie off the wound.

The ranking surprised me. Was I willing to risk exsanguination to grill Kit?

Apparently I was. And I didn't have time to argue with me.

My right arm wasn't going to be throwing any knives, though. I gritted my teeth to tug my handgun out of its holster. Hugging my forearm against my ribs gave me enough support to hold the weapon steady. My other hand tugged a knife from my bandolier, then I was stepping around the mercenary's body.

No time to waste bracing myself.

I almost leaped through the doorway.

The office was sybaritic even by my standards, even illuminated by those weak LED emergency lights near the floor. A U-shaped desk supported gigantic but sleek monitors, partially hidden by two cheap briefcases. The couch and chairs looked like they'd suck you down and never let you leave.

More magnificent than that imagined view, though?

Kit.

She stood before the desk, legs spread, automatic in a text-book two-handed grip. She'd never appear on the cover of *Sports Illustrated*, but seeing her alive almost stopped my hammering heart.

Those eyes glaring at me?

She was too far away, the lighting all wrong, but somehow I could see their rich brown.

I was still moving, my feet propelling me sideways as I turned, bringing the gun to bear, turning so I could throw but too slow, way too slow, the pain in my shoulder deepening and blending with that in my bicep, growing hotter with each beat of my heart but not cold, not yet, wrenching my gun hand around but I can't make myself turn quickly enough to get a line on Kit and tell her to freeze—

"Hold it!" Kit shouted.

For a second, she didn't shoot.

It was long enough.

My knife was ready to throw.

My handgun, lined up for the shot.

At that distance, I couldn't miss. A knife in Kit's gut, and she'd still be able to talk. For long enough, at least.

You want to talk about treachery?

My knife arm refused to let fly.

9

Illuminated only by lights shining up from below, separated by fifteen feet of plush carpeting, Kit and I stared at each other.

She was beautiful. Smudged and smoke-stained, hair disarrayed, blood trickling from a nostril, seeing her made my blood sizzle in my veins. Her every curve was perfect for me—you might not think so, but you're free to be wrong. She was proud and defiant, even in a bomb-tattered green pantsuit.

With my knife ready to throw, I had a sudden mental flash of ripping that ruined suit off of her. Seizing her in my arms. Being seized back. Kissing her so fiercely that my head whirls.

I cursed myself for ten types of screaming idiot.

Why didn't she shoot me?

I needed to know how she could use me like that. How she

could give me that soul-destroying dose of compassion, and rip it away right when I realized I wanted it.

But somehow, I can't get my mouth to form the words.

Kit spoke first. "Why did you do it?"

Her accent was sexy as hell. I needed to ignore it. "Because I'm paid to." Why else would I kill those men?

"I thought we had something."

"I didn't even know you were here." The gun quivered in my hand.

"I'm certain you did not." Kit raised her voice. "Because you thought you killed me!"

Wait—what?

I open my mouth but she shouted "Don't even try that with me. Don't you even try, Mister Stabbity Joe. That's what they call you, isn't it? You didn't find me in that bombed-out doctor's office. You picked me up there. You *used* me. You used me to get back into my camp. You left that bomb and walked away. If I hadn't been down by the well, you would have killed me too."

The heat in my injured arm and shoulder couldn't stand against the cold that flashed through me. I couldn't breathe. My gun was in my hand. My finger inside the trigger guard. Even in the weird upside-down lighting, the bore of her gun looked big enough to swallow my head, and I still couldn't fire.

Kit might not have been a killer. Not like me.

But anyone with that much rage coloring their face, that much fury in their voice? They're ready to kill.

My brain knows she's lying.

She's playing me.

Again.

Looking at her? Face-to-face?

I can't do the right thing.

Staring at Kit's tortured face I said, "I don't want any misunderstandings." I drew a shaky breath. "I'm dropping my weapons."

Kit didn't flinch.

I opened my hands.

A dull thud as my gun hit the carpet.

The knife dropped silently.

Her face was as open as a brick wall.

I fought for words. "I didn't plant that bomb. When I came back, the camp was gone. That blast didn't just take you away from me. It took away..." My brain grasped for what to say next—then it was there, spilling out of me, coming from somewhere deep inside. "When I lost you, I lost everything worth living for. My heart died with you. Seeing you now? Truth is, if I had to choose between living without you and you shooting me?" The words hurt as they burst out but I couldn't stop, I couldn't stop anything. "Put a bullet in my chest, because I'm already dead and I can't stand pretending I'm not anymore."

My mouth hung open.

I think I'd always known that. But hearing myself say it made it real.

Kit's gun shook.

Words aren't much good.

She was psyching herself up to pull the trigger.

Kit said, "Jackie. You can come out now."

10

My heart exploded. Again.

She'd played me. Again.

I'd been suckered in.

Again.

And I'd known it.

I was going to kill her.

Jackie Aspen stepped out of the attached bath, perfectly unmussed but with the expression of a piglet who's wandered into the Big Bad Wolf convention. Even if she lived through the night, her career in corporate espionage was finished.

I'd seen flung bricks that looked kinder than Kit. She had her finger resting right on the trigger of her gun. "Joe," she said. "Back up. Further. Keep your hands still and open. Right up against the wall. Now move left. Right in the corner."

I glared hot death at the woman who'd destroyed me.

But obeyed.

"Jackie," Kit said. "Grab his gun. From the floor."

Aspen glanced between the two of us.

I tried to will her to death, too.

"Quickly, now!" Kit barked.

Aspen scuttled forward, crouching to grab my discarded handgun by the barrel.

Kit smoothly shifted her gun to a single hand and held out the other. "Here."

Aspen scurried back, offering Kit the gun with a worried smile.

"Good." Kit took the gun in her left hand. "Get back a bit."

Aspen stepped back from the treacherous, deceitful, two-pistoled woman who'd destroyed me.

Giving Kit just enough room to raise my gun and put a bullet into Aspen's forehead.

II

I should have moved, but the sight of my target's body crumbling like a sack of bricks left me stunned. In that half-second of paralysis, Kit had the gun—my gun—aimed back at me.

That'll teach me to carry a gun.

"I was empty," Kit said.

I'd been suckered with an empty gun?

I swallowed. Stuck in the corner, with my wounded shoulder oozing weakness into me, there's no way I could close the distance between Kit and me before she'd shoot me too.

A quick move would have confused the issue. I could have grabbed a knife from my bandolier. Plant it in her throat.

My hands wouldn't move.

I'd spoken the truth. I'd rather swallow a bullet than kill Kit.

The thought...relieved me.

"I found the people who planted the bomb," I said.

Her chin tightened. "What happened?"

"They died." My lips were dry. I tried to lick them, with my parched tongue. "Bad. And slow."

Her shoulders loosened, just a touch.

We looked at each other.

"What now?" I said.

The gun wobbled in her hand.

With a hiss, she lowered it.

I didn't move.

"You hurt me." Kit shook her head. "You hurt me. And you being gone kept hurting."

"You haunted me," I said. "Every day without you was forever."

"It really wasn't you?" she said.

"If I'm lying, I'm dying." My nod makes my brain wobble in my skull. "No, I've been shot. I might be dying anyway."

She steps toward me.

The motion casts light into my heart, but I hold up my good hand. "No—don't!"

She stops, puzzled.

"I have a partner outside," I say. "The mission is, nobody

walks away."

Kit grimaces. "My job was to get the auction winner, then put Aspen and the buyer down." She glances at Aspen's cooling body. "Two months of infiltration, shot to hell. By *you*."

My laughter felt wonderful, despite the pain in my shoulder. "When did you start doing this?"

She rolled her eyes. "Just after some charming rogue told me what he really did for a living, and promptly tried to kill me."

Her words sobered me. "It wasn't...I didn't..."

"I believe you." Kit bared her teeth. "But it's been years. It's not that easy."

Her words shuttered the light in my heart.

Five years was a long time.

And five years of hate is a lot of hate.

I closed my eyes. "I get it." My mouth was impossibly dry now. I hadn't been hit anywhere vital or I'd be long dead, but a slow bleed is just as deadly.

But there was one last thing I could do.

"My partner's outside," I said. "If I don't come out, he's going to put an antitank rocket right into this place."

"Then let's go."

"No." The words tasted bitter. "The job is, I take those briefcases and everyone dies. You lay low. Give me...an hour. Dawson'll get me out as fast as he can. Oh, and don't take the road. He put grenade drones on it."

She nodded. "Can you make it?"

"I get to the kayak, I'll be fine." The rage still filled Kit's face...but it's not complete now. There's something else there.

I take a final chance.

"Listen," I say. "Next month...I'm going to be up in, uh, let's say Chicago. I have a standing reservation at the Five Seasons. I'll be there a couple weeks. Take in some shows. Eat some really good food." I swallow. "I won't be wearing a bulletproof vest."

"And what am I supposed to make of that?" she demanded.

I gave a one-shoulder shrug. "Whatever you want. But if I don't get out, we're gonna get blown up."

Kit licks her lips. She's still livid.

I can't blame her. First I destroyed her relief camp. Then I wrecked her job.

She lunged for me.

I didn't have time to brace.

She pressed up tight against me, hitting my hurt arm too hard but her lips on mine wash all that away. The sweet taste of her breath mingles with the dried blood from her nosebleed, and I don't care, it's Kit, and gunshot or not I'm more alive than I've been in years.

She broke the kiss too soon. "You need to go," she breathed into my mouth.

"Stop by if you like." The words stab my heart.

Before I could think, I rip my heart in half and stagger for the door.

Maybe she'd hire Dawson to put a bullet in me from a hundred yards away.

If she was truly angry, though? If she wanted to hurt me?

She'd let me sit in Chicago and wait.

I'd wait there forever.

I'd checked the briefcases and reached the door when Kit said, "Hey, Joe?"

If I look back? If I see her again?

I'll never leave. Dawson will blow us to cinders.

My heart is too full for me to form words.

I can't turn.

But I stop walking.

The love of my life says, "I'd rather see Chicago with you than walk around dead anywhere else."

FOG AND MEMORY

MICHELE DEAN

Michele Dean's story isn't as violent or as crime-filled as the previous two stories, but "Fog and Memory" does have an unexpected edge. It also has some wonderful atmospherics. The weather and strange motel in the opening leap off the page.

Michele came to writing romance through an unusual path. Her first short romance won first place in the New York City Midnight Short Fiction challenge, and that success led her to write more romance. She has since published short romances in the anthologies Love Among the Thorns *and* Love is Like a Box of Chocolates. *She's hard at work on her first romance novel. Learn more about her at www.micheledean.com*

They pulled into the parking lot at the same time, two weary travelers seeing the brightly-lit sign for the Overlook Inn as an oasis from the storm blowing in off the ocean and shrouding the Coast Highway in alternating waves of fog and rain.

At least that was why Leslie had stopped here, exhausted, nerves frazzled after a too-long, too-emotional day, body aching, hands cramping from the tight grip on the steering wheel.

She shouldn't have driven, though the long road from Santa Barbara to Oakland the day before, and a night in a too-expensive downtown hotel, had given her several hours of much-needed solitude and the time to prepare herself for seeing Michael again.

Michael.

Even after eight months, the mention of his name still tied her stomach in knots. But he had barely acknowledged her, cool contempt etched on his elegant features as she told the court about the disastrous end of their marriage. His expression never changed, even as she described how he'd beaten her almost senseless and left her laying in a pool of blood on the tile they'd chosen with such excitement three years before.

Seeing the photographs of her own battered and broken body, reliving the beating, had shaken her to the core. Leslie fled the courtroom as soon as the jury announced their verdict, barely waiting until Michael was taken away to await sentencing. She barely registered her attorney's glib reassurance that Michael would be locked away for at least two years, maybe as much as four, and this horrible part of her life was now behind her.

She drove aimlessly through unfamiliar streets, her wandering route taking her across the bay and toward the ocean. By late afternoon, Leslie was walking the beach in Capitola, the salt wind clearing her mind, restoring her sense of self.

She stayed too long, until well after sunset, loathe to leave. The ocean had always spoken to her in the pounding of the surf, the shushing of the small whitecaps that rolled over her feet, the cries of the gulls overhead. There were other places that she loved, but when she was sad, she came to the ocean.

In hindsight, it would have been better if she'd stayed the night, gotten a fresh start in the morning. The hours spent walking on the beach had been good for her soul, but not so great for her still-healing leg, which now ached from hip to knee where the hardware holding the broken femur in place had only recently been removed. But she wanted to put as much distance between herself and Michael as possible, so when the breeze coming off the ocean became too cold for her thin sweater, she left Capitola, missed the turnoff to the 101, and found herself winding her way south along the Coast Highway.

The storm had come up unexpectedly—or at least, she hadn't expected it. At this point, she wasn't even sure where she was. Marina? Seaside? It was entirely possible she'd passed Monterey and Carmel as well, the coastal towns all blurred together in the rain.

And then the Overlook Inn had appeared out of the mist like a lighthouse, a beacon of warm, golden light, guiding her off the increasingly treacherous road with the promise of a hot meal and a soft pillow, and she'd gratefully given in to its siren call.

The place was clearly popular—or simply the most visible refuge for weary travelers on this stretch of highway. Leslie eased her car slowly forward through the small, packed parking lot, the lights of another vehicle that had pulled in from the opposite drive shining in her eyes.

They moved as though drawn toward each other, both spotting the open space ahead at the same time, their glowing turn signals clicking like mirror images as each claimed the spot. Leslie was about to concede, when she realized that there were actually two spaces, side by side. With a tired smile she pulled into the nearest, the other driver taking the second one only a moment later.

She got out of the car, immediately regretting the lack of a hat, coat, or even an umbrella, as the wind blew her hair into her eyes and the rain began soaking into her thin sweater.

"We're going the same way," called a voice—rich, masculine, friendly. Leslie looked over to see the second driver standing near the end of his car, gesturing with a large umbrella. "No reason to get soaked."

Leslie clicked the car lock, then pulled her sweater tight around her. "Thanks," she said, her teeth already beginning to chatter. She moved to the end of her car and waited as the man came toward her, extending the umbrella so they could both walk under it without having to crowd close together.

She didn't look at him, saw only dark shoes topped by dark slacks; firm, quick steps as they moved across the parking lot and up the walk. He paused as they arrived at the covered porch, holding the umbrella behind him. Both reached for the door at the same time, but his longer arms gave him the advantage, and he pulled it open.

"After you," he said.

She could hear the smile in his voice.

"Thank you again," she said—or tried to say, her chattering teeth making her words all but unintelligible even to her. Stepping inside the restaurant, she spotted the sign across the small lobby indicating the ladies' room, and made a beeline toward it, the door closing behind her cutting off whatever it was the polite man with the umbrella had been saying.

If he hadn't stopped at the office, Jeremy thought, he wouldn't have gotten roped into the meeting, or the phone call after the meeting, or the farewell lunch after the phone call. Of course, it might not have mattered. Getting out of Los Angeles always took longer than he expected—he should know, after all, he'd only been trying to get out for six years, though there were those who would argue he hadn't really been trying all that hard.

But now he was out. Out of the city, out of a job that had grown stale. Out of the hillside house he'd shared with Monica for too many years, long after the relationship had devolved past even the point of convenience.

He'd hit the road right after lunch, tuning the satellite radio to a station promising three decades' worth of high-energy music suitable for road trips. Abandoning the Central Valley route for the Coast Highway as soon as he'd passed the areas closed by fire or mudslide, he'd relished the ocean view as he made his way northward.

Like most people in high-tech jobs, Jeremy was a combination of a realist and a dreamer, and as he headed toward his new job, new city, new life, he let the dreamer have full rein. Even the storm that had forced him to crawl forward through rain and fog for the past half hour hadn't dampened his spirits. So when the brightly-lit Overlook Inn emerged from the fog, perched lighthouse-like between the highway and the ocean, he turned into the parking lot with a smile. A hot meal would be welcome, and then, depending on the weather, he'd decide whether to stay the night or continue on.

The coincidences of timing flashed through Jeremy's mind as he opened his umbrella, and then saw the woman who had just gotten out of the car next to his, the wind whipping her long blonde hair around her face.

"We're going the same way," he called out to her. She looked over, and he lifted the umbrella slightly by way of a gesture. "No reason to get soaked."

It was a stupid thing to say, he thought, even as the words came out of his mouth. But there was half a parking lot between them and the restaurant, and she was only wearing a light sweater. He would have felt bad just walking off under the shelter of his umbrella without at least making the offer.

To his surprise, she agreed, but he could tell she was reluctant. He couldn't blame her, really, there were so many creeps out there, and he *was* a total stranger. Pulling up his coat collar against the rain, he held the umbrella to the side, so she wouldn't think he was up to anything suspicious.

She walked with a limp, and he shortened his stride to accommodate her pace, holding the door for her when they reached the building. She'd disappeared into the ladies' room almost immediately after they entered, presumably to dry her hair under the automatic hand dryer—or do whatever it was women did to repair themselves after being out in the weather. Monica had somehow managed to look absolutely perfect, at any time, day or night. He supposed it went with her being a model and aspiring starlet, but it had always seemed a little strange to him.

No, not strange. *Fake.* Like so many other things about Monica had turned out to be. In the beginning, he'd counted himself fortunate to have snared the picture-perfect beauty, her long limbs and luscious curves demanding his attention, just as they demanded the attention of every other man who saw her.

He'd been such a fool.

There had been too many other men—how many Jeremy didn't know, didn't want to know, though he suspected she'd never really been faithful. He'd been blind to it in the beginning. But there'd been too many parties, too many times he'd come home from work to find her laughing it up with a houseful of other Tinseltown wannabes, everyone drunk or high or both.

"Come play with us, Jeremy," she would say, putting on that little pout that had charmed him in the beginning but had so quickly grown tedious.

When an antique side table had been damaged during one of those drunken parties, he'd quietly removed it, along with several of the more valuable items he'd brought to the home they'd shared. His art collection followed, replaced by inexpensive, generic prints that could be discarded without comment after being knocked from the wall by a drunken party guest.

Signed, first-edition books were saved from being dropped in the pool. Crystal was replaced with shatterproof acrylic. Piece by piece, Jeremy relocated his most precious belongings to a storage unit, until one day he looked around the house and realized that he'd been moving out of it almost since the day he'd moved in.

That had been the same day he'd gone home to tell Monica that he'd been offered the job in San Jose, and found her naked— and not alone—in the hot tub. So he didn't tell her about the job, didn't ask her if she wanted to come with him.

Instead, he told her he was leaving.

"I'll throw away all of your things!" she had shouted, not bothering to get out of the water, just throwing her plastic champagne glass after him as he walked away. It had bounced ineffectually on the patio tiles, and he'd just laughed and kept right on going, out of the door and out of her life.

It was sad, he thought. They'd been together for almost five years, yet leaving hadn't felt like he was walking away from anything but emptiness.

So, as he sat there, at a window table in the Overlook Inn's cozy restaurant, looking over a menu that advertised simple, homestyle cooking, a small part of his brain registered the empty seat opposite him with a mixture of familiarity and regret.

"Oh...no. No, there must be some mistake," a woman's voice said.

Jeremy looked up. The blonde from the parking lot was standing near the empty chair, talking to the restaurant's host, who seemed quite confused.

"I'm sorry," she was saying. "We're not together." She looked past the host, scanning the crowded room. "Isn't there another table somewhere?"

"But you came in together..." the host began. Then he changed tactics. "As you can see, we're very busy tonight, with the storm and all. You can wait in the lobby for a table to open up." He gestured for her to move past him.

"I'm not using the second seat," Jeremy said, setting his menu down and standing. He gestured to the empty chair opposite him. "Please, there's no sense sitting in the lobby. Will you join me?"

The woman looked from the waiter to Jeremy and then again around at the other diners, many of whom had turned to look at her in return. With a sigh she nodded.

"If you insist," she said, seeming to collapse into herself, as though resisting was simply more than she had energy for.

They sat quietly, reviewing their menus, placing their orders. She'd told the waiter that they would be on separate checks, but he'd insisted that she was his guest, and once again, she had acquiesced without much of a fight.

"Long day?" he asked.

"The longest," she said. A tired smile touched her lips.

"Heading south?" At her nod, he continued, "There's still a big stretch of the highway that's closed between here and L.A. You'll be diverted over to the 101 about twenty miles from here."

She'd nodded, thanking him for the tip. "Do you always lurk around rainy parking lots offering umbrellas and travel advisories?" she asked, the smile finally reaching her eyes.

"No, but maybe I should more often," Jeremy said. She had the most beautiful blue-green eyes.

"People might get the wrong idea."

"Occupational hazard," he said with a shrug.

She raised an eyebrow quizzically at that. "Dare I ask?" she said, then quickly retracted the question. "No," she said, holding up a hand to stop him from speaking. "Don't tell me. I don't want to know. Everything about this day has been completely surreal, and this restaurant, you, appearing out of the fog, you're part of it. If we do the whole 'sharing names and business cards' thing, it stops being magical."

"Okay," he said, nodding. "I get that. I kinda like it." He smiled. "I would like to call you something besides 'parking-lot-lady,' though. I suppose we could go with Jane Doe and John Smith."

She shook her head slightly, wrinkling her nose. "Too generic. No magic."

They sat in awkward silence for a moment, before he said, "How about comic-book names? Not so generic, but still anonymous. And no creepy stalker-stuff later."

"Okay," she said, laughing. "That could be fun."

He saw the moment she relaxed, the tension in her shoulders easing as she breathed. It was as though she'd finally decided that being in a public place with him wasn't too threatening.

"I'll choose yours," he said.

He looked at her. Slim but not in an unhealthy way like Monica and so many of the women in her set, most in constant denial that they had graduated to their thirties. This woman struck him as more *real* than that. Blonde hair, long, straight, and still damp, pulled back in a ponytail at the nape of her neck, a few stray wisps curling around the sides of her face. She'd be embarrassed by that, he thought, because they softened her otherwise put-together look.

Her eyes looked tired. He supposed his own did, too—it had been a long day, and the storm hadn't made this end of it any easier. But there was a layer of vulnerability to her that made him feel protective. He squashed the instinct—he'd only just met her, didn't know a thing about her. Sensed that it would take only one wrong word to frighten her away. And for some reason, he didn't want to frighten her.

"Betty," he said finally.

"Like in the comic books? Or the television show?"

"Either," he said. "Though the television version is a little harder around the edges than the original. You choose."

He was probably right, she thought. She *was* more of a Betty than a Veronica, always looking after everyone else and usually letting people walk all over her more than she should. She hadn't realized she was so obvious, but there it was. He'd spotted it right away.

So what did that make him? A predator, that much was certain, but to what degree? Tall, with a runner's build and the tan to go with it. A few years older than her—maybe early forties?—if the gray strands at his temples were natural and not vanity highlights, which she thought doubtful. His smile was genuine, and reached his eyes, which were framed with small laugh lines that spoke of good times and close friendships.

But it was his eyes that captured her attention. Warm, intelligent, not glancing around the room, at his watch, or constantly looking at his phone. He paid attention to her when she spoke, to the waiter when he came to take their drink order, not dismissing them or treating them like background noise.

"Logan."

He raised an eyebrow, as a slow smile spread across his face. "I'm flattered...I think."

"You should be. If you like being compared to one of the most ornery, stubborn, hot-headed—"

"Hey!"

"—Hot-headed, superheroes I've had the good fortune to admire from afar through multiple late-night film-fests with my sisters."

His grin widened, "That's better. To Betty and Logan," he said, raising his glass.

She laughed, and raised her glass to clink against his. "To Logan and Betty."

He hadn't enjoyed himself so much in longer than he could remember. The meal was excellent, the conversation mostly small talk, starting with the weather, then moving to books and movies before brushing on politics just enough to discover shared frustrations. They talked about places they'd traveled or would like to visit, and hobbies they might someday pursue.

The restaurant gradually emptied, until only a handful of tables in scattered corners of the room remained occupied. Finally, when there was nothing left to eat and still far too much left to say, and none of it safe, he said, "I suppose this is the part where I invite you for a walk on the beach, seduce you, then, in true comic-book fashion, kill you and hide the body."

He'd said it lightheartedly, not even a trace of seriousness in his voice. Still, she stiffened, not moving a muscle, but at the same time withdrawing into herself instantly, like a rabbit suddenly aware that she was dining with a wolf.

"As pleasant as that all sounds—the beach and the seduction part, not so much the murdering," she said, the attempt at humor forced, "I'm going to have to pass."

"Already spoken for?" he asked.

"No." But she said it too quickly, trying to cover up that frightened rabbit look in her eyes with a casual, "We probably couldn't even find our way to the beach in all this rain."

"I'm sorry," he said, reaching out to touch her hand, the tip of his finger brushing against a thin scar that ran in a line from her thumb to her wrist. "It was just a joke. I didn't mean anything by it, really."

She snatched her hand away as if she'd been burned, and as the cloak of vulnerability that had faded during their conversation wrapped itself back around her, he realized that she *had* been burned—hurt very badly, probably by someone she had trusted.

He withdrew his hand. "I'm sorry," he said again, more gently this time. "Betty?"

"I can't," she whispered. "Please don't ask." She had turned away from him, looking out the window to where the rain and the ocean were no more than a single dark blur.

Abruptly, she reached for her purse, rummaged for some bills, and set them on the table. "I've got to go," she said. "It's been lovely, but...I'm sorry, Logan."

And then, before he could say anything, before he could stand and stop her or follow her, she was gone.

Leslie had to get away. Had to leave before Logan could see the tears she couldn't control, tears that mixed with the rain as she ran to her car, her leg screaming in pain.

She pulled onto the highway, heading south, smiling through her tears as she heard Logan's voice in her head reminding her of the upcoming detour. If she'd met him any other time...but not now. She couldn't open herself up like that...trust him...not while she was still so very raw. So why did she want to turn the car around and go back to the Inn, lean her head against his chest while he wrapped his arms around her...

She kept driving, following the detour and heading inland. Her mind gradually cleared as she drove into the night, the storm fading in the distance, wrapping Logan in fog and memory.

Leslie's tears dried and her grip on the steering wheel relaxed. Her sister, Jennifer, had been pestering her for months to come up to Seattle, get away from California and all the bad memories it held for her. Maybe it was time.

Three years later

With only a few minutes until the meeting was scheduled to begin, Leslie looked around the conference room to make sure everything was ready. Presentation packets at each place; check. Audiovisual equipment ready and functional; check. Water bottles, coffee, snacks on the sideboard for anyone who hadn't taken time for lunch; check. Now all they needed was for their clients to arrive.

Her sister had been right, insisting that she move to Seattle. While the last three years had had their share of difficulties, the new surroundings had been good for her, and the challenges of working in one of the city's premier advertising agencies had given her focus and direction that she'd lacked during that final, awful year in California.

It was as though she'd gotten lost during her marriage, and rediscovered herself since coming to Seattle. Now if Jennifer would just stop pestering her to start dating again. A man was the last thing she needed in her life.

Tension in the office had been high for the past three weeks, ever since one of the firm's major clients, Lumovation, had announced the merger with the Silicon Valley company, Unitechnics, and requested an entirely new approach to their marketing.

Leslie felt energized by the increased pressure—it was like drinking six cans of energy drink in one go. Exhilarated, heart racing, she dove into the task of creating the new campaign, working late into the night and over the last two weekends to craft the proposal, pushing her team to be more creative, more innovative, than they had been in the past. And as far as she was concerned, they had exceeded expectations. Even Charles Lawton, the demanding head of the firm, had signed off on the new plan, making very few of his typical changes.

Now, with nothing left to do but deliver the presentation, Leslie checked her watch, breathing deeply to clear the pre-meeting stage fright.

The sound of the elevator dinging in the lobby announced their guests' arrival. As the several suited men and women walked into the conference room, Leslie recognized all of the usual players, greeting them by name.

"Leslie," said Sam Tarbett, CEO of Lumovation, gesturing toward the tall man who had come up beside him. "Let me introduce you to Jeremy Richardson, who is here representing Unitechnics."

Leslie extended her hand, smiling as she looked up at the tall stranger, and suddenly her knees felt weak.

"Logan," she murmured.

Jeremy listened to the presentation, nodding in all the appropriate places, but his attention was divided. He hadn't imagined it. When the pretty advertising executive in charge of the campaign had been introduced to him, she had, in fact, whispered, "Logan."

He'd thought of her so many times. Whenever the fog rolled in across the Bay, he thought of Betty, and that half-magical evening, her taking off, Cinderella-like, leaving him standing there in the rain, watching her taillights disappear in the distance.

Had it really been three years? What had he been doing with his life in all that time? Rising in the ranks at work. Casually dating, but never really finding anyone who held his interest or he theirs for more than a few weeks.

Remembering a woman who had sat across from him, laughing and smiling as they talked; strangers taking shelter from the storm, pretending for a few hours to be friends.

And now here she was.

He watched her, listening as she fielded questions, handled objections, adapted the marketing strategy she had designed to suit the specific needs of her client. She was just as he'd imagined her—talented, self-confident—traits he'd only previewed during their conversation, but which had attracted him to her all the same. Then again, he'd known her for all of what, three hours? Now he wished he'd insisted on getting her real name, a phone number, anything.

Sam asked him a question, and as Jeremy turned to answer, he kicked himself for letting his hormones distract him from the business at hand. He would be in town for a few weeks, overseeing the merger; perhaps Betty—*Leslie*—would have dinner with him again. They could get to know each other as real people this time, without hiding behind comic book names.

As the meeting continued, Jeremy slipped one hand into his jacket pocket and pulled out the slip of paper with the name and number of the flight attendant who had flirted with him on the early-morning commuter hop from San Francisco. Crumpling the paper into a tiny ball, he dropped it and a used napkin into his now-empty disposable coffee cup, then replaced the plastic lid before giving his full attention to Ms. Leslie Burrows.

———

"So what did that California bigwig want?" Charles Lawton asked, coming up to Leslie after the elevator doors had closed on the departing Lumovation and Unitechnics executives.

"Nothing," Leslie said, her hand closing around the business card she'd tucked into her pocket as she turned toward her boss. "He thanked us for our time and said he'd contact me if he had any questions."

"Don't try to fool me," Charles said, scrolling through the messages on his phone as he spoke. He glanced up, pale blue eyes beneath shaggy gray eyebrows focusing on her. "I saw the way he was looking at you, Leslie. Couldn't keep his eyes off you through the whole meeting. Don't you go getting involved with a client and messing things up for us. You know my feelings on that sort of thing."

Leslie felt the color rising in her cheeks. "Of course not," she said, hating his good-old-boy demeanor. "I would hope you know me better than that."

"Just making sure we understand each other. I like you, Leslie; your work is top-notch. But I won't have personal entanglements getting in the way of business."

"I understand."

They went their separate ways, Charles toward his corner suite, and Leslie down the long hallway to her much smaller office. The meeting had gone exceptionally well, and she strode confidently, smiling to her co-workers as if she owned the world.

But when she closed the door behind her, she leaned against it, eyes closed, and let out a long sigh.

Of course Charles had noticed the electricity arcing between herself and Jeremy Richardson. He rarely missed much.

She'd noticed Jeremy's attention, too, and it had taken all of her energy to remain focused on the presentation. She was grateful she'd rehearsed the delivery enough times that it came automatically, even though part of her mind was reeling.

Logan.

She'd barely believed it was actually him at first, but each time she'd turned toward his side of the conference table and found him looking at her, she'd grown more certain of it. That infectious half-smile, the way his eyes followed the conversation, his attention fully fixed on the person he was speaking to; she'd never met anyone who had stayed in her memory in just that way.

But of all the things that had blurred together from that crazy day three years ago—the horrific morning in the courtroom, the calming afternoon on the beach, the Overlook Inn shining through the rain like a welcoming beacon—it was Logan, no *Jeremy*, she corrected herself, that had stood out from the fog of her memory.

She hadn't looked for him, not exactly. But in the weeks that had followed, whenever she'd seen a tall slim man jogging on the beach or walking on the opposite side of a busy street, she'd done a double-take, thinking that it might have been him.

Then she'd moved to Seattle, and packed the memory of dinner with Logan away, like one bright, final souvenir of her time in California.

Her phone beeped with an incoming message and she slipped it from her pocket to look at it.

Hey, Betty. Are you free for dinner? Logan

She couldn't help laughing. What were they? A couple of

teenagers? He'd barely had time to get downstairs and to the car with his colleagues from Lumovation.

I'm sure Sam has already made plans for you, she replied.

He'll understand if I beg off. Long day, and all.

Probably not the best idea, mixing business with pleasure, don't you think? she wrote.

Perhaps, was his immediate reply.

Leslie closed her eyes. Charles would be happy. Then her phone dinged again.

But Betty and Logan don't have any business entanglements that I know of. See you at seven?

Leslie looked at her phone, re-reading the message thread. Entanglements. It was the same word Charles had used. Probably for good reason. It would be so easy to become entangled with Logan...

She stared out the window at the tiny slice of the Sound just visible beyond the high-rises. Her sister's encouragement warred with her employer's warning, the two voices arguing the pros and cons in her head, while her heart served up memories of a magical evening overlooking a stormy sea.

Then she keyed an address into the reply field, hesitating for only a moment before pressing *send*.

As the Uber driver headed west across the city, toward the water, Jeremy decided that Leslie hadn't given him her home address, as he had at first supposed. His suspicion was confirmed when the driver let him off in front of a long low building, built on one of the city's piers.

Soft, jazzy piano music greeted him as he entered, and he smiled in silent approval. The ambiance was upscale, but not pretentiously so, and from where he stood, it appeared that every seat had a view of the water through the windows that surrounded the dining room on nearly all sides.

"Do you have a reservation?" the host asked.

"I'm meeting someone," Jeremy said.

"Under what name?" the host asked. "I can check to see if they've arrived."

Jeremy started to give Leslie's name, correcting himself at the last moment. "Betty," he said. "Or maybe Logan."

"Ah, yes, here it is," the host said, smiling. "It' doesn't appear that Mrs. Logan has arrived yet. But if you would care to follow me, I'll show you to your table."

Jeremy didn't correct him, just followed along quietly, smiling as he took his place at the cozy table for two near the window. He stared outside at the water, which was deep blue, tinged with gold near the horizon, where the sun was just beginning its evening show.

"Is this seat taken?"

He turned at the familiar voice. She stood near the opposite chair, hand resting casually on the back, smiling at him.

"I'm not using it," he said. "Please, join me."

She sat, but before he had a chance to say anything else, the waiter materialized. It took all his self-control to wait patiently through the routine as the waiter poured glasses of water, pointed out the specialties of the day, and took their drink orders.

"I was surprised to see you."

They both said it at the same time, then shared a laugh at the duplication of the thought. Jeremy gestured toward her, indicating that she should continue.

"You have no idea how hard it was to give that presentation," Leslie said. "I was so distracted."

"It never showed, not even for a minute," Jeremy said. "I, on the other hand, had to review the packet afterward, to make sure I hadn't missed anything."

"I can clarify..."

"No need," he said. "I didn't ask you here to talk business. In fact, I'd prefer to *not* talk business. I didn't know you were from Seattle."

"I'm not. I mean, I wasn't. I moved here three years ago. A few weeks after we met, actually."

"I was on my way to San Jose," he said. "I'd just taken the job at Unitechnics. I never thought to see you there, but whenever I went south, I always hoped I'd bump into you."

"Me, too. While I was still in California, I mean. I thought I saw you several times, but it was never you."

There was an awkward silence, broken by the return of the waiter bringing two glasses of wine. They placed their dinner orders, then, unsure what to say next, Jeremy turned the conversation to safe topics, like the weather and the sunset, which was painting the sky in brilliant oranges and pinks.

"Do you believe in coincidences? Fate? That sort of thing?" Jeremy asked, his eyes still on the sunset, half-afraid to look at her.

"I believe in serendipity," Leslie said.

He turned toward her. "I'd like to see you again."

"My company has a policy against..."

He raised a hand to stop her. "We'll be discreet. No one else needs to know unless we decide to tell them."

He saw that deer in the headlights look, the one that said, "I've been hurt before and I don't want to be hurt again," and he knew he had to tread very carefully.

"We'll take it slow, very slow," he said. "But I've been thinking of you for years, and I want to get to know you. I want to know if you're real or just a figment of my imagination."

"And if we find we just can't stand each other? What then? How will that affect our working relationship?"

Jeremy grinned. "That won't be a problem," he said. "I'm a very likeable guy."

Leslie laughed. "That's what I'm afraid of."

He sobered up instantly. "Look, we're both adults. If we click, it's all to the good. And if we don't...well, I'm sure we're both professional enough to not let it affect our business dealings." He paused, then plowed ahead, wanting to get the words out before he lost his nerve. "I'll be in town for a few weeks; after that, I don't know yet. But while I'm here, I'd like to see you. Often."

He waited for her to reply, half expecting her to jump up and run away from him as she had the first time. So when she didn't get up, but instead raised her glass and extended it toward him, he released the breath he hadn't realized he was holding.

"To Betty and Logan," she said.

"To Leslie and Jeremy," he replied, clinking his glass to hers.

Managing a secret relationship was complicated, Leslie thought a week and a half later, blocking out time on her schedule for a late lunch with Jeremy on the following afternoon. His office was a half-hour's drive across town in good traffic, and Sam always had him scheduled for so many meetings that it was a surprise that he was able to get away at all before late evening.

For her own part, she mostly wanted to avoid running into anyone she worked with. That meant looking for out of the way places, and trusting to ratings posted on internet review sites, since she couldn't ask her co-workers for recommendations.

How did people manage to have affairs and keep them secret, she wondered, laughing as she answered her own question. Because they were willing to go to the effort for the relationship.

Just like she was willing to take a chance and bend the rules a little—just a little—for Jeremy. Trusting him not to get her fired was the easy part. Trusting him not to hurt her was harder. But she was willing to believe that he might be worth the risk. That this might be the right man and the right time, at the *same* time.

They'd seen each other several times already, and the magic that had connected them before only seemed to be growing stronger. Their conversations had grown beyond simple generalities, and they talked about their lives, their dreams for the future.

But neither of them, she noticed, talked much about their pasts.

"I don't need to know, if you don't want to tell me," he'd said the previous evening, as they sat across from each other over a cheap Formica tabletop in a run-down diner that Leslie thought served the best fish and chips in town.

"Maybe someday," she'd replied. What Michael had done to her was not high on her list of things she wanted to talk about. Ever. Although if they did continue beyond this exploratory fling, or whatever it was they were doing, she knew she'd have to tell him.

"What about you?"

He'd shrugged. "We all have a past. Mine was...disappointing. Better forgotten." And then he'd neatly changed the subject, leaving her both curious and, strangely, understanding exactly what he meant.

"What shall we do tomorrow?" Jeremy asked. It was Friday night, and they'd just come out of the movie theater. She'd slipped her hand into the crook of his arm as they headed toward the parking lot, and though his Uber driver had messaged his arrival, Jeremy didn't want the evening to end.

"I don't know about you," Leslie replied. "But I'm babysitting. All day. Watching my sister's kids."

"What does your sister do?"

Leslie laughed. "Jennifer's a nurse," she said. "She's on the morning shift this month. So she'll get to the hospital about six-thirty a.m., work all day, and get home about four. Her regular sitter is out of town this weekend, which means I've got the kids."

"Her husband?"

"Army. Deployed to the Middle East."

"Ah," Jeremy said, nodding. "You're staying with your sister, then, while he's away?"

"Next door. They bought this old Victorian a few years ago, before they had kids, and renovated it. It's a duplex, so they live in one side, and rent out the other. I moved into the smaller half four months ago, just before Hank went overseas. So, yeah, it's like living with them, but not quite. Best of both worlds."

"I could come by."

Leslie said nothing, and Jeremy was afraid he'd crossed a line. "Look, forget it—" he began, but she cut him off.

"That would be nice," she said, her voice soft. "Jennifer keeps asking me to bring you around."

"She does? So that means you're talking about me? While binge-watching superhero movies?" He could feel the grin spreading across his face, and didn't try to stop it.

"Featuring a certain stubborn, comic-book character? Perhaps," she replied with a delighted laugh.

They'd reached her car then, and as she opened the door, he stepped closer, slipping an arm around her and turning her to face him.

"We're nothing flashy or fancy," she said, her voice catching a little as he pulled her closer. "Just ordinary people—"

"Ordinary is sounding very good to me these days," he said. Then he bent, his lips pressing against hers, and decided once again that nothing about this woman was the least bit ordinary.

Leslie could have kissed Jeremy when he showed up at the house promptly at noon with pizza and sodas. Instead, she called him her "white knight" and directed him to the dining table in Jennifer's cozy kitchen, three hungry boys trailing after him in slow motion.

"I think they're supposed to be zombies," she told him as the boys, ages four, seven, and eight, tore into the pizza.

"I thought zombies ate brains."

"Shh!" she whispered. "Don't remind them."

Jeremy watched the boys devour the pizza. "I should have brought two," he said ruefully. Leslie laughed, leaning against him as she pulled out her telephone and called up the pizza shop, whose number she had on speed dial.

"A woman after my own heart," Jeremy whispered in her ear as she placed the order.

"You know it," she said.

They managed to save a couple slices of the second pizza. Later, after Jennifer had come home, Leslie wasn't entirely sure if her sister's mumbled, "Good choice," was about the pizza or Jeremy.

"Well of course," Leslie said. "You love Guido's pepperoni, extra cheese."

"Not talking about the pizza," Jennifer said around another mouthful. "Was talking about that delicious-looking man out in my living room wrestling with my boys. He kiss you yet?"

Leslie turned away, reaching into the refrigerator for a soda so her sister wouldn't see the heat rising on her face. As though she really thought her sister would let her get away with that.

"Thought so," Jennifer said, snatching the can of Pepsi from over her shoulder. "If you want my advice, which I know you don't, you'll hold on to this one. He's got 'keeper' written all over him."

"I'm starting to agree with you," Leslie said.

After she finished her hasty meal, Jennifer shooed the boys upstairs so that the adults could all sit around the kitchen table and talk undisturbed.

"You ready for the interrogation?" Leslie asked Jeremy, wiping the condensation from a glass of water and handing it to Jeremy.

"Why not?" he said, taking a seat opposite Jennifer. "If I can face a board of directors, I'm sure I can handle a few simple questions."

The sisters looked at each other and laughed. "You have no idea—" Leslie began, but before she finished her sentence, the doorbell rang. "I'm up, I'll get it," she said. She tossed the dish-towel onto the counter and headed toward the living room, barely reaching the door before the boys, who were pounding down the stairs.

Leslie opened the door and froze, her heart leaping into her throat at the sight of the tall, sandy-haired man standing on the porch.

"Michael!"

"You're a hard woman to find," Michael said. He was twirling a knife in his hands, one of the pseudo-military style switchblades he'd always liked to collect. The wide, dark blade was folded back into the black handle, but Leslie remembered how quickly the blade could be triggered. "Lucky for me, I found an old Christmas card with your sister's address on it—"

"Who is it, Auntie Lessie?" asked seven year-old Johnny, trying to push his way around her.

"Go back inside," Leslie told him, catching him by the shoulder and turning him around. With a gentle shove, she propelled him back into the house. Three pairs of feet pounded across the living room floor behind her as the boys ran to tell their mother about the stranger on the porch.

"Well isn't this just charming," Michael said. "I never saw you as the motherly type."

"Why are you here, Michael?" Leslie asked, ignoring his taunting. In that, at least, he was still the same. But if she hadn't known him, she might not have recognized him. He'd lost weight, his always lean frame now almost gaunt, and a crescent-shaped scar curled around his right eye, marring his formerly elegant features.

"Who is it?" Jennifer called out from somewhere behind Leslie, gasping as she reached the door and saw Michael.

"Oh, my God!" Jennifer said. "What are you doing here?"

"Hey, Sis!" Michael said, waving at her with the knife. He popped the blade out for effect, laughing as she squealed in fright.

"Keep the children inside," Leslie said, not looking at her sister. "I've got this."

"I'm calling the police," Jennifer said, disappearing into the house.

"What's going on?" Jeremy asked, trading places with Jennifer.

"Oh, ho, what have we here?" asked Michael. "Should I be jealous, Les?"

"Go away, Michael," Leslie said. "You have no business here."

"Oh, but I do. We have unfinished business, you and I. You ruined my life—"

"You ruined your own life, Michael, the day you tried to kill me."

"—do you know what happens to a man like me, in prison?" He was almost screaming now, pointing to the scar by his eye. "They did this to me, and worse, because of *you*. So it seems only right that I should return the favor."

He had barely finished speaking before he lunged toward her, blade outstretched.

Leslie reacted automatically, twisting to the side as she stepped into his attack. Without even thinking, she swung her leg —the same leg Michael had shattered—in a roundhouse kick, her foot connecting with his jaw even as his knife swooshed past her, missing her shoulder by inches.

Stunned, Michael flailed for balance, staggering backward before toppling down the porch stairs.

As Leslie stood at the top of the stairs, looking down at Michael's unconscious form, Jeremy came up behind her. "Are you all right?"

"You know how we never really talked much about our pasts?" she answered, leaning against him, pulling the arm he looped around her waist just a little tighter. "That's mine."

While they waited for the police to arrive, Leslie told Jeremy about Michael and what he'd done to her, and how she'd just come from court the day she met him at the Overlook Inn.

"So when you said it was 'the worst' day, you weren't kidding," Jeremy said.

"Not by much. I suppose the day he beat me up was worse, but I don't remember much of it. Do you want some coffee? I think I need some."

Some time later, after the police had taken Michael away and Jennifer had managed to settle the children upstairs with cookies and a movie, Leslie, Jeremy, and Jennifer reconvened around the kitchen table.

"How did you know to kick him like that?" Jennifer asked.

Leslie shrugged. "Remember the self-defense classes I took, after the physical therapist said my leg was up to it? We used kickboxing as a warm-up"

"So your feet are lethal weapons?" asked Jeremy.

"Only when she takes off her shoes," Jennifer said. "Her socks...ewww!"

Leslie threw a potholder at her sister. "Don't listen to her. I'm glad I took the classes." She ran a finger over the scar on her hand, a long, thin line that ran from the side of her thumb nearly to her wrist. "I know what that knife can do, what can happen when someone confronts you and you freeze up. I never wanted to be that afraid again."

Jeremy reached out and took her hand, squeezing it gently. "We're with you."

They were all silent for a long, serious moment, before Jeremy spoke again. "So, there's someone else we need to confront..."

"Your ex?" asked Jennifer.

Jeremy's laugh was almost a snort. "I'm sure she doesn't even remember my name," he said. "No. I was thinking about Charles Lawton."

"My boss?" said Leslie, confused.

"The one and only. I'm tired of having to sneak around just to keep him happy—but I don't want to get you fired, either." He grinned, and Leslie saw a wicked gleam in his eye not unlike the spark that often glimmered in the eyes of her young, mischievous nephews.

"So what do you suggest we do?" she asked.

Jeremy leaned forward, resting his elbows on the table and tapping his fingertips together in front of his face. "I have a plan."

Three days later, on Tuesday afternoon, Jeremy joined the combined Lumovation and Unitechnics teams at the advertising agency offices. After a brief review of the changes they had made to the marketing strategy, and the pieces they had already begun to implement, Leslie turned to the assembled executives.

"Does anyone have any questions?"

Jeremy held up his pen, as though asking permission to speak.

"Yes, Mr. Richardson?" Leslie said.

"Will you have dinner with me?" Jeremy asked.

"Excuse me?" Leslie said, taking a step back as though caught off-guard. She was playing the part perfectly, just as they had rehearsed.

Charles stepped in, pre-empting anything Leslie might say. "We have a policy against that sort of thing, Mr. Richardson," he said, his bushy gray brows drawn together in a frown.

Jeremy looked across the table at Charles. "And I have a policy as well," he said. "*My* policy states that when I meet an attractive, capable, charming woman who I think I would like to get to know, and possibly spend the rest of my life with, I ask her to dinner."

"And how is that policy working out for you?" asked Sam, who was sitting next to him and grinning like a schoolboy.

"Don't know. I just decided to implement it today," Jeremy said.

A chuckle rippled around the room.

"We discourage employees from becoming involved with clients," Charles said gruffly.

"Discourage, but not outright forbid?"

Charles growled, but Jeremy knew he had him backed into a corner he couldn't weasel out of, and maintained his level gaze at the older man.

"No, it's not forbidden," Charles said finally.

"Very well." Jeremy turned to look at Leslie. "Ms. Burrows, would you do me the great honor of having dinner with me tonight? And possibly many more nights in our future?"

"I would be very happy to, Mr. Richardson," Leslie said, a warm smile lighting up her face.

That evening, as the sun sank over the Puget Sound, Leslie and Jeremy watched from their table in the Space Needle as the sky at the horizon changed colors from gold to red to deep purple. Closer to shore, a low cloud of fog shrouded the city, the lights glowing like fireflies through the mist below them.

"It's not the Overlook," Jeremy said. "But I hoped, since it overlooks everything, that it would do."

Leslie smiled. "I think I love you," she said, glancing toward the window as she said it, half-afraid of his reaction.

"I think I love you, too," he replied, reaching out and taking her hand.

She looked at him, then smiled and with her free hand raised her glass. "To Leslie and Jeremy," she said.

"To Jeremy and Leslie."

REUNION

KRISTINE KATHRYN RUSCH

There's no crime in my short story for this volume, "Reunion." Just a lot of loss and regret, so it matches the mood of the Michele Dean that came before it.

I write a lot of romance, and have done so under different names. Some of my shorter romances appear under the Rusch name. My light and fun romances appear under the Kristine Grayson name. To find out more about all of my work, go to kriswrites.com.

For the record, I've never been to my own high school reunions, although I've attended at least two of my husband's. Strange things, reunions. They lead to all kinds of interesting moments...

I

Ultimately, high school reunions were sad affairs. Jenn had noted something off at the ten-year, but hadn't been able to articulate it. Now, at the thirty-year, she knew.

People got together not because they liked each other or remembered each other or even respected each other.

They got together because they wanted to impress each other or because they had nowhere else to go or because high school had been the best time of their lives.

Jenn had come to all three of her reunions for each of those three different reasons. At the ten-year, she wanted to impress everyone with her high end Wall Street job—100K per year plus bonuses and she was only 28. At the twenty, she came because she realized she'd been happiest in high school.

At the thirty, well, she had nowhere else to go.

She walked into the badly decorated dance hall at the Moose Lodge in Neider Lake, Wisconsin, and stopped for only a half second to stare at the *Welcome Class of 1981!* She remembered hanging signs like those the summer between her sophomore and junior years, and thinking everyone who came to these things was so *old*.

Maybe she hadn't been wrong.

The registration area consisted of two folding tables, with large buttons scattered across the surface. The buttons had attendees' high school graduation picture in the center, their names underneath in a dark black font.

She searched for her name tag, getting help from the kid manning registration. He looked vaguely like Rudy St. Pierre— ruddy face, broad shoulders, too skinny—but at eighteen, half of Northern Wisconsin looked like Rudy St. Pierre. White, blondish, Nordic heritage. By twenty-eight, the beer gut started. By thirty-eight, the hair was gone. By forty-eight, there would be no recognizing anyone except for a select few.

And she—fortunately or unfortunately (only the night would tell)—was one of the select few. She still had her figure which, judging from the pudgy forms of her former classmates, was astonishing. Her hair was roughly the same color, and she hadn't gotten too many lines on her face.

Of course, she hadn't lived through as many harsh North Country winters either, since she spent half her life in Manhattan —and not the good half either.

Now she was home, if indeed, the place where you grew up could be called home, trying to sell a dilapidated house in a market that died long before the Great Recession of 08 hit, and of course, not succeeding. The real estate agent wanted her to paint the damn place, wanted her to recarpet, put in a new kitchen and a half bath, in other words, fix it all up so that someone would be comfortable living there.

Jenn hadn't been comfortable living there as a kid, so she didn't live there now. She rented an apartment in the fourplex on Superior Street, upper left-hand corner with a great view of the intersection. Five hundred dollars a month, including utilities which, considering how cold it got here in the winter, was a steal.

She needed the steal. She had some money, more than she probably deserved, enough to spend half a year taking care of her father, and another year besides. But she would have had a small fortune, if she hadn't believed her own damn hype. She shouldn't have invested as much of her money in the market as she had, and she should have pulled that money out quicker, and so many should haves that she hadn't discussed with anyone.

She went from a gorgeous apartment in up-and-coming Soho to this place. And found herself grateful for the cheap rent.

Her father had been dead all of two weeks. No one had come to the funeral, not even his drinking buddies. He'd been a mean old cuss by the end, not that he'd been nice to start with. It had been just Jenn and the priest, a truly nice young man who treated her with great kindness. He went through all the motions with sincerity, even though her father hadn't been to Mass since her mother died in 1980, and the priest offered Jenn comfort she claimed she didn't need.

Still, she'd spent that night on the cheap sofa she'd bought six months before, watching the flat screen TV, her eyes leaking tears. She had been convinced she wouldn't miss him. But something broke inside her, something that had to do with him, something she didn't want to examine too closely.

She liked to pretend the tears were relief—she didn't have to shepherd the cleaning lady, make sure her father took his medications, make sure he *ate*, for godssake—but that wasn't accurate. She missed him, frighteningly enough. She missed his occasional moments of clarity, the harsh wit, the too-true observations.

She carried them with her now, into this dilapidated hall whose exterior hadn't looked much better when she attended her senior prom here, thirty years before.

What a night that had been. She hadn't been part of the prom committee so she had no idea that they had somehow taken the hall, decorated then in late 1950s knotty pine, and managed to make it sparkle. Disco ball on the ceiling, excellent multicolored lighting, fabric over that hideous paneling. The place had smelled of perfume and beer, and somehow that had seemed romantic.

Along with the band—a young, energetic cover group from Duluth, who didn't mind the disk jockey who played records on the breaks.

Jenn had come with August DuLac, whom she had always thought of as the perfect man even though at that point he had been a boy. She still thought of him as the perfect man, even though she hadn't seen him in thirty years. He had kissed well, he had dressed beautifully, and he had made her feel so special.

Her mother had made Jenn's dress, filmy and gauzy, like something from the movies, and someone had told August that a regular corsage would not work, so he bought her a small wrist corsage, with matching flowers for her hair.

She felt pretty, she felt alive, she felt like her future was right outside her grasp, and she knew, she knew she and August would escape to the East Coast and run the world. Together.

Only he hadn't gone to Harvard despite his acceptance; he'd enlisted instead. She had gone to the East Coast alone. Worse, she'd gone to Columbia in New York City at a time when the biggest city she'd ever seen was Minneapolis, on one shopping trip with her mother, the summer before Jenn's senior year.

Jenn survived. That's what she needed now. A little button that said, "Hi, I'm Jenn Carlsen, and I survived."

She took her badge from the Rudy St. Pierre clone and pinned it to her dress. This dress wasn't filmy—she had given up filmy at thirty-five, thinking she was too old for that. The dress was black and practical and it flattered her pale skin. The dress was also expensive, unlike her open-toed shoes, which were scuffed, but were the only black heels she still owned. The rest had gone to consignment shops around the area, which brought her the occasional thirty or forty dollar check as someone found her beloved Manolo Blahniks and decided to shell out ridiculously small sums for her once horribly expensive shoes.

She stepped through the archway, under another banner celebrating the class. The hall looked more dilapidated than it had thirty years ago. Someone had replaced knotty pine with cheap 1980s paneling, and it hadn't worn well. There was no disco ball, but someone had thought to keep the fluorescents off, and to only use the wall and stage lighting, which made a small difference.

No dance floor except right in front of the stage. Tables decorated with dark blue runners over white cloths, the school colors, which she had nearly forgotten. In the center, fake candles, adding more light, and around the tables, chubby middle-aged rumpled people she didn't recognize.

Of course, he wouldn't be there—August. She didn't want him to be there either, didn't want to see the wrinkled ruin of the handsome boy she had fallen in love with, didn't want that image of perfection in her memory marred by reality.

She still had a few illusions. She wanted to keep them.

And that desire had almost made her stay away.

Except that she didn't want to look at the undecorated walls of her apartment or the flat TV screen playing crap or the paperwork strewn all over her kitchen table, the remains of her father's narrow little life. If she looked at that any longer, she'd realize yet again that her own little life was heading toward narrow, and she wasn't sure what she could do about it.

She cast about for familiar faces, and realized they were all familiar in that *I think I know you but I'm not sure* kinda way. She was rooted to the floor a few yards from the door. The music playing softly overhead—no speakers, no cover band, just a tasteful DJ hiding near the back (younger than she was now, and looking frightened and out of place)—was "Stayin' Alive" by the Bee Gees, which was sadly appropriate.

She couldn't quite gather enough nerve to plunge in, to grab a drink in the solid old glasses the Lodge had been using since she was a child, and to mingle with people she hadn't talked to for at least ten years.

A hand grabbed her arm, and she jumped so dramatically that if she had been holding a drink, it would have gone all over her and the fat guy in the ill-fitting suit two feet away.

"I'm sorry," a woman's voice said. "I didn't mean to startle you."

Jenn turned. She almost recognized the faded woman beside her. The eyes were bright, blue, familiar. Filled with compassion and covered with glasses so old that the lenses were scratched.

"I heard about your dad. Jase and I would have come to the funeral, only we had to be in Rhinelander that weekend."

Jase? Jenn used an old Wall Street trick to glance inconspicuously at the nametag. Arlene Magascar. Jenn didn't know an Arlene Magascar, but she had gone to school with Jason Magascar who dated Arlene Cummings, who had been slender and gorgeous and vicious. The ultimate mean girl before anyone had coined the term.

"Oh, Arlene," Jenn said as if she had known all along who she was talking to, "it's all right. I didn't expect anyone to come to my dad's funeral."

And the funeral had lived up to those expectations. But Arlene wasn't living up to Jenn's expectations of her. Arlene: brittle, funny, brilliant. Arlene: head cheerleader and track star, so fast that had she been born twenty years later, she might have gotten a college scholarship, and might have competed professionally.

Arlene: one hundred pounds heavier (which made her flat and square, not round), apologizing for failing to come to a *funeral* of a man she hadn't liked to support a friend she hadn't seen in decades. The mean girl would never have apologized. The mean girl would have made a pithy comment or forgotten the funeral had even happened.

Jenn felt off-balance. She had known the reunion would have *Twilight Zone* elements, but she hadn't expected to encounter them so soon.

"Jase is here too?" Jenn asked.

"Oh, yeah." Arlene nodded toward the podium. A tall balding middle-aged man was trying to find a way to keep the microphone upright. His suit fit, but his body didn't. Jase Magascar: captain of the football team, brilliant, and incredibly sharp-tongued, particularly to Jenn, whom he always kept at a distance. Jase had had a scholarship to Stanford, planned to be an M.D. like his father, planned to *escape*, like Jenn had.

She suddenly wanted to leave the Moose Lodge. This wasn't going to help. This was going to be worse than sitting at the kitchen table, staring at her dad's bills, wondering what had happened to her life.

Now she was wondering what had happened to all of their lives, and why it had happened so quickly. Thirty years seemed like a moment ago. A moment ago, they'd all been slender and filled with possibilities. Thirty years ago, they were going to escape—through their talents or their drive or sheer unadulterated ambition.

"C'mon," Arlene said, putting a hand on Jenn's elbow. "Let's get you something to drink."

And just that easily, Jenn moved into the crowd, heading toward the bar, with a woman who couldn't be Arlene Cummings, but somehow was. Arlene Cummings, whose dreams had always been impossible—no scholarship, no college, no college, no escape. So she had known she'd have to settle for marriage and kids.

She did settle. With Jase, who was still fiddling with the microphone, looking content.

Jenn stopped. She couldn't. She smiled at Arlene—at this Arlene, who had hidden the funny brittle Arlene in a fat suit and let her become Midwestern pleasant.

"I forgot my drink tickets," Jenn said, closing her right hand over them. "I'll be right back."

She slipped her elbow out of Arlene's grasp and headed back toward the door, her breath coming in tight gasps. One man—short, round, with short round glasses that mirrored his short round eyes—said, "Hey, it's Jenn!" and a bunch of other people made welcoming noises.

She smiled, waved, headed to the front where the young Rudy St. Pierre clone was handing out more badges to a group of people who looked like grandparents.

She skirted around them, through the entrance, down the stairs, and through the double doors into the parking lot, letting the mid-July heat encase her. No wind off Lake Superior tonight. Sticky humidity despite the darkness.

Her Mercedes was parked at the edge of the parking lot, the blue-and-white New York plates standing out as much as the shiny sleekness of the car itself. Didn't matter that it was ten years old. Didn't matter that the plates had expired. Didn't matter that she was too damn lazy to transfer her car registration and her driver's license and all the details of her life to Northern Wisconsin.

She could go back to New York now or anywhere. At sixteen, she'd dreamed of London. At twenty-two, she'd changed that to Paris. Then she went to Paris, and realized that much as she enjoyed it, it didn't suit her. She didn't like London either. It was too buttoned up for her. Too buttoned up and too alcoholic. She'd spent an entire childhood treading on egg shells. She didn't need to move to a city where egg shells coated the sidewalks.

One hand on the car's warm roof, one hand on her stomach. Queasy, tears—tears?—in her eyes. "Precious and Few" echoing from the dance floor inside, faint and sad, reminding her of that Christmas dance she'd gone to at fourteen, where she and Greg Everhart had talked about running away, just disappearing, and never coming back.

Jase Magascar married Arlene Cummings, and now they looked tamed. Tamed.

Jenn had married—no one anyone here knew—and divorced, and moved away, and was now here for no apparent reason except this was where she stopped.

"At least you went in."

Her heart rose. It recognized the voice before her brain did. August DuLac. Of course. She needed more disillusionment.

She turned, and there he was in the half light, looking like she remembered, only better, grown up now, his face angles and lines, his body thin, his shoulders broad. He wore a T-shirt that clung to washboard abs and jeans so old they looked like they might fall apart. He still had thick black hair, and dark black eyes, and a mouth that twisted into a near smile of self-loathing.

"A.G.," she breathed, wanting to run into his arms, wanting to hug him, hold him, lean on him, like the teenage girl she had once been, the teenage girl who still lurked inside.

"Jennifer Carlsen Tate. Tate, right?" he asked, apparently the only person in town who knew her married (formerly married) and therefore still legal name. "More stunning than ever."

She let out a half laugh. "Not stunning, A.G. Not by half."

The car was holding her up. Her ten-year-old car with expired plates. Her shoes felt wobbly, her stomach still queasy, her eyes still damp. She wasn't stunning. She was a mess.

"I don't know, babe," he said, using the endearment she had tried to break him of at eighteen. "You look stunning to me."

She'd learned long ago not to argue with a man handing out compliments. Not only was it churlish, it sounded like begging.

"How come you can't go in?" she asked.

"You're out here," he said.

She tilted her head. She remembered the easy charm, had missed it in fact, thought so many of the men she'd met in New York bars after the divorce could learn a thing or two from the high school student who lurked in her memory as the perfect man.

"Yet you couldn't go in when I was inside," she said.

"Touché," he said, then ran a hand through his hair. "I haven't been able to go in for thirty years."

"You stood in the parking lot at all three reunions?"

His smile softened. "You looked gorgeous at the tenth, but brittle. At the twentieth, you seemed—I don't know—a little wistful."

"And now?" she asked, a bit unnerved that he had seen her at all of those reunions but she hadn't seen him.

"I told you," he said. "Stunning."

She shook her head, tried to speak, then shook her head again. If she spoke, the tears would come, and she would collapse, right here, in the Moose Lodge parking lot in Neider Lake, Wisconsin, the place she had escaped from, and then returned to like a whipped dog.

Then his arms were around her, her eyes pressed against his shoulder, her head still shaking. She wanted to move away, but she didn't. His left hand slid up her spine, then cupped the back of her head, holding her in place—a familiar movement. An old movement. A comfortable movement, as comfortable as calling him A.G., as letting him hold her while she struggled not to cry.

She swallowed, took a deep breath—realized he smelled the same: his shirt, washed in Tide; his hair, faintly lemony; his skin, soap and leather and something indefinably him. She made herself step back, rubbed two fingers under her eyes, glad she wasn't wearing mascara because she found moisture there, more of it than she would like.

She kept her head down, but she wasn't shaking it any more.

"Sorry," she said.

"Your dad just died," August said as if that was the reason for the tears. And maybe it was. Maybe her emotions were right on the surface because her dad's death surprised her (even though it hadn't); because she missed him (even though she didn't); because she was alone in the world (even though she'd been alone from the moment she drove out of this town, thirty years ago).

"Yeah," she said, and gave August a watery smile. "So, you were going to tell me why you can't go in."

He frowned at her, then glanced over his shoulder. "I didn't like those people thirty years ago."

"So why show up at all?"

"You have to ask?" he said.

She nodded.

"Silly girl," he said, tucking a strand of hair behind her ear. "You forgot who we were."

2

She hadn't forgotten:

That first moment—all the confusion of the first day, new school, *high* school, the pinnacle or so it seemed, the beginning of the end, three more years and escape. She wore a summer dress, heels—it was hot, too hot for a school with no air-conditioning—and she felt wilted as she got out of the car, her mother (her mother! Dead before high school ended) wishing her well.

Inside, clutching her schedule and her notebooks, not wanting to wear a backpack because it would mess the line of her skirt (oh, she was probably a mean girl too, and didn't know it, certainly hadn't cared), looking for her locker, the combination lock weighing down her purse. The locker was easy, right near the cafeteria, not too far from the principal's office, stash everything inside except one notebook, pens, and lock the whole thing with the combo lock—whose combination she had actually practiced until she had it by feel.

Then she turned around and there he was, leaning on the stairs, arms crossed, watching her, hair black and thick, too long even then, boyishly thin, but he already had the shoulders and the promise of those angles in his face, wearing a T-shirt, and jeans so old they looked like they might fall off, and she walked over to him and touched his arm and it felt like sparks of lightning exploded in the room.

Oh, she remembered, she remembered it all, and—

3

She shook herself out of it, backed up until she hit her car, ran a hand over her face, feeling foolish and fifteen and terrified and sad all at the same time.

"I'm sorry," she said for what? the third time? "I need to go home."

"An apartment's not home," he said. "Especially that apartment."

She felt cold, despite the heat. "Are you stalking me?"

"It's a small town, Jenn, and you took an apartment on the main drag."

She did and she kept the drapes closed at night. Even when she opened them in the morning, she hadn't seen him.

Maybe she hadn't wanted to.

He threaded his fingers through hers, another movement she

remembered, then pulled her forward. His dark eyes questioned her—*is this okay?*—and she leaned toward him, her answer in her parted lips.

He kissed her, gingerly at first, but then his arms went around her, pulling her close. He tasted familiar, like a favorite food she hadn't had in decades, and she wanted more of it. Their tongues met, their bodies pushed against each other, and she fumbled behind herself for the door to her Mercedes. She managed to pull it open without ungluing herself from him, and they eased wordlessly into the back seat just like they used to do.

He pulled the door closed as she reached under her dress, removing her panties, and he stopped for just a moment—those eyes, questioning again. Then he eased his legs upward, grabbed his wallet from his back pocket, and fumbled inside.

The New Yorker in her was offended, but the teenage girl remembered that move; she'd seen it dozens of times. He found what he was looking for, tossed the wallet aside, and held up a condom between his index and middle fingers.

"How old is that thing?" she asked.

"Younger than us," he said, and leaned forward to kiss her again. She unbuckled his pants, slid them down, helped him with the condom, then sat on him.

The sensation felt familiar—*he* felt familiar, and she felt alive for the first time in years maybe. Her first orgasm was so fast it caught her off guard. Him too, because he laughed, then slid his hands under the dress and up, cupping her breasts. He tilted his head back, his face smooth in the faint streetlight, his cheeks flushed.

Her hands were under his shirt, against his ribcage—that flat skin—but there were ridges, scars, maybe, and she didn't want to think about that or the years. Instead, she moved and he moved, all without much more than the rustle of skin.

She bit her lower lip to remain quiet, and somehow he

managed to stay soundless even with his mouth open. Unlike their teenage selves, though, they didn't scan for anyone else in the parking lot. Let some observer get a thrill. Or one of their classmates say, *Jeez. Just like old times. Saw Jenn and A.G. steaming up a car.*

Only there was no steaming. It was so hot that sweat ran down her back and she didn't care.

Her entire body felt like a live wire. She leaned in, kissed him, and that did it for both of them. He shifted, she moved, and tipped them over, their mouths catching each other's cries of passion, and keeping them somewhat quiet.

It ended as fast as it started. She finished the kiss, then fell against him, his heart pounding as hard as hers, her breath as fast as his.

"I haven't done that in years," she said, startled at the confession.

"In a car?" he asked.

"Yeah," she lied. She meant all of it, but he didn't need to know that. "What the hell, A.G.?"

They were a sticky mess of sweat and fluids. The condom was probably going to ease off, if it had even held up. She had nothing in the back of the car to clean up with, unlike the old days, when she drove with towels.

Dunno why a girl needs towels in a car all the damn time, her father had said once, watching her put some in the backseat.

I'm a girl, *Daddy,* she said, a phrase she always used to shut him down. Let him imagine what he wanted—an out-of-control period, or some other mysterious girl thing. She never elaborated, and he never asked.

"I don't know about what the hell," August said. "That was more like an old dream coming true."

She laughed awkwardly, then slid off him. The condom wilted. She handed him her panties.

"What am I supposed to do with those?" he asked.

"Clean up," she said. "I have another pair at home."

He let out a small bark of laughter, grabbed the condom with his two forefingers, and clamped it shut. Then he opened the car door with the other hand, and slid the condom onto the parking lot.

"A.G!" she said.

"It's a reunion," he said. "They had to expect it.'

"Maybe at the five-year," she said.

"There was a five-year?" he asked.

"No," she said. At least, not one anyone had told her about.

She wiped her hands against her dress. He wiped his against his pants, then handed her the panties back.

"You'll probably want those to preserve the leather up front," he said.

"I don't remember you being practical," she said.

"Yeah," he said, and sounded sad.

She slid off him, put the panties back on, and wanted to ask, *Now what?* but she knew what. This was a reunion fuck, something that people did when they saw old lovers, nothing more. A way to recapture a bit of that magic they'd had at the beginning of the relationship, before the memories of what fell apart crushed them.

"You're quiet," he said.

"Yeah," she said, and that sounded sad, even to herself. She had no way to end this. He was in her car. She would have to initiate a conversation.

Or maybe he had expectations. Maybe he thought they were going to repair to her apartment and stare at the bills on the table. Or discuss what happened with his life, and how he ended up here. Maybe even reminisce.

She opened the door beside her and slipped into the

extremely warm night. Usually, it wasn't this hot in Neider Lake. There was usually a wind.

At least the parking lot was empty. Apparently, she and August were the only ones who felt like channeling their youth enough to end up in the parking lot.

It didn't look like anyone had left; there were a lot of cars here. Music still echoed from the well-lit dance hall. More Bee Gees, whom she had hated for a very, very, very long time.

August spent a few more minutes inside her car, tidying himself up. She didn't bother with tidying. There was no way she could go back inside even if she wanted to. She wasn't comfortable seeing her former classmates when she reeked of sweat and sex.

Not that she wanted to go back inside anyway.

August got out on the other side of the car, then folded his arms on the roof, and put his chin on his forearms.

"You want to go for a drink?" he asked.

"I don't drink," she said. He should have known that. She had been the only kid in their class to avoid all kinds of spirits, although she'd probably gotten contact highs from the pot everyone had smoked around her.

"Still?" he said, then nodded as if answering his own question. "Your dad."

"My genetics," she said, although she just as easily could have said, *my parents* and he would have understood.

He watched her, as if he couldn't get enough. "See you tomorrow?"

The reunion continued with a golf outing, something she never would have expected from the Neider Lake Class of 1981. Golf was something old people did, or bigwigs in New York brokerage firms that would eventually go under due to incredible financial mismanagement.

Then there was a sit-down dinner tomorrow night back here

at the Moose Lodge. The dinner was supposed to be catered, but probably not in the way she was used to from her New York days.

"I don't know," she said. "What's going on here, A.G.?"

He smiled slowly. "I think you're old enough to—"

"Don't be flip, A.G." She felt tired. And old, suddenly. And wrung out. And cheap.

He nodded, then pushed away from the car. He bowed his head, ran his hand through that marvelous mane of hair, and nodded again—some kind of acknowledgement of something or other, what she didn't know.

Finally he looked at her, the car a barrier between them.

"I never married, Jenn," he said.

She waited. What was she supposed to say? He knew her last name. He knew she had married, and he knew it hadn't worked out.

"You were always the one," he said.

"Jesus, A.G," she said, mostly to cover that little surge of joy that made her heart rise. "We were in high school."

"Yeah," he said. "That's what I keep telling myself. But what just happened here—"

"Was a lot of fun," she said. "And frankly, I needed the relief. It's been too long, and the stress has been awful. So I thank you."

His face shut down, almost as if she had slapped him. Then he said, hollowly, "You once told me that you should never thank anyone for sex."

"I was sixteen," she said, and wished she hadn't. Because saying that made it clear she remembered the conversation too.

Another back seat—his mother's car, seat covered with a scratchy wool blanket that Jenn couldn't figure out how to wash— and the look on A.G.'s face. Rapt, almost, as if he had discovered the path into heaven.

That was...oh, wow, he had said, his voice shaking. He was naked and chilled enough that he was shaking. The perfect body was a bit too thin then, not like it was now, all muscle and strength. But with hints of that to come.

Thank you, Jenn, he had said, and the tone was reverential. *Thank you.*

She didn't know how to react to that. It had been good for her, strange, but good. But his tone frightened her, and the look in his eyes was too intense. Her mom had just died. Jenn didn't have the room for intense.

So she said to him, *Never thank anyone for sex*, as if she'd had sex before. As if she knew anything there was to know about sex.

He nodded like she had read the first line of Catechism to him, and he was going to absorb the lesson, learn it so well that he would be absolutely perfect, the best at everything.

He didn't seem to care about her fake worldliness. He accepted it, like he accepted the admonition, and he never thanked her again, although afterward he would often take a strand of her hair, tuck it behind her ear, kiss her gently, before telling her she was absolutely beautiful.

She stared at him for a minute, and she realized that she had always misjudged him. The perfect man, when he had been a boy —a needy boy who spent a lot of time with her, and made her feel special, yes, but declared love too fast, and tried too hard, and maybe cared a little too much.

"Yeah," he said. "But being sixteen didn't make you wrong."

There was hurt in his voice. Maybe there had been the first time she said it to him as well. Her *thank-you* had been curt, dismissive, deliberately so. And now he was old enough to know it.

The words "old enough" caught her, made tears well again (dammit). She closed her eyes gently so that the tear wouldn't fall, wondering if he'd even be there when she opened them.

He was, and still watching her. And she realized that she didn't want this to end after all.

They had been in high school, and now they weren't, and they had experience and a lot of living behind them.

She opened the driver's door. "Get in."

He frowned at her, his face all angles and shadows in the half-light of the parking lot.

"I changed my mind," she said. "Get in."

She didn't wait for him to answer. Instead, she slid into the buttery leather seats—soft and unchanged from the moment she bought the car, unlike everything else in her life. The interior still smelled of sex, and was much too hot.

She revved the engine, turned on the AC, and wondered if she would have to drive away from him after all. Because she wasn't going to repeat her invitation a third time.

The passenger door opened, and he climbed in, his long legs folding as his knees brushed against the dash. He slid the seat back until it clicked, then reached for his seat belt.

She didn't wait for him to latch it. She backed up, and peeled out, as if the Mercedes were a sports car instead of what she had considered practical when she was looking at houses in Connecticut, back when she thought she was going to be promoted, that the old boys' network didn't apply to her, because she was the best sales person in the entire company by a mile.

Sales aren't a measure of management skills, one of the Old Boys told her at that year's performance review.

Five years later, as the feds were shutting the company down because of the massive amount of fraud and insider trading that had come to light during the financial crisis (not that the company would have survived anyway), she passed that same Old Boy, and sneered at him.

Looks like you didn't have management skills either, she said, and he scurried past her like some kind of bug in a thousand-dollar suit.

She drove, not to a bar, but to Karl's, the all-night diner that still ruled the highway that ran parallel to Neider Lake. She and

August used to spend half the night there on weekends, commanding a booth with nothing more than a shared cinnamon roll and two "bottomless" cups of coffee.

Since she'd been back, she had thought of going inside, but she hadn't. Too many memories. Besides, there were a half dozen takeout options on Superior Street, options that hadn't been there when she was a kid.

The old parking spot was still there, underneath an elm that somehow made it through Dutch Elm disease unscathed. The tree looked the same, although it probably wasn't, but its arching branches and thick leaves provided shade on hot summer days, and great cover for late-night make-out sessions.

She drove past that spot—she didn't want him to think she was angling for another make-out session—and parked closer to the door.

There were a dozen cars in the lot, all with "foreign" plates, as the locals used to say. She almost assumed that meant no one else had flaked on the reunion and come here, and then she realized that half the attendees could have come from out of state.

She hadn't remained long enough to know if anyone else had escaped this decaying old town.

She got out. Wind teased her hair, and made her skirt flare just enough to remind her of the drying sweat along her back. She probably should have offered to meet him, gone home and changed clothes. But if she had done that, she would have never seen him again.

She knew that as clearly as she knew her name.

The breeze had the beginnings of a chill. The wind was shifting. Within an hour or two, the breeze would be off the lake, just like it was supposed to be, and this solid old dress of hers would be much too flimsy.

Although she would welcome the cool right now.

August got out as well, and started to walk toward her, as if he would take her hand like he used to do.

But he stopped, maybe remembering that chilly *Thank you*, and swept his hand forward in an archaic, but very August *ladies-first* gesture.

Younger her would have chided him for it. Forty-eight-year-old Jenn didn't feel like chiding anyone. She stepped up the curb and went through the front door.

The interior had the same layout, although a newer, upgraded palate. The dual pie cases, each large as a booth, were to the left, and to the right were tacky postcards and holiday cards, along with some hand-drawn art by artists who barely deserved the name.

The restaurant didn't quite smell the same. The overpowering stench of cigarette smoke had faded to a suggestion of it. Apparently years and repainting hadn't been enough to get the smell out of the walls. The scent of bacon and gravy and freshly baked pie still couldn't cover the ghostly old smell—not entirely.

But she found it comforting, just like she found the layout comforting. The big round booth in the corner, the one that didn't have a good view of the lake, used to hold Jenn, August, and all of their late-night friends. She'd laughed a lot in that booth— the demented I-can't-stop-laughing-at-every-little-thing that happened with too much caffeine and not enough self-control.

She let the moment sweep over her, while August spoke to a server who had to be not much older than Jenn had been the first time she and August had come here.

The girl, in her brown and green uniform, clutched two plastic menus to her chest and walked toward a booth on the parking lot side of the restaurant, just like August had asked.

And Jenn was glad he had. The rest of the diners sat on the lakeside of the restaurant, even though, technically, they had a better view of the highway than they did Neider Lake.

Jenn and August sat, ordered—coffee and strawberry pie for her; coffee and a burger for him—and then, as the server left, stared at each other.

In the clear light of the restaurant, his face looked different. Not as young. Crow's feet around the eyes, a slight spray of silver near his temples, and deepening lines around his mouth.

They gave his face character that he had lacked as a young man, but also a wisp of sadness, something he'd never had before.

"You know all about me," she said, even though that probably wasn't true. "But I don't know anything about you."

"Jenn," he said, and his tone made it clear he was going to contradict her.

"Last I heard," she said, speaking quickly so he couldn't finish that sentence, "you had joined the military. How did you end up back here?"

She was proud of herself for not having an edge in her voice, for not sounding accusatory, even though his service still set her teeth on edge. Not because he served, but because he had abandoned her without even consulting her. One day he was there; the next, he had vanished, taking all of their dreams with him.

His cheeks flushed. He looked away, and then he twisted his head just a little, as if mentally forcing himself to look her in the eyes.

"We had it all mapped out, didn't we?" He sounded almost breathless. "I came to the ten-year to apologize to you. Then the twenty, and now this one. It's a lot harder than you'd think, apologizing. Because the military was good for me. It turned out to be a good decision."

"I had no idea you were even thinking of it," she said.

"Yeah." He rubbed his hands on the edge of the booth, then adjusted the salt and pepper shakers. "I didn't talk a lot in those days."

"You're not talking a lot now," she said.

He nodded, and she could see his cheeks move. Apparently he had smiled, but she couldn't see his lips so that she could actually tell.

"Harvard," he said. "Full ride. Boston. I think about that a lot, and sometimes I think I was really stupid."

You were, she almost said, and caught herself.

"But I...um...didn't belong with the rich kids. The recruiter, he came to our double-wide, and he said, maybe thinking I couldn't hear, that charity cases didn't do well at the school because 90% of what happens to undergrads was networking, based on who your parents were."

She froze in place. Columbia hadn't been like that, only because it was in Manhattan. The city was too diverse and the university in the middle of it all. It was impossible to ignore all of humanity streaming around the campus. There was no island, like she had heard about when she talked to the other Ivy League students.

"I was already scared," he said. "I didn't apply anywhere else. I couldn't afford it. I suppose, now, I guess, that I could've gone downstate, Madison maybe, or used reciprocity with Minnesota, but that never even crossed my mind."

He smoothed the napkin, adjusted the silverware on top of it, and then looked up at her. His eyes were sad.

"I was so mad that night," he said. "I called, and your dad hung up on me."

She closed her eyes. Of course her dad was involved. He'd always said he never talked to August, but she had known even then that might or might not have been true. On a binge, her dad was a blackout drunk. He didn't remember half the stuff he had done, and he never remembered any of the things he had promised. The blackouts were convenient. They allowed him to lie about the things he did remember.

"So..." August was saying, "I just drove, and saw the recruitment office—right next to a bar—"

"I remember," she said, and she did. She used to shoot daggers from her eyes at that center, those months after August had left. The entire summer between her senior year in high school and her freshman year at college, she'd poured every bit of hate she could muster on that one little building, hoping they could feel her loathing inside.

"I almost went into the bar." He half-smiled. "You kept me out."

"Me?" she said.

He nodded. "I didn't want to turn into your dad."

She let out a small breath.

"The recruiter was locking up. He turned around, saw me just standing in the parking lot, staring at that bar, and he asked me if I needed someone to talk to." August smiled. "Now I know that was his pitch. Seem casual, offer help, be nice even if it's refused, be an ear if it's not. It was effective. He was the only person who ever listened to me."

"I listened," Jenn said.

August shook his head. "*I* listened. So I could be the person you wanted me to be. *You* wanted that big Ivy League education, not me. *You* wanted New York, not me. *You* wanted to get as far from here as possible."

"You didn't?" she asked, stung.

"Maybe then, yeah," he said. "But I served. I did well. I came home. I like the lake and the community and knowing everyone. I used the G.I. bill to go to school, got an engineering degree—"

"Engineering?" she asked. He had hated math and science in high school, just hated both of them with a flaming passion.

"Yeah." He let out a small self-deprecating laugh. "Turns out I'm good at it."

She felt off-kilter. "You live here?"

"Yeah," he said. "In a house on Mansion Hill."

Which, she knew, sounded more impressive than it was. Mansion Hill was named for a single mansion, the Neider estate, which was now a tourist spot. Housing developments had been built up and down the hill in the big real estate boom after the turn of the century, but most of those houses were empty, thanks to the housing crisis from the past few years.

There must have been something on her face, a look of shock or bewilderment, *something*, although even she wasn't sure how she felt.

"Neither of us ended up the way we expected, huh?" he asked.

The server brought his burger, and Jenn's pie, which looked gorgeous, but she no longer wanted it. This had been an escape, a lark, and instead, the entire evening had turned out to be filled with surprises, most of which she didn't like.

Although the orgasm had been nice.

She smiled just a little, hoping he thought that was because of the pie, and not the deliciously filthy memory she had just conjured up from only an hour ago.

She wondered if she could let go of him, that perfect man she'd carried in her head, the one she had compared every other man in her life to.

And now, she was comparing the real man, August DuLac on the downhill slide to fifty to the boy he had been, and finding him —she'd briefly thought *wanting* but that wasn't accurate. She was just as attracted to him as she had always been, and the sexual chemistry might've been better.

And, truth be told, even with her fine education and her high-falutin' career (as her dad used to say) she was wanting too. She wasn't that girl, and nor was she the person that girl had wanted to become. That girl would've been appalled at her future self, returning to this place, enslaving herself to the father who had verbally abused her from the moment she drew breath.

August reached out his right hand, palm up. "I said you looked stunning tonight," he said quietly. "I meant it."

She let out half a laugh, then raised her gaze at him. "You are filled with blarney," she said, using one of her mother's phrases.

"No," he said just as quietly. "I'm not. You've grown into your face. You look like a woman who has actually lived her life, and learned something from it."

She shook her head. "I didn't learn anything. I'm back where I started."

"Home is a touchstone," he said. "It lets you see where you came from, and where you want to go."

She took a deep breath. That was the question she hadn't asked. Not once, not since she came here to care for her dad, not since she had lost so much in that damn economic collapse. She'd blamed herself for that, for the losses, the fact that she had only some money rather than a lot of money.

But she never really cared about money, not like those creeps who had brought down the company. She had used money to keep score, and she had won the game—until the game imploded.

She'd come home because there was no game. And even if there had been, she was done playing.

She put her hand in his. His fingers were warm, his eyes were kind.

"I don't know if I'm going to stay here," she said, and they both knew she wasn't talking about the restaurant. She was talking about Neider Lake.

"I'd be surprised if you did," he said.

She would be too. But stranger things had happened. *He* had stayed here.

"But I'll be here a while," she said. "I have to put my dad's affairs in order, get rid of the house..."

And rest. She really had to rest. Take the kind of breather that she had never allowed herself after high school, after college, maybe not ever.

"I'd like to…" Her voice trailed off. "I'm…I enjoyed tonight."

He smiled.

"Not just the—nostalgic part." Was it all nostalgic? She wasn't sure. "But the…this. I haven't had anyone to talk to for a long time."

Maybe ever, but she didn't say that either.

"Talking's good," he said. Then he clasped his fingers around her hand, and raised it to his lips. "It's all good."

And it was. For the moment, anyway. For what she needed, right now. Maybe there'd be more over time. Or maybe she would figure out what drew her to this place, what drew her to him, what she actually wanted to do, instead of what the world—from her long-dead mother to her professors to her awful bosses—wanted her to do.

Maybe this was what reunions were for. This reckoning. This once-a-decade examination of where she was and where she had been. A chance to pat herself on the back or realize that she had missed something important or to just celebrate the fact that she had survived.

August was still clutching her hand. She unfurled her fingers, and used their tips to trace his cheek. It was a bit scratchy with stubble, and the stubble was coming in gray.

She liked that. She liked him. Not the imagined him. The real him.

She would like to get to know him better.

She used her free hand to wave at the server.

"I'd like a burger, please," she said. "And he wants more coffee."

He smiled at her. That was an old ritual, ordering coffee for each other. It signaled a long night of conversation in a booth they once rented for coffee and pastries because they had nowhere else to go.

Now he had a house and she had an apartment, and there was no one waiting at home for either of them.

This was a waystop, not a haven. But it would give them a safe place to talk, to get to know each other, to rediscover things, not just the sexual chemistry, which, she had to admit, thrilled her to find again, but things they had in common, things they could share besides their history and their attraction.

She had been wrong. This wasn't a sad affair. They weren't trying to impress each other or even relive old times. Maybe they hadn't been ready for each other thirty years ago. Maybe they needed time and seasoning.

Maybe they needed to figure out who they were individually, before they could ever think about who they were together.

She was ready to move forward, to think about the future, just a little bit. To contemplate who she was and who she was going to be.

He kissed her hand again, and then their hands untangled. He went for the burger, and she sipped her coffee.

And weirdly enough, it didn't feel like old times.

It felt like now.

And that felt really, really good.

ABOUT THE EDITOR

Kristine Kathryn Rusch

New York Times bestselling author Kristine Kathryn Rusch writes in almost every genre. Generally, she uses her real name (Rusch) for most of her writing. Under that name, she publishes best-selling science fiction and fantasy, award-winning mysteries, acclaimed mainstream fiction, controversial nonfiction, and the occasional romance. Her novels have made bestseller lists around the world and her short fiction has appeared in eighteen best of the year collections. She has won more than twenty-five awards for her fiction, including the Hugo, *Le Prix Imaginales*, the *Asimov's* Readers Choice award, and the *Ellery Queen Mystery Magazine* Readers Choice Award.

Publications from *The Chicago Tribune* to *Booklist* have included her Kris Nelscott mystery novels in their top-ten-best mystery novels of the year. The Nelscott books have received nominations for almost every award in the mystery field, including the best novel Edgar Award, and the Shamus Award.

She writes goofy romance novels as award-winner Kristine Grayson.

She also edits. Beginning with work at the innovative publishing company, Pulphouse, followed by her award-winning tenure at *The Magazine of Fantasy & Science Fiction*, she took fifteen years off before returning to editing with the original anthology series *Fiction River,* published by WMG Publishing. She acts as series editor with her husband, writer Dean Wesley Smith.

To keep up with everything she does, go to kriswrites.com and sign up for her newsletter. To track her many pen names and series, see their individual websites (krisnelscott.com, kristinegrayson.com, retrievalartist.com, divingintothewreck.-com, fictionriver.com, pulphousemagazine.com).

FICTION RIVER

Doorways to Enchantment
Edited by Dayle A. Dermatis

Stolen
Edited by Leah Cutter

Chances
Edited by Kristine Grayson

Dark & Deadly Passions
Edited by Kristine Kathryn Rusch

Broken Dreams
Edited by Kristine Kathryn Rusch

A subscription to *Fiction River* saves you money and ensures that you receive the very best short fiction from some of today's best authors. Subscriptions are available in electronic and trade paper formats and begin with the very next volume. Don't wait! Subscribe today at www.FictionRiver.com.

Missed a previously published volume? No problem. Buy individual volumes anytime from your favorite bookseller.

Unnatural Worlds
Edited by Dean Wesley Smith & Kristine Kathryn Rusch

How to Save the World
Edited by John Helfers

Time Streams
Edited by Dean Wesley Smith

Christmas Ghosts
Edited by Kristine Grayson

Hex in the City
Edited by Kerrie L. Hughes

Moonscapes
Edited by Dean Wesley Smith

Special Edition: Crime
Edited by Kristine Kathryn Rusch

Fantasy Adrift
Edited by Kristine Kathryn Rusch

Universe Between
Edited by Dean Wesley Smith

Fantastic Detectives
Edited by Kristine Kathryn Rusch

Past Crime
Edited by Kristine Kathryn Rusch

Pulse Pounders
Edited by Kevin J. Anderson

Risk Takers
Edited by Dean Wesley Smith

Alchemy & Steam
Edited by Kerrie L. Hughes

Valor
Edited by Lee Allred

Recycled Pulp
Edited by John Helfers

Hidden in Crime
Edited by Kristine Kathryn Rusch

Sparks
Edited by Rebecca Moesta

Visions of the Apocalypse
Edited by John Helfers

Haunted
Edited by Kerrie L. Hughes

FICTION RIVER PRESENTS

Fiction River's line of reprint anthologies, edited by Allyson Longueira.

Fiction River has published more than 400 amazing stories by more than 100 talented authors since its inception, from *New York Times* bestsellers to debut authors. So, WMG Publishing decided to start bringing back some of the earlier stories in new compilations.

The Unexpected
Darker Realms
Racing the Clock
Legacies
Readers' Choice
Writers Without Borders
Among the Stars
Sorcery & Steam
Cats!
Mysterious Women
Time Travelers

PULPHOUSE FICTION MAGAZINE

Pulphouse Fiction Magazine is returning twenty years after its last issue. The first issue came out in January 2018, and the magazine will be quarterly, with about 70,000 words of short fiction every issue. This reincarnation mixes some of the stories from the old *Pulphouse* days with brand-new fiction. The magazine has an attitude, as did the first run. No genre limitations, but high-quality writing and strangeness.

For more information or to subscribe, go to www.pulphousemagazine.com.

www.ingramcontent.com/pod-product-compliance
Lightning Source LLC
Chambersburg PA
CBHW020236260626
47156CB00002B/695